MOON BURNED

THE WOLF WARS SERIES: BOOK 1

H. D. GORDON

For all the brave & beautiful women of the world.

1

The summer sun blazed down over Dogshead and the surrounding lands as if it had been personally insulted by the mere existence of the place. I leaned against the squat wood structure that housed a bar and gambling den, stealing some of the shade cast by the wretched building, drawing deeply of the smoke balanced between my first and second fingers.

The clank and clatter of someone striking a tin bell rang through the square, and people began to emerge from the wooden edifices. The unpaved, dusty street—not having seen a good rain for nearly two weeks—sent up plumes of dirt as children and stray dogs darted here and there. Others gathered under the shade cast by the squat structures, leaned on fence posts, and sat beneath the awnings of hotels, hostels, and various dens of iniquity.

I remained where I was, smoking my square. It was the first of the month, the time when the new Dogs would be brought in, which was always a spectacle.

It was also a fight weekend, and I was one of the unlucky Dogs on the roster. When the unforgiving sun set tomorrow evening, I would step into The Ring for the eighteenth time—a number that matched my approximate age. I would be forced to shift into my Wolf form and fight another to the death.

I knew he was behind me before he spoke, and I tilted my head in the slightest to let him know it was so.

"You got a fight tomorrow, don't ya, Rook?" His voice was gravelly and somehow inherently offensive. I turned to see Murphy step out of the shadows cast by the adjacent building like a scarecrow come to life—which was actually an apt description of the male.

He limped toward me, his broken gait as familiar as the stench that floated off him and carried on the wind. In the dirt square before us, the procession of incoming Dogs had begun. Wagons with large cages full of newly acquired slaves began to roll through, guided and guarded by Hounds and Sellers, whips hanging ever coiled at their hips.

"You know the roster," I replied after taking time to drag from my square, my body subconsciously angling away from him. Murphy was the kind of Wolf that females knew well; the kind that set instinctual alarm bells ringing in the stomach.

But the Masters protected him, so it was best to just ignore him, to keep my mouth shut and opt for being civil.

Murphy sidled up beside me, the scent of death and fresh-turned earth lingering on him like cheap aftershave, his beady eyes fixing on the procession of wagons. After the fights, Murphy's job was to take out the dead Dogs and bury them, their bodies nourishing the soil for the crops of the coming seasons. It was a lucky job for a Stray, an easy ride that those like me, who were forced into The Ring, resented.

In the hierarchy that was Werewolf society, the Gravediggers were a step above the Dogs, but that one step may as well have been a leap.

Gravediggers didn't have to fight to survive, after all. Dogs did.

"You thinkin' about running?" Murph asked, and I could

sense the brown-toothed grin that was tugging up his lips without having to look at him.

I didn't respond to this. I drew on my square, held in the smoke, and released it.

He moved a bit closer, and the hair on the back of my neck went up, the Wolf in me raising its hackles. It would be no large matter for me to sink my teeth into his neck and tear his throat out, no issue I'd lose sleep over.

But as much as being a Dog taught one to live by violence, it also made it imperative to choose one's battles wisely.

"Because you know," he continued, his warm breath brushing over my cheek, making the rabbit I'd consumed for breakfast gurgle wretchedly in my belly, "they catch every Dog that desserts. You know that? Every. Single. One... Then they bring you back here and make an example outta you. Strip you naked and string you up." His eyes roamed over me. His voice lowered. "When it's done, I get your body." A wet sound as his tongue slithered over his lips. "I get to do what I please before I bury you in the fields."

My only response was to inhale deeply of my cigarette, hold it in my lungs for a tic before blowing it coolly into his face. His nose scrunched up, making his nostrils flare, and a little Wolf-Gold lit up his glassy, probing eyes. Werewolves—even those as old and perverted as Murphy—had highly sensitive noses.

As he waved at the air in front of him, a low growl emanating from his belly, more wagons full of slaves continued past. The sound of whips cracking made my jaw clench. It was a sound every Dog who made it past their fifth year of life knew well.

A stray Wolf could become a "Dog"—sentenced to a life and death in The Ring—one of two ways. The first way was the most common; they were bred into it. Birthed solely for the purpose of being trained, sold, and fought. They were named "Dogs" after the lesser beasts, as creations meant for nothing but servitude.

When we were not fighting and killing, we were working the fields to pay for our "living expenses"

"Lookie there," Murphy said, leaning closer to me still, his posture highly hostile while I remained unmoved, leaning carelessly against the wall. He pointed a bony finger at one of the wagons crossing the square.

"I do believe they call that one the Bear, because she's the biggest She-Wolf anybody's ever seen..." He coughed into his hand, phlegm rattling in his chest. When he was finished, he added, "And because I *do* know the roster, I know that she's your opponent tomorrow night. How do you like that, *Rook the Rabid*?" The laugh that followed was vulgar and insolent.

My gaze followed his line of sight. The wagon to which Murphy had been referring held only one person, unlike most of the other wagons, which had been stuffed to the brim with as many people as they could hold. The Werewolf they called the Bear stood alone in the center of her own cage, and she was indeed as large as a mountain, even in her human form.

It had been a while since I had felt real fear, as it was an emotion I had grown mostly numb to, but a bit of it spiraled through my stomach now.

The Bear was corded with muscle, veins pulsing through her arms and legs like vines crawling up the trunks of sturdy trees. Her skin was smooth ebony, her eyes darker still, like two black holes. Her head had been shaved and it gleamed in the summer sun. The look in her eyes was one I also knew well—that of a Dog finally succumbed to their animalistic side. It was a gaze that lacked faith or reason. The gaze of a hopeless, half-mad slave.

I'd seen the look in my own reflection on the worst of nights.

When Murphy lifted his hand to stroke his fingers down my cheek, I snapped.

It was like the flipping of a switch with me, as it always had been. One moment I was in control, and the next I was... Well, *rabid*.

I gripped Murphy's wrist tight enough to make his bones creak, slapping my other hand over his mouth to cut off his squeal while spinning our bodies so that he was the one with his back against the wall.

In the following instant, my knee came up and slammed into his most tender spot, and he sputtered a sound that was half gasp and half choke as I shoved him harder against the unforgiving wall of the building, holding up his weight easily with my supernatural strength.

My eyes glowed Wolf-Gold as I released my hold on his wrist, transferring my grip to his throat. I squeezed just hard enough to make him panic for air.

As calm now as the countryside moments before a tornado, I leaned in and held the Gravedigger's gaze so that there could be no mistaking my next words.

"I will kill you if you ever try to touch me again," I told him. "I'll slit your throat and leave your body in a ditch for the carrion to find if you even *look* at me, and I will gladly take the lashings for it. I'll *smile* while they whip me."

My grip on his throat tightened a fraction, his pockmarked face turning a sick shade of blue. I asked if he understood me, and he managed an enthusiastic nod while his eyes bulged from his head.

Shoving Murphy back into the wall for final punctuation, I allowed him to slump down to the ground and cradle his private parts while gasping for air. As he did so, I searched the ground for the half-smoked square that I'd discarded unwittingly in my rage, found it, and dusted off the filter before placing it into the corner of my mouth and striding out into Dogshead square.

I did not turn around to look at the Gravedigger where I'd left him slumped in the shadows, but I could feel his angry gaze on my back, and I wondered if it would have been wise to just kill him right then and there and take the consequences.

Choices, after all, always led to consequences...but I'd worry about that after my fight.

Because whatever retaliation Murphy the Gravedigger might seek was nothing if I couldn't survive in The Ring tomorrow night against the Bear.

2

I allowed the final wagons to finish their procession before crossing the street, eyes fixed on a bar called the *Blood Moon*. It was a place where many a Dog, Hound, and Stray came to drown their sorrows, lose their earnings, or pay for a roll in the hay with one of the working ladies of Dogshead.

As the last wagon trundled by, I forcibly kept an apathetic look on my face. The wagon was full of pups ranging in age from three to ten years old, half of them destined for slavery as Dogs, the other half doomed for an early, violent death.

There was always a demand for a supply of new fighters, because every fight in The Ring was to the death. This was where the Collectors and Sellers (Werewolves who made a living in the capturing, buying, and selling of their own kind—the worst kind of Wolves, in my opinion) came in. They snatched up Strays wherever they could find them, and because the world of a Wolf was a violent one, this left plenty of pups running around without anyone to care for them. Easy prey, as one might call it.

This was how it had been with me. Fifteen years ago, *I* had been a pup riding into town in a cage hitched to the back of a horse-drawn wagon.

As this thought flitted across my mind, my eyes locked with one of the pups in the final wagon. I wanted to look away, but was captured by the gaze of the little Wolf in the cage. The pup's eyes were a striking shade of hazel—a rainbow of colors, not so different from the shade of my own eyes. In them, I could see the terror I knew so well, masked by a stubborn defiance I also found relation to.

My ruined heart gave a tug in my chest, and now I *really* wanted to look away, but still found myself unable. The Wolf pup rested her little brown head between her paws, her gaze holding mine as though unawares of the spell it had cast over me.

Before I could think better of doing so, I found myself sending a thought to the girl in the telepathic manner Wolf-kind were capable of sharing with one another.

"Do not be afraid, little one," I thought.

I knew I had been heard when the pup in the cage lifted her head, her ears perking and swiveling. Her hazel eyes gleamed with unshed tears as the summer sun beamed brightly down from above, and I wished foolishly that I could offer more than empty words of solace to the child, that I could offer more to the world than a fight on a Friday night that ended in my death or that of another.

But that was not the way things were. That was not the reality we lived in.

The wagon continued its slow trundle until it was out of sight.

The smell of booze, sweat, and Werewolf filled the *Blood Moon Bar and Tavern* even though most of last night's customers had left hours before. I suspected the stench had permeated the walls, and no matter how much polish Bernard the bartender rubbed over the bar's gleaming wooden surface, or lemon-scented cleaner he used to mop the floors, the underlying scents would always be evident to a Wolf's nose.

Bernard offered me a smile that revealed his multi-colored, crooked teeth. As always, he wore slacks and a button-up collared shirt tucked tightly into his pants and rolled up at the sleeves. His thick black eyebrows sat low over his dark brown eyes, and his mustache twitched as he breathed through his nose.

"There's my favorite fighter," Bernard said, pouring a glass of apple juice and sliding it down the bar to me before I had to ask.

I pulled out a stool and sat down before taking a long swig of the sweet juice. "You say that to all the female Dogs," I said, running the back of my hand over my mouth.

Bernard held up a finger, his crooked grin stretching up nearly to his ears. "But I only *mean* it when I say it to you," he claimed, and winked.

I rolled my eyes and shook my head. "What are the numbers looking like tonight, Bernie?"

He quirked a thick brow, meeting my gaze square. "You're not gonna like 'em," he said.

I only returned his stare unblinkingly.

Bernie sighed. "Twenty-to-one you lose to the Bear."

I took a swig of my apple juice and considered asking him to add a good shot of moonshine, but decided not to. "So little faith in me," I mumbled, making sure my tone held no inflection.

The bartender sucked at his multi-shaded teeth. "It ain't like that," he said. "You see her roll by earlier? That bitch is *huge*. Hell, *I* wouldn't even want to fight her." He let out a chuckle, his mustache twitching. "She's probably bigger than I am in Wolf form."

I did not disagree, but said, "You should be an inspirational speaker. Seriously. I think you'd be great at it."

He huffed a tight laugh. "There's that sense of humor we all love. But, anyway, the odds have been against you before," he said. "Hell, you've been the underdog since you was a pup. They had you slated as a Bait dog, and you proved them wrong then." He chuckled again, but there was no humor in it. "I still remember how shocked Lazar was when he came in here that day. Going on and on about the runt that killed his most promising pup."

I tapped the edge of my glass with two fingers, reconsidering that shot of moonshine. Bernie uncapped a bottle and obliged, watching me as he poured the amber liquid.

"And that son of a bitch has hated me ever since," I mumbled, and downed the glass in one deep gulp. I hated the taste of it, but the alcohol settled warmly in my belly, loosened some of the tension stringing my shoulders.

"That's what happens when you're as lacking as Lazar in all the places that matter," said a sultry voice behind me.

I looked over my shoulder to see Goldie, her ginger hair tousled from a long night. She wore the same slip of a dress she always wore. It stopped several inches above her knees and hung over her thin shoulders as if clinging for purchase. Her teeth were straight and white as she grinned at me, her blue eyes twinkling like sapphires and perpetually full of mischief.

"Morning," I said, and my eyes caught on the bruises on the girl's neck. I nodded toward them. "You gonna tell me who did that?"

Goldie's brow quirked and she placed a hand on the curve of her hip. "If I do, you gonna go start a fight that ends in a crippled Dog and more lashes to the back for you?"

I considered this a moment, then shrugged.

Goldie sighed and slid onto the stool beside me, her full lips pursed. "We have to choose our battles," she mumbled, quiet enough so that only I would hear. "I shouldn't have to tell you that. And, besides, I'm not watching you get whipped on my behalf again. Not a chance in hell."

As I studied the ring of bruises around my friend's neck, my jaw clenched. "Just tell me who did it, and I'll go have a little chat with him."

Goldie snorted and rapped her knuckles a couple times on the bar to get Bernard's attention. He slid her a neat of her preferred poison before moving down the bar to finish stacking clean glasses. After she took a slow swig, Goldie said, "This is our life, love. They use your body in The Ring, and mine in the bedroom." She took another swig, her mouth turning down into a grimace. "We all have our roles to play."

As much as I hated to admit it, I knew Goldie was right. We were both slaves, both property of Master Bo Benedict, like the rest of the people in this gods-forsaken town, as the black collars around our necks boldly pronounced.

Despite the awful reality that was life as a Dog, I was thankful that I hadn't been chosen for the life Goldie had endured. I would rather face a million rounds in The Ring than one night as a working girl. I really didn't know how Goldie did it.

"We could run away together," I whispered.

"We wouldn't get far. They'd catch us."

"I know."

"Then why say things like that?"

I met my friend's gaze. "So that you know there is always another option."

"A choice between crap and poop is just a shit choice."

"You're a true poet."

Goldie winked, her red lips curving up. "I am a woman of many talents."

"That, you are, buttercup," said a rough voice from the front of the bar. My back stiffened as I tilted my head to take in the new arrival.

I would have known they were Hounds even if they hadn't been wearing their uniforms, whips coiled at their waists. The bastards had a way of carrying themselves that was unmistakable.

The one who had spoken was a beefy Wolf who walked with his chest puffed up and his arms tensed outward at his sides as if he thought he was just too buff for the world. I resisted the urge to roll my eyes. The other two Hounds that had arrived with him sauntered over to an open table and plopped into seats, snapping their fingers at Bernard the bartender. But the one who'd spoken approached Goldie and I at the bar.

As he got closer, I could smell fear bloom under the floral scent of Goldie's perfume. Without having to ask, I knew this was the Wolf who was responsible for the bruises on my friend's neck.

Of course it would be a Hound. *Of course.*

"Hello, Mekhi," Goldie said, her voice the soft purr she used for all of her customers. Goldie was a master at hiding her feelings beneath a cool mask. She had no choice but to be.

Mekhi, his brown eyes gleaming, picked up one of Goldie's ginger curls and let it slide through his fingers. "Hey there, honey," he said. "You miss me?"

I felt a growl trying to bubble up from my belly and swallowed it down. I kept my gaze on the empty glass between my fingers, my jaw clenched tight enough to ache. An image of my hand smashing the glass into the Hound's head flashed through my mind, and a crooked grin pulled up my lips at the thought.

"Of course I did," Goldie replied, rapping her knuckles on the bar again for a refill—the only outward indicator that she was not comfortable with the Hound's presence.

When his gaze settled on me, I felt it slither over my skin. "Who's your friend?" Mekhi asked. He moved a little closer to me, and his nostrils flared as he took in my scent.

Sensing the shift in me, Goldie tried to reclaim the attention of the Hound. "She ain't nobody," Goldie said, running her fingers down the Hound's shoulder in a suggestive manner.

He would not be deterred. His hand snaked up and brushed aside my dark hair, revealing my shoulder and neck. Though I did not give him the satisfaction of acknowledging him, I could *feel* the grin stretching over the Hound's lips as he looked at the brand there.

Like all Dogs, I had been branded years ago. A crescent moon burned onto the top right shoulder blade of my back. The skin there was tan and scarred, and the moon was purplish and raised enough that one could trace the shape of it in the dark. Like all the others, I'd received the brand on the same day I'd received the thick black collar around my neck, both symbols of my slavery.

Now I had no control over the deep growl that rumbled through my belly and up my throat. My eyes lit up Wolf-Gold, and the tiny hairs on the back of my neck stood on end.

Because he was a fool, the Hound named Mekhi laughed, a grating sound that rang in my ears. Goldie's voice echoed telepathically through my head, but I hardly heard her.

"Just let it go, Rukiya. For gods' sake, just let it go."

My friend was deadly serious, which was evident by the use of my full name, if not by her tone. But as far as I was concerned, the gods had never done anything for *my* sake, so I would *not* just let it go.

3
_____

If the Gravediggers had a step above the Dogs and the working ladies, then the Hounds had a whole flight of stairs. The Masters also dictated their lives and actions, but they were like the police of the Wolf world. Hounds kept the Dogs (and everybody else) in line. When there was punishing to be done, it was the Hounds who enacted it. They did what they were told first and foremost, and otherwise, what they wanted.

Inevitably, this led to the abuse of their power (evidence of which could currently be found on Goldie's neck). To say the least of the matter, I had a rocky past with Hounds, and the evidence of *that* could be found among the various scars that marred my otherwise golden skin.

So when Mekhi the Hound placed his filthy fingers on the crescent moon on my back, and traced the raised skin there as if he were my long lost lover, that switch inside me snapped to its alternate setting.

In the next moment, my movements as fluid as liquid, I'd broken the fragile bones in Mekhi's fingers. The snap that echoed through the bar set the Wolves' teeth on edge. Before this could be processed, I twisted the Hound's arm up hard, causing his body to lurch forward. With my free hand, I slammed the side of his head to the shiny surface of the bar, still wrenching his arm up behind his back at an unnatural angle.

For a split second, silence fell over the room, but I was unaware of it. All I could hear was the rushing of blood in my ears and all I could feel was the fire coursing through my veins. My eyes blazed Wolf-Gold, and my lips pulled back in a Wolfish grin as I leaned down to whisper in Mekhi the Hound's ear.

In a voice so calm it chilled my own heart, I said, "You know what kind of males beat on females? Cowards, that's who."

"Rook! Watch out!"

Goldie's voice echoed in my head and I released my hold on the Hound in time to duck the blow of one of the other Hounds who'd risen from their seats at the table. The Hound's baton sliced through the air just above my head, the breeze of its wake stirring my hair.

The beast in me that relished the fight awoke like a dragon from a light slumber. It was always there. Always close. Always at odds with the other parts of me. On many long nights, when I would lie awake, unable to find dream's doorstep, I would secretly worry that one day all that would be left of me was the beast within. With each life I took, it was like something essential was chipping away inside me.

But in the heat of the battle, when I yielded to that beast, these things made no matter. I ducked the blow of the Hound who'd snuck up on me, sweeping my leg out and knocking him off his feet. He hadn't even landed on his tailbone before I had taken out the third Hound, punching him hard enough in the solar plexus to leave him gasping for air.

Mekhi was recovering by then. His lips were pulled back over his teeth, his eyes aglow, and his mangled fingers set at an unnatural angle. A deep growl issued from his throat.

"You *stupid bitch*," he snarled, snatching the baton from his belt with his good hand and raising it into the air. "You're gonna pay for that."

He swung—hard enough to knock teeth out, but I was too fast for him. I danced back, the baton cutting through the air where my head had been just moments ago, and kicked a barstool with the sole of my boot. The stool skidded fast across the hard floor and knocked into Mekhi, the air rushing out of him in an *oomph!*

The other two Hounds circled, calculating and coordinating an attack now that they understood the degree of threat they were facing. One side of my mouth pulled up into a crooked grin, and I settled into a fighter's stance, my right leg shifting back and my muscles loose and ready.

I met the Hounds' gazes with the burning challenge in my own. It was too late now; I would pay for this dearly either way.

So I might as well make it good.

～

"Enough."

The command echoed through the bar, drawing the attention of the three Hounds to the door, where the person who had issued it stood.

I could feel a presence there, standing before the swinging double doors, blocking out most of the light with a tall, wide form. But I didn't dare flip my gaze away from the other Hounds, not when my body was still thrumming with the rhythm of battle, my tongue thick with the need to taste their blood.

However, as the three Hounds snapped to attention like children caught out of line, I realized that one of their superiors must have entered, and my gaze slid to the door at last.

His eyes were bluer than any Wolf's I'd ever seen, and his hair was a shade of golden brown that nearly glistened in the sunlight. He was tall and lean and muscled, his skin a shade that suggested many kisses from the sun. By the way he carried himself, I knew he was indeed a Head Hound. Judging by the black uniform with the blue anchor sigil over his right breast, he belonged to Reagan Ramsey, Master of the West Coast Dog fighting ring, no doubt in town for the fights this weekend.

"What happened?" he asked, his voice deep and low.

Mekhi the Dipshit spoke first, jerking his chin in my direction. "This bitch was causing trouble," he said, his chest somehow managing to puff out more. "We were handling it, though."

My teeth ground together, and beside me, Goldie cringed, anticipating my snide remark. But the Head Hound spoke again before I could.

"Looked to me like *she* was handling *you*," he said.

If I hadn't been so stunned, I might have laughed. Mekhi, on the other hand, looked mad enough for steam to billow from his ears.

"Go back to your posts," the Head Hound commanded, his tone allowing for no argument.

The two Hounds whose names I didn't know started toward the door, but Mekhi held up his mangled fingers. "She did this," he snarled. "She has to be whipped for it. It's the law... *sir*."

The growl that issued from the Head Hound's throat was laced with enough warning that my stomach muscles clenched.

"I know the law, Mekhi," was all he said.

Mekhi cast one more burning glance at him, during which I had to resist the urge to stick my tongue out at him like a child, before shoving out the double doors to join his weak ass companions.

The Head Hound with the golden brown hair and crystal blue eyes remained unmoving.

I pulled out a stool and slid atop it, giving him my back—an obvious show of disrespect.

From behind the bar, Bernard flashed me a warning look, and I could smell the fear floating off Goldie, who had apparently given up trying to talk sense into me. I appeared relaxed, but I fully anticipated an attack of some sort.

Instead, the blue-eyed Hound approached the bar and stood beside me, close enough that his large form towered over me in a way that made the hackles of my inner beast rise.

For a moment, he said nothing, but the clean, masculine scent of him filled my nose with his proximity. Still, I was tensed for an attack.

He ordered a neat of moonshine from Bernard, who poured the drink with watchful, anticipatory eyes. The Head Hound swallowed the alcohol in one deep gulp, set the glass down, and turned to look at me.

I kept my eyes forward, dismissive and unconcerned. I took a slow sip of my spiked apple juice and pretended not to notice his attention or location.

"You're lucky I walked in when I did," he growled, voice low and threatening.

My brow quirked, my eyes flicking toward him and away again in utter dismissal. "Pretty sure your boys were the lucky ones," I said.

The look that flashed behind his eyes was so intimidating that I almost flinched, but managed not to. The shade of his gaze had turned to that of ice.

"Stay away from those males," he said, too calmly. "I don't know how things work here in the middle of nowhere, but those are not Hounds you want to mess with. So don't be stupid, and stay in your place, *Dog*."

With that, the Head Hound shoved away from the bar and exited.

I wasn't aware of clenching my fist until a sharp pain shot through my palm where the glass that had held my moonshine and apple juice lie shattered between my fingers.

4

My blood fell in thick red droplets to make a small pool on the surface of the bar, the room utterly silent. I welcomed the stinging in my hand; it tempered the rage sizzling through me.

I was aware of Goldie approaching me slowly from my right side, her hands held out and up, like a tamer courting a lion, though she surely knew I would never hurt her.

Goldie's sweet voice sang a familiar tune low and gentle in my head. *"Hush, little Wolf, don't go chasing after doom... Save your spirit, stoke your fire, give your troubles to the moon..."*

Slowly, I felt the wave of anger subsiding, pulling back like a tide. I breathed deeply through my nose and rolled my neck. Opening my hand, I surveyed the damage and let out a low sigh.

Goldie stepped up beside me and took my hand, inspecting the cuts. She clicked her tongue. "You're going to get yourself killed," she mumbled.

I met my friend's gaze. "No matter what, that's pretty much how this thing ends."

Goldie rolled her eyes, but a small smile pulled up her lips and she leaned in to give me a quick kiss on my cheek. "Always my hero," she said.

I shrugged.

"Yeah, well, you owe me another glass," Bernard chimed in, his face scrunched up and mustache twitching as he swept the broken glass into a trash bin and wiped down the bar. "You sure know how to pick 'em," he added.

"Who was that?" Goldie asked, her eyes going to the door as if she could still see the Head Hound standing there. "He was very... handsome."

I snorted, and Bernie shook his head. The bartender made it his business to know everyone who passed through Dogshead. In fact, he made it his business to know things in general, which was why I never fully trusted the male.

"I'm pretty sure that must have been Ryker," Bernie said. "He's Reagan Ramsey's Head Hound. They say Ramsey raised Ryker himself, took him in when he was just a pup. I'm actually surprised he didn't drag you outta here and whip you in the street."

Goldie had moved closer to the bar, and she leaned forward now, giving the bartender a little gander down the front of her dress. Goldie and I both knew that Bernie favored her, and that he would give information more freely if she flirted with him.

Despite me having told Goldie not to do this, my friend used the bartender's affection whenever she could to get what she needed. With the life that Goldie had been forced to live, I refused to judge her for it. Actually, I refused to judge Goldie for anything, and Goldie returned the favor. It was part of the steel that had forged our friendship.

"Why do you say that?" Goldie asked.

One side of Bernie's mouth pulled up in a crooked smile. "He's as loyal as they come to his Master. And there's a reason he's Head Hound... They say he sold his brother out to Ramsey, and then murdered him while the male slept." Bernie shook his head. "What kind of Wolf does that?"

A small stone settled in my gut, and Goldie shuddered beside me. "Apparently, a handsome and heartless one," Goldie answered.

"Or a crazy one," Bernie added. He looked at me now, his eyes as serious as an undertaker's. "He's not someone you want to go messing with, Rook. And by the looks of 'em, neither are those other Hounds."

I would never admit it, but the warning shook me slightly. But then I looked back at Goldie, at the dark bruises around my friend's neck.

"You let me know if that pig touches you again," I said, and there was no yield in my expression. "Promise me, Goldie, because I'll kill him if he does."

Goldie's face went slightly pale, a reaction to a memory and an understanding. She knew for a fact I would do what I said I would do.

It would not be the first time.

Goldie sighed, the sweet scent of her filling the space. She rubbed the spot between her eyebrows with her palm and squeezed her eyes shut. "Let's just get through today and tomorrow, my friend," she said. She opened her eyes and gave me a small smile. "We'll worry about murdering abusers after you win your eighteenth fight tomorrow night."

Bernard nodded. "And if you manage to beat the Bear, you'll get to go to The Games this year, since you're finally of the age, and the Bear is the West Coast Champion."

He didn't add that no one expected me to win it, that the odds were stacked against me, and that the rosters for this year's Games had already been drawn up. He didn't need to.

The Games were an annual event that had been taking place for nearly five hundred years. Like so many other terrible things, their start came shortly after the disaster that was the Great War and the subsequent Dividing of the Territories.

The rules of The Games were simple, two Wolves went into The Ring, and one came out. The victors would continue to be matched up over the course of a week until there were only four Wolves left. Two females, and two males. The final matches were held after a big banquet, where the richest of the Wolves dressed in their finest and placed bets on their favored Dogs.

Out of one hundred competitors, two would remain at the end of the week. One male victor, and one female. Their reward would be twenty-five points added to their Count, which was no insignificant amount.

Outside of the annual Games, each fight in The Ring—like the fight I faced tomorrow night—was worth one point toward the winning Dog's Count. Reach one hundred points, and a Dog could win his or her freedom.

In five hundred years of history, only two Dogs had ever earned that freedom. And neither of them had been female.

As if reading my mind, Goldie's sultry voice sounded in my head.

"There's a first for everything, love," she said. *"If anyone can do this, it's you. Mind over matter, remember?"*

I had never outright told my friend how many times I'd drawn strength from her, but I had a feeling Goldie knew. If the barely-adult young woman standing before me could put mind over matter in the bedrooms above this hellhole night after night, I could do that in The Ring tomorrow night and find a way to beat the Bear.

And for Goldie, there was no Count, no hope for an exit ticket; her sentence was for life.

As if to prove the point, a rather disgusting male with a beer gut, baldhead, and odor that reeked of sweat and onions sauntered up to Goldie. Without ceremony, my friend took the fat

Wolf's hand and led him toward the staircase lining the back of the bar.

Goldie only glanced back once at me over her shoulder, giving me a small, sad smile before disappearing up the stairs, the balding male trailing hungrily behind her.

~

N ight was falling as I finished up my workout in the woods near the edge of Master Benedict's property. Sweat drenched my shirt, making the cotton fabric cling to me, and my bangs stuck to my forehead.

I felt good, though. Strong and capable and hungry. I was a stickler about keeping my body as honed as possible, more so than most of the other Dogs of the Benedict plantation. As a Wolf that fell on the smaller side physically, doing so had no doubt helped win my current survival.

I had managed to push the image of the Bear sitting all alone in the back of that wagon from my mind as I climbed the high trees of the forest, leapt over rocks and streams, and ran through the acres of Benedict's land until my muscles were screaming from exhaustion and my lungs begging for air.

But as I stepped out of that mindset I slipped into while working out, the unpleasant thoughts swooped back in like bats to a belfry, and I leaned back against one of the tall oaks, studying the dapples of sunlight peeking through the green canopy above.

My chest heaved as I sucked in the clean oxygen, my skin glowing with moisture as a small breeze rustled through the trees. I closed my eyes and willed my mind to clear.

I was interrupted a moment later when I heard the snapping of branches and crunching of leaves underfoot someone who was moving. Someone who was moving *fast*.

My senses snapped to high alert and I crouched, maintaining

my position behind the tree and peering carefully around it in the direction of the commotion.

The sounds of crushing leaves and twigs grew louder, and I lifted my nose to the wind and tested the air, picking up a young female scent followed by that of three older males. I closed my eyes and tilted my head, concentrating on my powerful hearing as the fleeing Wolf and her three pursuers pulled nearer.

When the Wolf pup from the carriage this morning—the one with those hazel eyes that were so like my own—came crashing through the brush, I didn't have to question what had happened.

Somehow, the child must have slipped past the handlers, and was on the run.

And once they caught her, they would whip her or put her down. While the habitants of Dogshead stood and watched.

Don't do it, warned a voice in my head. *It's got nothing to do with you.*

I let out a quiet curse as my body disobeyed my mind's orders.

~

My muscles were tensed and ready to strike, like a snake assuming a coil. I waited until the perfect moment, just as the pup was passing, and spun around the tree behind which I was crouched, scooping up the pup like a fish in a net.

Shift, I commanded telepathically, and set the pup on her paws. She only stared up at me, ears flat on her head.

I resisted the urge to shout the command again, but sensing that this would only accomplish scaring the child, I kneeled before her and gripped her brown muzzle gently but firmly in my hand, forcing the pup to hold my gaze.

"If you want to live, you'll have to trust me," I said. *"Now, shift."*

Whether it was because the child had a keen sense of preservation, or because she was too frightened to disobey, finally, she shifted into her human form.

The transformation took precious seconds, faster than that of a full-grown Wolf. Standing before me now was a small girl of no more than five, dirt streaking her face and caked into her brown hair. Hazel eyes stared up at me, terrified, but defiant.

I removed my sweaty shirt and pulled it over the girl's head. I snatched a handful of muddy earth from the ground and quickly rubbed it over the child and myself in an effort to mask our scents. Once that was done, I scooped the girl into my arms, and slid her around so that she was on my back, her arms keeping purchase around my neck. Her small weight was nothing for my supernatural strength.

"Hold on," I told her.

Closing in fast, I could still hear the three Hounds crashing through the forest. I bent my knees and leapt up to grip the lowest hanging, sturdy branch of a large oak, pulling the child and myself up into the canopy with ease.

Then I started to climb.

5

It was not a feat a mere human could have easily managed, but I was no mere human.

For helping the child, however, I was certainly a fool.

Through the green canopy below, I could see the Hounds searching. So many Wolves used these woods that I knew it would be difficult to pick out the scent of the child for all the overlying smells—difficult, but not impossible.

The Hounds' ears, however, would still be as sharp as ever, and one whimper from the child could alert them to our position. My heart was pounding so hard in my chest I thought it was a wonder they didn't hear *that*.

I had climbed as high as I could go, the floor of the forest forty feet or so below. The wind blew more heavily up here, and the smaller branches surrounding us swayed with its direction. Overhead, the day was dimming by the minute, the skies growing a deeper blue with each passing breath.

The child was utterly still and silent in my arms, her head tucked into my chest as her big hazel eyes stared down through the branches below. The Hounds, still in their human forms, roamed about, their noses testing the air and their heads tilting this way and that in an unmistakable Wolf-like manner.

When the Head Hound from the bar earlier appeared through the surrounding brush, I scarcely dared to breathe. Those blue eyes shifted and scanned, his golden-brown hair stirring slightly in the breeze. His heavy boots hardly made a sound as he moved through the forest.

The Hound prowled nearer and nearer to the tree in which the child and I were hiding, coming within ten feet... eight... three, until he was standing directly below us.

I swallowed hard, my arms tightening in the slightest around the child between them. I'd been a fool, a *damn fool* for trying to save the child. Even if the Hounds didn't find us, how would I get her to safety? What could I offer her that was better than her prescribed fate?

Nothing—that was the answer. But as the Head Hound with the blue eyes moved nearer to the trunk of the tree in which we were perched, and bent his head to sniff at the bark I'd scaled only moments ago, I decided I'd save later troubles for later.

The world stilled for all of three heartbeats, both the child in my arms and I staring below at the Head Hound sniffing around the trunk of the tree where we were hiding.

Then the moment passed, and the Hound's head cocked to the side in that Wolf-like manner. His blue eyes lifted to the canopy, and found my gaze waiting there.

I cursed the gods, same as they'd done to me so very long ago.

~

Think. Don't panic. *Think.*

I watched with increasing horror as the cruel Hound from the bar—Mekhi, his name was—appeared a handful of paces to the south, asking if the other Hound had found anything.

I needed to move. We were sitting ducks up here, and this had been the worst idea ever, and the child and I would likely be beaten for this, or worse.

Think, damn it.

Shield us from direct sight, that's what I needed to do. I spied a branch ten feet or so below and fifteen paces to the left, around the wide trunk that might just be thick enough to screen us from the Hounds' sight line below.

But if I set my weight in the wrong place, if a branch groaned or a leaf went twirling to the forest floor below, it could draw the eyes of Mekhi the Hound. For whatever reason, the Head Hound named Ryker didn't seem eager to reveal us, but I had no questions about what a Wolf like Mekhi was capable of.

I fought against the shudder that ran through me as I thought about what Mekhi would do to the little girl in my arms. More often than not, it was the runaways who got made into brutal examples, reminders of why one obeyed.

Sending up a silent prayer, I adjusted the girl in my arms and eased into a crouch, hardly daring to breathe as I did so, all concentration centered on maintaining balance. Below, Mekhi prowled closer to the tree, and for reasons wholly unknown to me, the Head Hound still didn't alert his inferior to our presence above.

Holding my focus in an iron grip, I was able to edge closer to the thick trunk of the oak, my hand reaching out to use it for balance. On the ground, the two Hounds were having what seemed to be a clipped exchange, and though my powerful ears could hear them easily, I could not devote any mind to the exact words.

I began to edge my way around the trunk, all of my weight and that of the child poised on the balls of my feet.

Somehow, in a handful of seconds that stretched on for an eternity, I maneuvered to the other side of the tree and onto the thick branch there. Moving as smoothly as water through fingers,

I brought up my legs and eased onto my back, lying flat on the branch with the child flat on top of me. I rolled my shoulders inward and crossed my legs at the ankles, making myself as small as possible.

I didn't dare move or look below again until the scents and sounds of both Hounds had long faded on the wind.

~

Later, after the sun had fallen and the almost-full moon had risen over the Benedict plantation, the child and I crouched within the corn stalks ringing Dogshead, moonlight making our almost-matching hazel eyes appear silver.

As we crouched there, I tried to let my mind catch up with the turn of events. I had a big fight in The Ring tomorrow night, and that was what I should be focused on, certainly not trying to figure out how to save a pup that had been doomed from the start.

The girl shifted beside me, and I turned my head to see big hazel eyes staring up at me, an intelligence behind them that suggested she knew what was passing through my head.

Pushing away the discomfort this incited, I focused on my ears, listening intently to determine when to step out of the cover of the corn stalks. When all was clear, I took the child's hand and gave a silent command that she remain quiet as the two of us darted across the clearing and toward a row of squat, wooden buildings flanking the main street of Dogshead.

When we reached the targeted cabin, I snuck around to the back, where I knew a window waited. Standing on my tiptoes, I peered inside, finding the washroom dark within. Knowing that the latch on the window had been broken for months, I gently pushed on the glass, swinging it open just wide enough to squeeze the child, and then myself, through.

I sent my thoughts out telepathically, and a moment later,

Goldie opened the bathroom door and flipped on the light. Her red-gold hair was set high on her head, long curls flowing down to dangle over her bare, dainty shoulders. Makeup that was in need of reapplication smeared her pretty face, and the scent of various Wolves clung to her skin, her breath. I would never stop wanting to murder someone every time I saw my friend in such a condition. But now was not the time for all that.

Goldie's brow was creased in confusion, and she spoke before she took in the situation. "What are you doing?" she asked.

And then her sapphire eyes drifted down to the child standing behind my back.

Next, Goldie posed what was not at all an unreasonable question.

"Have you lost your gods damned mind?"

I couldn't exactly confirm or deny this, so I swallowed, and said, "We need your help."

6

Apparently, the question warranted repeating.

"Have you lost your gods damned mind?" Goldie asked again.

I tried not to cringe at the validity of it. "We need your help," I repeated.

For Goldie, I knew, there was no decision to make. I had asked for her help, and she would give it, because that was how it was with us.

But that didn't mean she wouldn't grumble about it the whole time.

She did so as she ushered us out of the washroom and into the main room of the cabin. The smell of explicit acts still hung in the air, but a scowl from Goldie had me snapping my mouth shut. Goldie grabbed a small vial of perfume from the dresser against the wall and squirted it around the room. Both the child's and my strong noses crinkled.

Goldie rolled her eyes, crossing her arms over her chest. She gave the child still hiding behind my legs a gentle smile, then looked sharply at me.

"What did you do?" Goldie hissed.

"She ran," I said, not knowing what else to say but the truth. "They would've beaten her... so I... stepped in."

Goldie gaped. "You 'stepped in'? Are you out of your gods damned mind?" A little shame crossed Goldie's pretty face as the child glanced up at her, but she shook her head at me, and switched to communicating telepathically.

"They'll whip or kill you both for this. What were you hoping to accomplish?"

I couldn't keep the slight snap from my telepathic tone. *"I wasn't 'hoping to accomplish' anything. I just acted. I know it was stupid, but it's too late to go back now. They'll put me down quick if they think I'm assisting runaways."*

For a moment, silence hung between us. Goldie stared at me, and I stared back at Goldie.

I cleared my throat, but spoke again silently. *"That's not all,"* I said.

"Oh dear gods," Goldie grumbled aloud. "*How* can that not be all?"

A chill snaked down my spine, but I didn't allow myself to shudder beneath it. "That Head Hound from the bar earlier... He saw us."

Goldie threw her hands up, her arched brows practically kissing her hairline. "What the hell do you mean, 'he saw you'?"

If the situation weren't so tense, I might have laughed at all the parroting. Instead, I explained what happened in the woods, and again, silence fell between us.

Goldie's voice was barely more than a whisper as she glanced down at the child and back at me again. "Rook... Remember what Bernie said about what that Hound did to his own brother?" She paused, as if the words needed to sink in. "What if he wasn't *really* letting you go?"

I could feel my face slowly drain of color, and as if in answer to my friend's question, there came a harsh rap upon the cabin door.

~

All three of us in the cabin froze like dew on a winter's morning. Three sets of eyes went to the cabin door, and three hearts skipped beats as that harsh rap sounded again.

"Hide," snapped Goldie's voice in my head, and this broke whatever panicked trance had befallen me. I scooped up the child and slipped back into the washroom, sliding the door shut behind me at the same time as a third knock sounded on the cabin door.

Pressing my back against the washroom wall and holding the child against me as though that might keep her silent, I held my breath.

Beyond the thin wall separating the washroom from the main room of the cabin, my sensitive ears picked up the sound of the cabin door swinging open.

~

I was cursing myself like a Witch as I sat cradled with the child in my arms, her heartbeat rapid within her small chest. The moment seemed to stretch on for an eternity, and I ran through scenario after scenario, trying to find a best-case candidate.

Nothing I could think of fit the bill. I couldn't imagine a way that this didn't end badly.

Assisting runaway Dogs was a crime punishable with death. Not only would they kill me for harboring the child, they would make sure that my execution was made publicly. They would draw it out. My blood would flood the dusty streets, its evidence remaining until the next real rain.

And the child. I shuddered. I couldn't think about what they might do to the child.

When the door to the washroom opened, I nearly leapt out of my skin, so lost I'd been in my own morbid thoughts. Though my fists rose in a gut reaction to fight, I saw that it was only Goldie standing in the doorway.

"It was just Bernard," she said. "I got rid of him, but he'll be back." She looked between the child and me, unwilling to tell us to go, but terrified of letting us stay.

I realized only then that this move of mine had not been fair to her, and I once again picked the child up, this time to take my leave.

"Thank you," I told her silently. *"I'll figure this out. Don't worry."*

I began to pass the child through the washroom window and set her down on the outside, having no idea where we'd go from there.

"Don't be ridiculous," Goldie snapped, and the look on her face indicated she already regretted what she was about to say. "Keep her here tonight. In the morning, we'll figure out our next move."

The air rushed out of me, a breath I hadn't realized I'd been holding.

Before I could profess my gratitude, Goldie knelt before the child where she was curled up against the washroom wall and asked a question I'd been avoiding since I'd intercepted the pup in the woods.

"What's your name?" Goldie asked, her voice gentle and almost... motherly. Unlike I'd ever heard it before. For whatever reason, it made my cold heart ache.

The child was silent for so long that I thought she wouldn't answer. But her hazel eyes met mine as she said, "Amara."

She was so small, her voice so young, that something I'd long suppressed reared its angry head within me. At the horror of it, at the *injustice* of it all. It was such an ugly world we lived in, and I cursed the gods who'd created it.

"That's a pretty name," Goldie said, still using that soothing voice. "This is Rook, and my name is Goldie, and we're going to try to help you, Amara... but you're going to have to trust us. Can you do that?"

Amara's eyes darted between the two of us. At last, she nodded her little head.

It was cowardly of me, and I knew it, but I almost wished she hadn't. I almost wished I'd never come across her out in those woods.

Because it felt like the start of something, like the first yank on a thread that would lead to an utter unraveling.

And some instinct within me knew that once unraveled, this was not a tapestry that could be rewoven, but rather, something that would need to be strung anew.

7

We left Amara in Goldie's cabin, making the child swear upon the gods that she would stay put and remain silent until we returned.

Goldie would conduct her night's work in the rooms above the *Blood Moon Bar*. This would cost her a percentage of her earnings (on top of the percentage our Master, Bo Benedict, already took), but it was a sacrifice Goldie made without batting an eye. If I hadn't already loved the young lady, I would have done so just for this.

After my friend double-checked the lock on the cabin door, sealing Amara inside, she turned to me, her pretty face grave. With so many prying ears, she only dared to speak mind-to-mind. While Wolves were not mind readers, we had the ability to speak to each other telepathically as long as the communicating parties let their mental shields down enough to do so. This, of course, required a certain amount of trust, but it was an ability that came in particularly handy when in Wolf form.

"We have to get her out of Dogshead. Maybe to one of the coasts."

I considered this. *"But where?"* I asked. *"Where can she go that she won't be picked up by one of the Collectors or Sellers?"*

"Perhaps that is something you should have considered before *you decided to assist a runaway."*

I swallowed at the tone, and was too aware of her correctness to respond in kind. *"I'm sorry,"* I said. It sounded lame, inadequate. And that's because it was.

Overhead, the nearly full moon had risen, casting its bluish glow over the countryside, dimming the stars in its brilliance.

Goldie sighed through her nose, her red lips pursing. *"No,"* she said. *"Don't be sorry. What's done is done. And this wretched world needs more acts of kindness, so don't ever apologize for adding to them."*

"I've put your life in danger," I said. *"I've put both our lives in danger."*

The sound of Goldie's sultry laugh echoed in my head, though there was no humor in it. *"Wake up, love. We're always in danger, and if we're being honest, our lives aren't so great as to matter should we lose them... Where would you rather die, in The Ring, or in the attempt to commit a kindness?"*

A real smile formed on my face, as rare as a snowstorm in summer. My head tilted in a manner I knew was Wolf-like.

"If I liked females that way," I told her, *"I'd probably ask you to be my mate."*

Goldie's pretty face lit up in an answering grin. An image of her linking her arm through mine passed through my head; a display of friendship that we'd never been allowed in our lifetimes, not with so many eyes and gainful people around. To love in this world was the ultimate weakness, and one that could get you killed.

Goldie's response was the last of the evening as we slipped through the double doors of the *Blood Moon Bar,* soon to feign total indifference for each other.

"And if I liked females that way," my friend told me, *"I'd probably say yes."*

~

O n the nights before a big fight, Dogshead turned into a place that gave definition to the saying *howling at the moon*. With Reagan Ramsey, Master of the West Coast Wolf Pack, in town with all of his slaves, servants, and lackeys, the shear number of new faces alone was enough to set the town in frenzy.

The Midlands Region, where I had been born and slaved, and which Dogshead was the center of, did not have major cities, as there were rumored to be on the coasts. This meant excitement was hard to come by, with the land being mostly fields of lavender wheat or forests and rolling hills of vibrant green. The Midlands Region was the vastest amongst the five Regions, and people whispered tales of great beasts and wicked creatures roaming the lands that made those from outside stumble and hesitate before entering.

In the late spring and early summer months, mighty tornados ravaged region, ripping trees from the roots and houses from the foundations, claiming the lives of those too poor or too stupid to have prepared and taken cover. On the coasts, Mother Nature pillaged with roaring waters from the surrounding seas and tremors on land. Here, She purged with mighty winds and raging fires started by lightning striking down from the heavens. Fires that burned for days, wiping large slates bare and clean.

I had never been beyond the borders of Dogshead, knew nothing about the world save for what I'd heard in whispered stories. Odds were, I would die before ever going beyond this dreadful place, but this was a fact I'd accepted long ago.

Around midnight, I stumbled out of *Blood Moon*, bleary-eyed and more than a little drunk on moonshine. It was not a habit I was proud of—the drinking, but it was one almost every Dog and working lady acquired by the age of ten. It was how we dealt with the reality of our lives. Our addiction was part of the poison that kept us chained to our stations, same as the moon-shaped brands on our shoulders and the collars around our necks.

The world was swaying, the dusty street outside the bar tilting as I made my way into the moonlit night. I hadn't seen Goldie for the last three hours, as she'd disappeared up those stairs with two hungry-looking Wolves with leering faces. My friend was no doubt in the throes of her own liquor-induced stupor, the burning drink likely the only way she got through these long nights.

My boots trudged over the dirt street, kicking up plumes of dust and sending pebbles tumbling out of my path. A cool night breeze swept through the square, kissing the sheen of sweat clinging to my forehead, my neck.

My vision adjusted to the gloom with more of a delay than when I was clear-headed, my eyes at last adapting to see in the dark. The sounds of fighting, laughing, arguing, and fucking rose up into the night, creating a symphony alongside the night bugs and creatures that occupied the surrounding fields.

Both Wolves and Vampires prowled about the town square, the latter no doubt in town for the fights tomorrow evening, their faces among those that would look upon me when I faced down the Bear. They would place bets, shout praise or vulgar disappointment, and thrust their arms into the air with excitement. The eyes of the Vampires would dilate, going so dark as to appear wholly black when the irony tang of Dogs' blood rent the air.

When the Territories had been divided among supernatural kind nearly five centuries ago, the Wolves and Vampires had been allotted shared lands, but there was no love lost between the two races. Both felt inherently superior to the other, though Wolves seemed to hold the lower station within the culture.

I passed a group of Vamps huddled around the circular fountain that depicted a pack of howling wolves and marked the center of the town square. One of the males turned to watch me as I did so, but I met his gaze with the predator in my own, and he soon found his companions once more appealing.

Snorting and stumbling, I rounded the corner of a three-story inn and sauntered down the alley beside it. I was exhausted, but figured I should go check on Amara before crawling back to my own hut near the kennels and passing out cold.

The thought of my warm pallet of straw and old horse blankets beckoned me, the idea of escaping into dreamland beyond alluring. Even in my drunken stupor, I was distantly aware that this could be the last night I did so.

And it was this thought that kept me from realizing I was being surrounded by three Wolves on a mission until it was already too late.

A familiar voice snaked out of the shadows, the words somehow simultaneously sharp and slurred.

"Just the bitch I was looking for," it said, and Mekhi the Hound stepped into a shaft of moonlight that illuminated his Wolfish grin.

8

I went utterly still.

My stomach twisted, and the tiny hairs on the back of my neck stood on end. Mekhi took another step forward, standing directly before me, legs spread wide and arms folded over his perpetually puffed out chest. "You've found yourself in quite the predicament," the Hound said.

With a smirk on his ugly face, Murphy appeared out of the shadows to my right. "A predicament, indeed," the Gravedigger said.

To my left, a third Wolf whose name I didn't know, but whose face I recognized from the bar earlier, slipped into the moonlight.

A curse clanged through my head, but I tilted it to the side, feigning indifference. "You shouldn't use words you probably can't even spell," I replied.

From the look that took over Mekhi's square-shaped face, I knew the insult hit its mark. He reached for his belt and snatched up the baton attached there, holding it tightly but letting it dangle down by his thick leg.

"You know what I'd like, brother?" Murphy said, drawling my eyes toward him for a moment. He held a long metal shovel in his dirty hands, the head of it made of iron and forged both sharp and flat. "I'd like to see what else that pretty little mouth is capable of besides all the talk."

With these words, I felt a lethal sort of calm settled over me. It was always the same, one of my oldest friends, perhaps. The killing calm that became me, the monster that awoke and reared its head. My inner Wolf was aware of impending death at every moment, and unlike the human side of me, it did not fear it.

I spat at the ground between Murphy's feet, my lips pulling back from my teeth in a snarl. "I would bite your puny dick clean off if it came anywhere near my pretty little mouth," I said. Rolling my shoulders, I added, "Get on with it, then."

My invitation was instantly met. The three male Wolves began to circle around me, decreasing circumference inch by inch.

～

Three sets of eyes glowing Wolf-Gold stared back at me, three sets of teeth bared in grimacing snarls. The smell of sweat, anticipation, and unchecked testosterone rent the air, and my jaw clenched in revulsion.

Before Mekhi lunged for me, there was only a handful of heartbeats, and within them, the world slowed. In that short space, I was intensely aware of the air in my lungs and the blood rushing through my veins. The fog that had been over my mind cleared, leaving my stomach tight but my mind sharp and focused. I likely would not walk out of this alley, but I would drag at least one of these bastards to hell along with me.

Mekhi moved first, as I'd known he would, the black baton clenched in his fist sailing through the air aimed right for my temple. I ducked, my movements fluid and balanced, and slammed the heel of my palm as hard as I could into his solar plexus. A sound like vacuumed air gasped out of him, but as it did, Murphy the Gravedigger swung that flat-headed shovel hard enough to knock the life out of me.

I danced back only fast enough to avoid the brunt of the damage, the metal making a clean incision through the air and similarly slicing the tender skin of my right cheek along with it. Oddly, I didn't feel the pain, but I did feel the warm trickle of blood as it slid down my face.

The third Wolf was moving. Instead of the baton, he'd chosen the whip that was the partner to the baton; two weapons every Hound always carried. There was a special compartment in my black heart where I stored my hatred for those whips.

And I accessed that compartment now.

Moving faster than Wolves of their size were capable, I spun around the third Wolf and launched into a leap, running up the side of the wooden inn, using the surface of the building to propel myself high into the air. This move put me behind the whip-wielding Hound, and I slammed my fist into the back of his neck, driving him to his knees as though I'd used a hammer.

A small crunch echoed up through my hand, but I did not have time to watch the Wolf slump to the side, paralyzed.

Mekhi's face was a mask of cold fury, his eyes glowing like vengeful golden suns. Spittle foamed between his slanted teeth, and he barreled at me in a way that was more bearlike than Wolf.

As he did this, Murphy the Gravedigger charged in from my opposite side. I dropped into a roll and thought for a heartbeat that I had escaped the collision, but was yanked up hard by the back of my shirt, the fabric constricting to choking-tight around my throat.

In the next moment, I was sailing through the air. Then I was colliding with the wall, my body striking the old wood hard enough to tremble the structure. My teeth rattled in my head, the breath going out of me in a rush. I hit the ground a second after, choking on the cloud of dust my body sent up from the dry earth.

When I lifted my head, my vision was fuzzy and I spat blood onto the dirt. It was thick and hot and dribbled down my chin.

I pushed up onto my knees, gripping that unforgiving wooden wall for support, but as Mekhi and Murphy prowled closer, I knew that my body had lost the edge of speed. The Hound had tossed me hard enough to kill a mortal. I had no doubt a weaker Wolf would have been knocked clean unconscious.

Mekhi's knuckles were bone white as he moved in for the kill, gripping that baton as though it anchored him to the realm. My hands went up to block his blow, but instead, he slammed his knee into my midsection.

This time blood sprayed from my mouth in a thin rain of crimson. I sputtered. For what felt like an agonizing eternity, my lungs could not grab hold of a single atom of air.

My body hit the earth again, and I moved slowly—too slowly, trying to pull myself back to my feet. With a sudden rush of panic I realized that I did not want to die here—not like this, not this way. After all the fights I'd faced to still be here, after all of the things I'd overcome, and the narrow escapes I'd made from The Ring over the years... Dying like this, at the hands of these sadist males, just seemed so... tragic.

I shifted.

One moment I was woman, the next I was Wolf. It was a skill I'd honed over the years, the ability to shift in the space between heartbeats, and situations like this were precisely the reason why. It took most Wolves nearly a whole minute to make a full shift, and a wise mentor had once told me that a whole lot could happen in a whole minute.

I was not most Wolves, however, and I hadn't lied about taking one of these bastards with me. Both Mekhi and Murphy paused at my sudden changing, but my back was against the wall, both figuratively and literally, and so the two did not back down.

Mekhi only said, "What a neat trick," before raising that heavy baton back into the air.

I released the power coiled in my canine muscles and launched myself at him in a flash of fur and teeth.

∼

The taste of Mekhi's blood filled my mouth as I latched onto his leg. I'd been aiming for the soft spot of his lower belly, but he'd twisted to the side at the last minute, and I'd been forced to clamp my powerful jaws down on his leg or risk not making contact at all.

Blinding pain shot through my back, rippling all the way down to the pads of my paws, like a strike of lightning through my veins. I whipped my head to the side, taking a good chunk of his thigh with me.

But that blinding, lightning strike of pain fell down upon me again, this time the blow aimed directly at my temple. A high-pitched whimper escaped my throat, swallowing the growl I would have preferred to bellow.

This time, as the blackness swirled in my head, my vision, and devoured up the world, the scene did not fade fully back to reality. I was slipping away into unconsciousness, or worse. And once that blackness fully consumed me, there would be no escaping it.

Despite the inner protest that occurred at the thought of this, there was nothing I could do to shake out of the fog that was encasing me, steady tightening its grip.

There was a brief image of Mekhi's leering grin, and then that of Murphy hoisting that heavy shovel over his head.

Right before the darkness claimed me, I thought I heard a familiar male voice break through the gloom.

But there was no way to be sure as my grip finally loosened on the ledge of consciousness and I slipped smoothly away.

9

Pain greeted me upon awakening.

It was a familiar train to ride out of unconsciousness, and I was a frequent passenger.

My eyes peeled open slowly, and it took me a moment to recognize that I was still in my Wolf form, sprawled out on my side, the smell of blood caked into my fur. I tried to lift my head, and sharp pain soared through it like a star across a night sky.

A sound to my right had me lifting my head too swiftly, but I clenched my jaws against the pain to assess where I was—and *who* had removed me from that alleyway.

Because I wasn't dead. And I should have been. Even with the fog that was slowly lifting from my mind, I was sure of this fact.

"Take it easy," said a deep voice, my eyes clearing just in time to see Ryker the Hound sit forward in the chair he was occupying nearby. "You're still healing."

I felt my ears go flat on my head, the fur near the back of my neck rising. Though even this small movement hurt, my lips pulled back over my fangs in a snarl that started low in my chest.

The Hound set aside the papers he'd been looking over and

held both hands up, palms out. "Easy, girl," he said. "Is that how you say thank you to the Wolf who saved your life?"

I surveyed my surroundings, taking in the plush carpet and comfortable furniture, the bay windows on the eastern side of the room, the pile of thick blankets I was still sprawled across. Questions flew through my aching head, but I didn't want to speak them directly into the Hound's mind. Telepathy between our kind was common, but also much more intimate than verbal communication. It required some degree of trust.

As if he were reading my thoughts, the Hound jerked his chin toward a door behind me. "That's the washroom. I took the liberty of finding you some clothing. You can go shift and get dressed, if you so wish. Though you'll heal faster in Wolf form." He shrugged, as if he couldn't care either way.

For a moment, I only remained where I was. What the hell was going on here? My eyes darted toward the door, assessing the chances of escape. The Hound watched me the entire time, a smirk pulling up his lips as he sensed my intentions. But even if I made it out, where would I go?

These thoughts had me padding toward the washroom, wondering how much time had passed and if everything was all right with Amara and Goldie. As I approached the closed door of the washroom, I shot an annoyed glance back at Ryker, who knew I could not turn the doorknob with my paws.

The Hound rose from his chair, prowling toward me with all the grace of a predator. He towered over me at his full height, which had to be over six feet. The soft light beginning to leak in through the bay window caught on the gold in his hair, the muscles under his shirt shifting with the movement.

I snapped my gaze to the carpet, releasing a little snarl at the smug look he'd given me when he'd caught me staring.

Bastard.

He gripped the doorknob to the washroom in a large hand

H. D. GORDON

and turned it, pushing the door so that it swung open. "There you go, little Wolf," he said.

I hesitated before stepping over the threshold. For all I knew, there could be an uncoiled whip and chains waiting on the other side of that now gaping door. But then light flooded the small space, and I looked up to see Ryker still wearing that smug smirk, his hand shaking out the match he'd used to light the torch affixed to the washroom wall.

His smooth skin appeared golden in the flickering flame.

I snapped another snarl and the Hound huffed a deep laugh before shutting the door gently behind me.

What the actual fuck? I thought to myself, and then shifted back into my human form so as to find out just what was happening here.

~

Since the rules were unclear, the situation unprecedented in my experience, I used the washroom to its full capacity. It was rare that I got to bathe in running water that wasn't moved by a stream or waterfall, as Dogs' huts didn't come equipped with actual washrooms.

And though I knew there were other matters that required my attention, blood was still coating my skin, matting my hair to my head.

So I stepped into the bathtub and marveled at the sight of water falling from a faucet as if by magic. When I moved into the spray, I let out a low groan at the feel of the warm water hitting my skin, my face. Of all the luxuries Dogs were denied, this was the one I envied the most. In all my lifetime, I'd only ever bathed in an actual washroom three times. All three of those times had been following a roll in the hay with some Wolf who'd strolled in from out of town and allowed me to use his hotel's facilities before I slipped away to never see him again.

48

I was not ashamed of the fact that all three of those times I'd enjoyed the hot shower even more than the sex.

Ten minutes later, after I'd lathered myself with what had to be the Hounds' sandalwood-scented soap and rinsed clean, I dried off with the fluffy towel that had been set out for me, frowning down at the metal comb and toothbrush that had also been set out.

Beside these toiletries sat a pile of clean clothes, the styles of which I knew belonged to Dogshead. I lifted the toothbrush and sniffed it. New. Then the comb. Also new. As if he'd gone out and purchased these items while I'd been passed out. I continued frowning the entire time I made use of the items, my jaw clenched in confusion and anticipation.

I had not forgotten about the fact that Ryker had seen me in the woods with Amara. The fact that he had information that would easily get me killed.

Heart pounding as though I was stepping into The Ring and not a modest hotel room, I gathered my courage around me and opened the washroom door.

The Hound had resumed his seat in the plush chair near the bay window. His head tilted toward me as he met my eyes. He snorted at the change in my appearance.

"You clean up all right," he said.

My lip curled at the not-quite compliment.

"What the hell is going on here?" I asked, and didn't care that there was a certain snap to my voice.

The Hound only smirked. "My name is Ryker. I'm Reagan Ramsey's Head Hound." He waved a hand to the chair beside his, again suggesting I sit. "And who are you?"

I made no move to follow his instruction. "I'm a Dog who should be dead. So why aren't I?"

He shrugged, his wide shoulders rising and falling just once. "My men were out of line," he said. "I'd told them at the bar earlier to stand down. If I'd wanted to punish you, I would've done it then." Another shrug, as if the matter of my life were no thing.

He's a Hound, snarled a small voice in my head. *Your life is no thing.*

I continued cautiously. "You saw me in the woods," I said.

One of his gold-brown brows arched up. "Yes, I did."

I threw up my hands, tired of this game. "And so I ask you again, why am I still alive?"

His bright blue eyes seemed to darken, though the crystalline shade of them didn't really alter. "Is it so hard to believe that even Hounds grow weary of all the killing—all the death?"

I sputtered a bitter laugh, my answer clear enough in the sound.

Ryker the Hound let out a sigh, and I shifted uncomfortably at the honesty behind it.

My voice came out softer than intended when I said, "You can't possibly think I would trust you."

I would never, ever admit it aloud, but the sad smile he gave me made his face undeniably handsome.

"Come now, little Wolf," he replied. "You can't possibly think you have a choice."

10

Teeth gritted, I took a seat. The world outside the windows before the chair I now occupied was shifting from the bluish gray of predawn to the pinkish blue of early morning. By the time the sun rose to its apex, Dogshead would be hot enough to fry eggs on the roofs of the buildings.

By the time the sun sank toward the western horizon, I would be readying to step into The Ring and face the Bear.

"If you're not going to whip me, and you're not going to turn me in," I said, "then let's make this quick."

The Hound's gaze was locked on me, head tilted and eyes as blue as sapphires pinning me to the seat. "You have somewhere more important to be?" he asked.

The words he did not speak, but which hung between us nonetheless, were: *Perhaps helping a runaway pup get out of Dogshead and toward gods-knew-where.*

"I need to prepare. I'm on the roster tonight," I replied tightly.

From the look on his face I gleaned that he already knew this. He nodded as if in confirmation. "Against the Bear, and now, you're injured."

I said nothing. If he already knew everything, what was there to say?

He continued staring at me. "You won't beat her. She's the West Coast Champion."

I returned his gaze unflinchingly. When it was clear he wanted some sort of response, I sighed and shrugged, the look on my face asking what of it.

"I helped train her myself," he added.

I knew the wise choice was to remain silent, but as usual, my silver tongue got the best of me.

"If you trained those Hounds from the bar, I'm not sure I have anything to worry about," I said.

To my utter surprise, he laughed, and there was not a trace of malice in it. I hadn't been aware Hounds were capable of making such sounds. But it did not fool me. He was the enemy. No amount of unwarranted familiarity or handsome smiles could change that.

The Hound leaned forward in his chair, the muscles under his black shirt shifting with the movement. His blue gaze still held mine, and one side of his mouth pulled up in an almost-smile. When he noticed that he had my attention, he sat back slowly, again making those tanned muscles flex and contract.

"Your name is Rukiya, no?"

"Rook," I corrected. "Everyone calls me Rook."

"Well, Rook, would you like something to eat?"

My traitorous stomach growled in answer, but I said, "I'd like to know what you want from me, and don't try to claim that you don't want anything. I wasn't born yesterday, and I really do have other matters to attend to."

The Hound's straight white teeth showed just barely as he grinned. "Why? Is there something you feel inclined to give me?" he asked.

The low growl that tore up my throat had him chuckling again. He held up his hands, which were flecked with various scars. "It was a joke, little Wolf," he said. "Relax. I really don't want anything from you, and I'm not going to turn you in."

My eyes were narrowed to slits. "Why. Not."

The Hound absent-mindedly ran a hand through his trimmed golden-brown hair. "I already told you. I grow tired of all the death, and the truth is, you won't survive The Ring tonight, anyway, so what difference does it make if I kill you now, or if the Bear kills you tonight?" As if to prove the point, his large shoulders lifted in a shrug.

The sunlight growing steadily stronger through the windows travelled over his handsome face as a lazy cloud passed over the sun. He was still staring at me in that pinning, intense way, and I shifted in what I wouldn't admit was discomfort.

"And what of the child?" I said quietly, my even tone that of a stone cold killer.

For all of three heartbeats, he said nothing, but just when I sensed the electric energy filling the room about to break, he said, "I take no joy in punishing children."

His tone was deep, unyielding, his handsome face gilded by the soft gold leaking in from the windows.

I decided to push no further. I knew when to fold my cards and run.

"So... I'm free to go?" I asked.

The Hound gave a single nod, a slow smirk following after. "Unless you'd like to stay."

I rose from my chair and was halfway to the door before I turned back to face him. He had rotated in his seat, his azure gaze tracing my every step.

"What if I win in The Ring tonight?" I asked. "What if I defeat the Bear?"

His head tilted, his eyes traveling the length of me in a way that was too intimate. "I suppose then we'll have to have another wonderful conversation," he said, and waved a hand in dismissal before turning back to the window.

I stared at the back of his head for a moment before slipping out, feeling as though I'd just escaped a snake's den.

But for whatever reason, no matter how many steps I took after leaving, I couldn't shake the feeling that I hadn't *actually* escaped.

~

"Where the hell have you been?" Goldie snapped, practically hauling me inside her cabin by my shirtfront. She shut the door behind me and double-checked the locks. Her red-gold hair was a mess of curls on her head, her makeup left over from the night. "I was worried sick."

"I'm sorry," I said, wincing as I took a seat on the bed, and then cringing a bit again as I reconsidered and stood. "I got caught up."

Goldie scanned my face for all of two seconds before placing a hand on the curve of her hip. "You got into a fight," she corrected. "With who? That Hound, Mekhi? It was, wasn't it? Have you lost your gods damned mind?"

I sighed. "Maybe I have." I looked around. "Where's Amara?"

In answer, the door to the washroom creaked open and Amara stepped out. A bit of tension flooded out of my shoulders, though I'd been unaware of its presence until just then.

Right, I thought. I still had to figure out what to do with the slave child I'd stolen.

"I've already taken care of it," Goldie said, as if she could read my mind. "She'll have transportation to the northeastern coast by moonrise tonight."

I gaped, my mind reeling to catch up, which seemed to be the trend of the day. "How?" I asked.

Goldie shrugged. "I asked Bernard for information, and he gave it to me."

My gaze narrowed. "What kind of information?"

"The kind someone might need in order to secure safe passage for a runaway. The kind that is never spoken of again after the initial relaying."

I gave a slow nod. "And what did Bernard want in return for this information?"

Goldie's red lips pursed into a thin line. Speaking directly into my mind, she said, *"What do you think he wanted?"*

My mouth opened to argue, to say she shouldn't have done that.

But Goldie held a hand up and beat me to the punch. "Save it," she said. "It's done. And after you didn't return last night, I wasn't even sure if you were alive, so I... handled it." She blew out a puff of breath. "You're welcome."

In a move that was as rare for me as two full moons in a single month, I wrapped my arms around Goldie and squeezed her tightly.

Thank you, I told her silently.

I looked back to the child still standing in the darkened mouth of the washroom doorway. I'd yet to hear her speak other than when she'd uttered her name yesterday. Then I looked back to my friend.

"Okay, then," I said. "Just tell me what I need to do."

~

The plan was simple, easy. Perhaps too easy. I made Goldie say it twice, and despite my unvarnished trust in her, I almost couldn't believe it.

She was equally disbelieving of the story I told about Ryker the Hound.

"So he just let you go?" she asked for what had to be the tenth time. "He's that certain you'll lose to the Bear?"

I twisted my thick brown hair up into a messy bun,

suppressing a sigh. "Everyone in this whole damn town seems sure of it."

Goldie gripped my hand, her small fingers pale, smooth, and polished. A sharp contrast to my own tanned, scarred, and callused hands. "Not everyone," she said.

"I'm not at my full strength, and the Bear is twice my size." These were not insecurities I would've shared with just anyone. I simply couldn't afford to.

"You've faced tougher odds before," Goldie said, and her blue eyes lingered on the right side of my face, where a thin scar ran from my temple down to my chin, separating the outer edge of my eyebrow in a small cut where no hair would grow.

I nodded, forcing myself to focus on the tasks at hand. Spending time worrying about my fate in The Ring in a handful of hours would do me no good.

While we talked, eating some of the cold meat Goldie had scrounged up for us, Amara sat silently on the threadbare rug, chewing on a piece of meat as well.

"How do we know we can trust Bernard?" I asked Goldie silently.

Goldie gave me a humorless smirk and echoed a sentiment that had been stated to me earlier that morning. *"What makes you think we have any choice?"*

11

Darkness fell, the now full moon making its reliable ascent into the night sky. Huge bonfires had been lit, torches erected along the dirt street, surrounding the fountain in the town square and lining the walls of the squat structures.

The air was hot and thick with the stench of anticipation. Wolves and Vampires prowled through the streets of Dogshead and lurked in the fields and forests beyond. The whole of Bo Benedict's plantation was crawling with creatures large and small, prey and predator.

Especially predator.

Of course, I counted myself among that group, but then again, so did everyone around me. I stood in a line of Dogs, arranged in the order in which we appeared on the roster; the bigger the fight, the closer to the end of the line. We would first march through the square to be examined. Then, bets would be placed. After that, the Dogs would fight one-on-one to the death in The Ring. Winners would crawl off to heal somewhere or drink to their victories at the *Blood Moon*. Losers would be dragged away by Murphy and his goons.

I had not seen the Gravedigger, or the Hounds who'd nearly

killed me, since the incident. As I stood in the procession of Dogs, I realized it probably didn't matter anyway.

Across the square, on the other side of the Howling Wolves Fountain, stood the Bear. She towered over the white sculpture, her dark eyes pinning me with deadly intent. She had to stand over six feet tall, her waist as thick as a tree trunk, shoulders as wide as a house. Her bald, ebony head shone in the moonlight, flecked with scars that told a silent story of all the battles she'd endured in the past. I held her gaze indifferently, aware of every pair of eyes on us, refusing to let an ounce of the dread circling my stomach show.

The pounding of drums began, and the procession followed on its footsteps. The line in which I stood began to march forward, our hands bound behind our backs—an effort more for show than anything else. The magical collars around our necks and the Hounds surrounding the area ensured that we would never run.

It was all part of the sick ritual, all elements of the show.

A platform with wooden ramps on either end had been constructed. On one end of the structure stood Bo Benedict, Pack Master of the Midlands, and owner of the invisible leash connected to the collar around my neck.

Benedict was a short, bulky man with a face tanned from constant exposure to the sun. He wore his usual wide-brimmed hat, his boots with spurs on the backs of them, an old cotton shirt tucked in at his large silver belt buckle. He looked more like a farmer than a Pack Master, but everyone knew him to be as deadly a Wolf as any of the others. Beneath the brim of his hat, Benedict stared out over the crowd gathered in his square, a lazy smile revealing too-white teeth, and deep rivets spreading from the corners of his sharp green eyes.

On the opposite side of the platform stood Reagan Ramsey, visiting Pack Master of the Western Coast (and Master to a certain Head Hound I'd met earlier). In tailored slacks and a finely woven white collared shirt, he was the opposite to Bo Benedict's farmer's appearance. His shoes were black and gleaming, matching the thin belt that hugged his muscled waist. His skin was darkened from the sun, but not in the over-cooked way that Benedict's was. Ramsey's tan was golden, as if cultivated with carefully timed exposures on a sandy beach somewhere along that Western seaboard. Though his position as a Master made him an inevitable bastard in my mind, even I had to admit Reagan Ramsey was handsome, his face and appearance styled like that of a wealthy gentleman.

A veritable Wolf in sheep's clothing.

At least with Benedict, what one saw was what one got. I was not too proud to admit that Reagan Ramsey scared the shit out of me.

Around the platform where the Masters awaited, the crowd of gathered spectators practically pulsed with animalistic excitement. The Vampires could be spotted among the Wolves from the unnaturally unmoving manner in which they stood—as still as pale stone statues. The Wolves, on the other hand, paced and prowled, some in human form, others having shifted and now stalked through the crowd with glowing golden eyes and perked, swiveling ears.

The pounding of the drums grew louder, the vibrations moving up from the soles of my bare feet to the tips of my fingers and top of my head.

I'd been dressed in the short brown skirt and tank top (made from old sacks that had once held potatoes), every muscle and scar on my arms and legs bare for display. My skin was tinted brown from the summer sun, my body still aching from the beating I'd taken the night before, though no one would know it.

Wolves heal fast, but the invisible internal damages always outlasted the visible external damages, and the internal were the ones that could kill you.

Goldie had braided my thick brown hair all the way down my

back, as was our personal ritual on the days of a fight. She'd placed a small kiss on my forehead afterward, pleading with her eyes that I survive tonight. I'd given her the slightest of nods, promising without words that I would sure as hell try.

The line in which I stood began to trudge forward, and before I knew it, I had reached the end of the platform with the ramp leading up to where my Master, Bo Benedict, stood waiting in his wide-brimmed hat. At the other end of the structure, the Bear also waited to make her ascent and stand before her Master, Reagan Ramsey.

Overhead, the moon and stars watched on indifferently, ever the spectators to the earthly show.

Behind the platform, standing as still as the Vampires among us, were Benedict's and Ramsey's Head Hounds.

I refused to look over and acknowledge Ryker or Lazar. Ryker was likely playing games with me by letting Amara and I live, and Lazar—Benedict's Head Hound—was just an asshole. I had the scars on my back to prove it.

Soon enough, it was my turn to step forward. The announcer —a fat Wolf with a tucked in white tank top and striped suspenders hitching his pants—bellowed the usual introduction.

"Now... this next Dog is a real survivor," the announcer said. "She was the runt of the litter, slated as Bait since she was born, bought for the smallest of prices."

As always, my fists clenched a fraction at the sound of my story, but I watched the gathered crowd with cold, unfeeling eyes.

"After killing the Dog she'd been Baited for," the announcer continued, "she faced her first opponent in The Ring and caused a serious upset. She survived, however, though her face was nearly ripped off on the right side." He gestured toward me with a hand that was holding a piece of parchment with stats and averages, and added, "As you can see by the scar running down the side of her pretty face."

Countless sets of golden eyes glowed back at me, the Wolves

and Vampires all but licking their chops. I let a bit of my teeth show in a silent snarl, and someone in the crowd howled up at the moon, causing a ripple of laughter.

"Standing at just under five feet and five inches and weighing in at one hundred and thirty-five pounds, ever the underdog and underestimated fighter, ladies and lupines, feast your eyes upon... *Roooook the Rabid!*"

The hoots and hollers and leers and crude comments ensued as if on cue. I'd heard it all before, and it no longer affected me— not like it had the first few times I'd stepped onto this stage. When I'd been a child, they'd thrown heads of cabbage and tomatoes at me after I'd killed a prize Dog. Once I'd begun to step into womanhood, the comments and taunting had taken on a different nature.

And it was this part I hated most of all.

It was not enough just to force us to fight to the death. No, we had to be *demeaned* in the process. And the females had it worse than the males, of course. At every station in life, the females *always* had it worse than the males.

I was shoved from behind, having gotten lost in my own thoughts, and I stumbled up the platform toward the center of the structure. The eyes of the two Pack Masters traveled over me uninterestedly, clearly not impressed with what they saw.

The announcer moved his attention to my opponent. "And facing Rook the Rabid in The Ring tonight is a Dog with a reputation as large as she is, a soul as dark as the color of her skin... Standing at six feet and three inches and weighing in at two hundred and twenty-two pounds, your West Coast Champion... *The Bear!*"

The wooden planks of the platform shuddered under my feet as the Bear made her way over to stand beside me—*tower* beside me.

I'd known she was big, but hearing the stats and standing in the shadow cast by her wide shoulders, I realized how ridiculous my odds were, and that Ryker the Hound had probably been right.

Why do the dirty work when he could let the Bear do it for him and allow his Master to earn money on the fight? Money paid for with my blood.

From the humored faces of the crowd, I knew no one on this blasted plantation expected me to win.

Instead of cowing me, this only made me think of how spectacular a victory on my part would be. How the loss of their money would be sure to knock the amused smiles right off all their leering faces.

Bet against me, you bastards, I thought. *Bet against me... and* lose.

12

There was exactly an hour between the ritual of the viewing platform and the actual fights, giving people time to mull over and place their bets.

And me just enough time to disappear into the stalks of high grass and execute the plan Goldie had hatched to get Amara out of Dogshead and toward someplace that would hopefully be better. Despite the fact that I had a hard time imagining such a place existed—(when one has only known misery, one only *knows* misery)—it had to be better than staying here. There was no reversing what had been done. Too much time had passed since she'd escaped. The child would be whipped and hanged upon capture, no questions asked, no trials held. They would leave her battered body in the square until the crows came to pick at it. And only then would Murphy the Gravedigger carry her away.

I shoved these thoughts aside and focused on the task at hand. I moved as silently and swiftly as I dared, careful to appear nonchalant and unhurried. Many Dogs had personal routines and rituals they took part in before a fight, including myself, so my absence shouldn't be seen as too odd.

Still, my heart was pounding like a drum in my chest, my senses perked for any obstacle that might impede me. Hours seemed to pass in the handful of minutes it took me to make my way back to Goldie's cabin from the town square. Another small eternity passed between the time it took me to make it from Goldie's cabin to the rendezvous point we'd determined earlier.

At last, I entered a line of trees thick with mossy growth and dangerous deadfalls. I debated shifting into my Wolf, but decided against it since I would have no way to carry my clothes. I pushed onward, and as the inky shadows of night were truly beginning to permeate the Midlands, I made it to the clearing where Goldie and Amara should be waiting for me.

I paused at the threshold, like a visitor to an unknown house. My sensitive ears and night-adjusted eyes scanned the area for life or movement, my body going as still as a bloodsucker.

Something gripped my shoulder, causing me to react in the only way I knew how. I pitched forward, gripping the arm attached to the hand that had grabbed me, and tossed the assailant over my shoulder.

A familiar scent flooded my nose at the same time Goldie let out a small squeak.

There was no stopping the arch of my throw, but I caught my friend around her back with both arms, grinning down at her as though I hadn't just flipped her over my shoulder.

"How many times have I told you not to sneak up on me?" I asked.

Goldie gave me a small shove before I set her to rights again. With a sigh of relief, I whirled and found Amara standing behind me, her eyes wide at my display of strength.

"You brute," Goldie snapped, keeping her voice low. Silently, she added, *"You know what to do. Don't waste any time. Don't stop for anything. You've have to move fast if you're going to get back in time for the fight."*

I gave my friend a small smile, teeth flashing in the budding darkness. *"Then stop wasting my time with sappy goodbyes—you're looking at me like you'll never see me again."*

To this, Goldie said nothing.

I gripped my friend's hands, knowing time was short, that the child and I needed to go. *"I will see you again, Golds. I'll see you tonight, on the other side of that ring. I'll expect you to have a drink waiting for me afterward."*

In response, Goldie took my face into her hands and kissed me gently on the lips. There was nothing sexual about it, only the love of the only friend I'd ever had.

"You make sure of it, Rukiya," she replied, and jerked her chin for me to go.

Neither of us cried, because that was not something women like us were afforded the luxury of, but sometimes a soul can cry out without shedding tears, sometimes pain can cut deep without even scarring.

Because despite my words, it felt very much like a goodbye.

∼

I'd removed my clothes and shifted into my Wolf. Shiny, dark chocolate fur—the same color as my long hair—now provided a nice coat over my muscled and deadly body. The child remained in her human form, her tiny body clinging to my back, her fingers digging into the fur of my neck.

We moved much faster in this way, and time was certainly of the essence. If I didn't return in time for the fight, I'd have some serious explaining to do.

I knew that Goldie had given herself the task of distracting Bo Benedict's main Overseer, and though I hated to let her use her body again in this task I'd thrust upon the both of us, I trusted that she could get the job done.

Still, I hesitated as I reached the edge of Bo Benedict's land. There were no fences marking the territory, but there was a definite boundary, nonetheless. I felt the ripple of magic as I neared it, felt the instincts that had been beaten into me since childhood rear their ugly heads.

Everything in my mind and body urged me to turn and go back the other way. Just coming this close to the edge was punishable by death.

Then again, pretty much everything in the life of a Dog was.

Where would you rather die, in The Ring, or in the attempt to commit a kindness?

I let Goldie's words steel me as I held my breath, my head held low between my haunches. We'd long passed out of the moss-covered trees and emerged in rolling fields of lavender wheat, the stalks high enough to conceal my predator's body. Shadows clung to every crevice and corner, the silver glow of the full moon not nearly enough to banish them. In the daytime, this land was quite a wonder to behold, with its rolling hills of violet punctuated with trees of emerald green.

But, at night, this place was whispered of in nightmares.

The creatures beyond Benedict's invisible border were legend, and across the realms they were rumored about for their vicious nature. With the plantation's magic in place, and the fact that so many Wolves and Vampires roamed through, most of the nasty creatures steered away.

But out there... Beyond...

Atop my back, small hands digging a bit deeper into my fur, Amara let out a little whimper.

"Be strong, girl," I told her. *"Do not let them see you tremble."*

The child fell still and silent once more.

Carefully, I crossed over the invisible magic boundary and into another world.

~

The air shimmered. A small zap of energy shot through my veins and seeped into my bones, and then I was on the other side.

I glanced around, my head still held low and my body coiled to strike or flee should either be necessary.

Never in my eighteen years of life had I stepped beyond the confines of Bo Benedict's lands, and I wasn't sure what I was expecting, but... nothing really happened.

Or even seemed different. I felt Amara's head lift from my shoulders, could sense rather than see her scanning our surroundings same as me.

The child spoke in my head for the first time since I met her. *"Is this... the human world?"*

"It is part of their territory, yes."

Again, her little voice surprised me. It was small, but strong. *"This is where you're taking me?"*

"Would you rather I take you back to Dogshead?"

To this, she said nothing, only sighed and rested her head between my shoulders.

I began moving again, heading quickly in the direction Goldie had given me. The fields on this side of the veil were golden rather than lavender, and the trees had lost some of the vibrant luster they'd possessed as well. It was an effort to keep focus, to not slow and drink in the novelty around me. It was ridiculous, but I felt as though I could sense them here—the humans. I had never met one, had only heard tales. Despite myself, I wondered what their world was like, what lay beyond the vastness of these fields.

When I looked back at where I knew Bo Benedict's land to be, there was only more of the same surrounding me, nothing to see out of the ordinary. The illusion was so strong, and the feel of that repulsive magic so insistent, that I bet humans and creatures alike passed through here all the time and were none the wiser about what lay just on the other side.

In fact, if I wasn't careful, I could easily get lost here. Goldie had said Bernard had warned her about this possibility.

I passed a large boulder that was a marker Goldie had mentioned and didn't allow myself a moment to sigh in relief. Using my strong nose, I lifted my muzzle to the wind, and sure enough, just as my friend had said, I picked up the scent of running water nearby.

Even the scent of water was different here. Duller, somehow.

Again, I wondered what lay beyond.

Again, I reminded myself of the task and pushed onward.

Soon, I reached the edge of a wide river cutting through a range of big hills that were not quite large enough to call mountains. I stopped when I reached the bank of the rushing water, lapping at it with greedy thirst. The journey here from Dogshead had only taken me twenty-five minutes or so, but I had spent every second of that time in a full-out run, and I was winded.

After I'd drunk my fill, setting Amara down to cup some water into her own hands, I scanned the quiet lands around us. Where was the damn escort? They should've been here by now.

A minute passed. Then another. And another. If I'd been in human form, I would have started to sweat.

What if they didn't show? I couldn't take Amara back to Dogshead, and I couldn't just leave her here, either... Could I?

Amara's hazel eyes met mine under the moonlight, as if she were reading my mind. I wished to the gods that the child would stop looking at me like that. That capturing gaze was what had gotten us into this mess in the first place.

Just as I was getting ready to make a very difficult decision, a dark figure swooped in from above, making me yelp and snap blindly with my jaws at the air. Amara tucked herself behind me, and I shielded her little body with my own.

A moment later, a large figure landed in front of us, its impact making the ground shudder beneath my paws. The hair on the back of my neck stood on end, and a low growl ripped up my throat as I bared my sharp teeth.

The dark figure that had landed before us was a male—larger than any male I'd ever seen, with the sides of his head shaved and a long brown braid hanging in a thick cord down his back. His attire was that of an assassin or soldier, all black with metal armor guarding the most vulnerable spots of his enormous body.

I stared up at him, even though I was no small beast in my Wolf form, my head lowered between my haunches and teeth still bared.

The male grinned, and I noticed that his teeth were fanged and the tips of his ears pointed. Not that it mattered one bit, but he was also as handsome as a devil, with deep brown eyes and porcelain smooth skin.

The warrior held up his large hands in a signal that said he meant no harm. In a deep voice, he said, "Easy, girl."

A rumbling snarl was my only answer.

The warrior put a large hand over his wide chest, where the metal of his armor gleamed in the moonlight. "I'm Yarin," he said. "I'm here to transport the child."

Though I could hear time ticking away with every second, I made no move to yield Amara.

The warrior sighed and waved a hand at me. "Why don't you shift so we can talk about it?"

Shifting would require precious energy, but he was right. I just couldn't hand over the girl without questioning this stranger first.

With a wink that earned another snarl, the male turned his enormous back to me, a pretty strong statement of trust on his part—to turn his back while I was in this form, or any form, really.

But I wasted no time in switching back into my two-legged self, and like a true gentleman, the warrior unclasped the black cloak hanging from his back and handed it back to me without looking.

I wrapped it around my shoulders, soaking up the warmth that lingered in the material, and said, "You're Fae." It was not a question.

The warrior grinned as he turned back to me. "Half Fae," he corrected, and ran his tongue over an elongated canine. "Half Vampire. And I have a name. It's Yarin, as I've already told you."

I knew that it was rude, but I couldn't help it. I stared at Yarin as if he had two heads. I'd never met an actual Halfbreed before. Such interbreeding was taboo among the supernatural races. But... I had to admit that the results were not esthetically displeasing.

Yarin smirked, a look coming into his deep brown eyes that suggested he knew what I was thinking.

"You're kind of attractive yourself," he said, and winked again.

A ridiculous rush of heat flushed my cheeks, and I cleared my throat. "Where are you taking her?" I asked.

"Somewhere safe," Yarin said.

"Where? With whom?"

"Well, now, those are mighty valuable secrets. Just let me have the child and we'll be on our way." He raised a dark brow. "Unless you want to take her back to that shithole they call Dogshead."

"Where are your wings?" I asked.

"Half Fae don't have wings."

"But you can fly?"

"One does not need wings to fly."

I was wasting time. These were unnecessary questions. But...

As if sensing the reluctance from me, Amara stepped slowly out from behind my back and toward the Halfbreed warrior. She looked so very tiny standing in the large shadow of him. To my ultimate surprise, Yarin dropped down smoothly into a crouch, resting his large forearms on his knees, and gave the child an easy smile.

70

"Hey, there, sweetheart," he whispered quietly, though I picked the words up easily with my strong hearing. "You're going to be okay now. We're going to take care of you."

Amara glanced back at me, and from the look on her face, I could tell that she already trusted him. My eyes narrowed just slightly, wondering if he'd used some of the persuasion ability Fae kind were known for, but made no move to stop her when she said, "It's okay, Rukiya. I'm ready to go with him."

Hearing my full name spoken in her tiny voice tugged at that cold muscle in my chest. I swallowed once and met the warrior's eyes.

"Give me your word she'll be safe," I said.

"I give you my word," he said with a small bow of his head.

He opened his arms to Amara, but to my utter shock, the child ran toward me and threw her arms around my legs, as she was not tall enough to even reach my waist. Now, my eyes burned, but I blinked back any traitorous tears.

"Thank you for saving me," Amara said.

I ran a hand through her hair, not trusting my voice not to break should I attempt to speak. Amara pulled back and stepped into Yarin's muscled arms.

"You could come with us," Amara added. She looked to the warrior that held her, his handsome face gentle and kind. "She could, couldn't she?"

Yarin's brown eyes went to the collar around my neck, surely knowing as well as I that the magic in the thing would strangle the life out of me once the Master noticed I was gone. Amara had escaped while they'd been about to brand and collar her. If it had been after, I likely would not have even intervened.

Once you were stamped and collared, you were owned. There was no escaping after that.

"She could," Yarin mumbled, the two words carrying the weight of all the others that had just gone through my head.

H. D. GORDON

"You made me a promise," I said to the warrior. "I suggest you keep it."

This earned a small tilt to Yarin's mouth, but I shifted into my Wolf form in the next heartbeat and slipped out of his cloak so that he could reclaim it. In a move that could have lost him a couple fingers, he surprised me again by patting my chocolate head and scratching behind my ears before clasping the cloak to his shoulders.

"Hold on," he told Amara, and then the two of them shot upward into the night sky, the blast of their departure stirring the fur around my face.

I didn't have the time to watch them disappear into the darkness.

I turned back in the direction of that invisible boundary... and ran.

13

S hift, fight, survive.

Those were the rules of the game. Two Wolves entered The Ring, one came out. It was simple, brutal, and sometimes, lightning quick.

It was worse when it lasted longer, a drawn out execution.

I could hear the crowd, could feel the excitement and anticipation hanging in the air, before I reached the area where the fights took place. My tongue lolled out of my mouth as I slowed my pace at last, gulping down air like a just-surfaced swimmer.

For a few moments, my head spun, my heart beating rapidly near my throat. The streets of Dogshead were quiet and empty as I padded through, heading in the direction of that wild energy. For the past two days I'd been able to avoid the reality of my fight with the Bear, had been able to push it to the rear of my consciousness in order to focus on other matters, but as I drew nearer The Ring, there was no way to ignore it.

My side ached, lingering pain from the fight with the Hounds and Gravedigger, and on top of that, a stitch had formed from my long run out to the edge of Bo Benedict's land and back. I stopped at the waterhole near the kennels and lapped at the foggy, stagnant water for as long as I dared.

Time was up. As if to punctuate the point, a high-pitched whine tore across the night, the final death scream of a dying Dog.

I wondered who it was, but supposed it didn't matter.

I just needed to get back to the kennels in time to hear my name called for the fight.

As I padded closer and closer, slipping between squat wooden structures and over low wooden fences, I picked up an unfamiliar scent on the air and stopped dead in my tracks. My ears flattened on my head and my glowing eyes scanned my surroundings for the source. I was being watched by someone... or *something*, and I could feel it.

A low warning growl rumbled up my throat from deep in my belly. My tail was held still and low, my head lowered between my haunches.

I was just about to head on my way, knowing that if the watcher was any real threat, whoever it was could just get in line behind the threats directly before me. But then I looked to my left and saw duel flashes of red staring back at me. The eyes were just two scarlet-glowing orbs in the shadows of a nearby structure. Unblinking and utterly transfixing.

They were the eyes of a predator, their beauty disturbingly enthralling.

I sent a low snarl in that direction, and just before I entered the kennels (little more than a few rows of mud huts where the Dogs slept) there was a flicker of white beneath those glowing red eyes, as though the owner had flashed a smile.

There were only a handful of stolen moments to contemplate this mystery before the thoughts of glowing eyes and flashing grins in the darkness were swept away by the deafening roar of the crowd, and the sound of my name being called on the other side of The Ring.

No time to rest, then.

It was time to kill or die.

~

The announcer, still wearing his striped suspenders and stained white shirt from earlier, gave me a semi-suspicious look as I came running up in my human form, having snagged my clothes on the way back out of the forest.

"I was about to call the Hounds," he hissed, the cards listing names and stats fisted in his fat hands. "You just barely made it, girl. Now get up there so I can announce the fight." His gray eyes darted toward where the Bear was already standing beside the enormous metal cage that was The Ring and then back to me. He snorted and added, "Good luck."

I barely heard him. I was already zoning out, stepping into that space where survival was pushed to the forefront. The atmosphere surrounding The Ring added to the feeling. Metal bleachers were lined up around the chain-link, octagon-shaped cage where the body of the Dog I'd heard shriek moments ago was being dragged away by Murphy the Gravedigger. Following him, the water boys would come with a bucket of water and splash it over the mats that made up the center of the octagon in a half-assed attempt at washing the blood away.

Now I stood on one side of The Ring, and the Bear stood on the other. The crowd around us, full of stone-still Vampires and drooling Wolves, murmured their anticipation at the match up. My eyes scanned the gathered for Goldie, but I did not see her among them. I sent up a silent prayer to whichever gods might be listening that she had pulled off her part of the plan without falling into danger.

And just as I was finishing the silent plea, the Announcer pulled open the door that led into The Ring, and waved an impatient hand at the two fighters to enter. The Bear approached from her side, circling the octagon cage so that those in the stands could get a good look at her. I did the same on my side.

We reached the cage door at the same time.

The Bear shoved me to the side and entered first, earning laughter and shouts of approval from the crowd.

I gritted my teeth and followed after her. The metal door of The Ring clanged shut behind us. A thick metal chain was wound around the opening, sealing us both inside. From the raised wooden platform constructed around the cage, the Announcer paced back and forth, beady eyes scanning the crowd, revving them up with his introductions.

Inside The Ring, I stood face-to-face with the Bear.

She was even bigger than I remembered, as if she had somehow grown wider and taller and darker in the last handful of hours.

The last handful of hours, when I'd been running myself ragged helping a slave child escape Dogshead.

The booming voice of the Announcer interrupted that rogue thought and forced me back to the here and now.

"Shift!" he bellowed, and the Wolves in the audience tipped their heads back and howled at the moon.

Inside the cage, I shifted into my Wolf form, the process taking a half minute or so longer than the usual instantaneous shift that I'd trained myself to be able to do. After, I shook myself free of the rags I'd been wearing, leaving them in a dirty brown pile against the chain-link wall of the cage.

That left only the task of watching the Bear make her slow, painful shift into her Wolf form, and though it was of course something I'd seen many times before, it was nothing short of gruesome.

She bent double, dropping to all fours and back arching as though a demon were trying to force its way out of her. Her bald, ebony head gleamed under the harsh torchlights that had been lit around The Ring. A deep, rumbling noise escaped her, the sound resonating through the mats and up my paws. I remained where I was, my chocolate brown fur raised along my back and my tail held low and still.

I wanted to look away, but knew that to do so would be considered weak. So I watched every bit of her painful shift. Every second.

Thick, black fur sprouted from her elongated snout, knuckles, and inverted knees. A bushy black tail grew out of the bottom of her back. Another pained grumble erupted from her mouth, where teeth as sharp as daggers had grown and were dripping long ropes of silver saliva.

After what seemed an eternity, the Bear completed her change. Standing before me now stood the biggest black Wolf I'd ever seen. In this form, she was easily the size of any of our most impressive male counterparts.

For the briefest of moments, my attention caught on something over her shoulder, on a pair of hypnotizing red eyes I'd seen only moments before, staring out at me from the shadows.

I only had time to notice that those eyes were set in a terribly beautiful pale face, though the grin I'd glimpsed in the darkness before was gone.

Then the Announcer yelled, "Fight!"

~

I gave myself to the beast within me, maintaining only the essential cognitive parts that made me woman. There was little room for the girl I was when I walked upright, and no space for doubts or insecurity. Those things in The Ring meant certain death.

The Bear wasted no time moving in, clearly not a fighter that had to rely on speed or stealth. She was all size and brute strength.

She charged me—teeth and thick black fur flashing. I slipped to the side and nipped at her flank before she spun around again to face me. Somewhere far away, I heard the surprised response of the crowd, but paid them no mind.

My focus was pinpointed on the beast I'd been locked into a cage with, as well as the beast that had been released within me.

Speed would be my greatest ally against this behemoth. I could not afford to be caught between her powerful jaws.

Just as the thought crossed my mind—as if the idea had created the reality—the Bear caught my left rear flank and tore easily through fur and flesh. A squeal almost escaped my mouth, but I clamped my jaws together and tore free of her grip.

The scent of my own blood floated up into the night.

I dashed to the side just in time to avoid the powerful clamp of her jaws once again. Her mouth snapped shut in the exact spot my throat had been only moments ago.

That bite had been a deathblow.

In response to my continued evasion, the crowd hissed and booed.

She struck, I moved. Again and again.

Until various objects struck the outside of The Ring from all around—tomatoes and heads of cabbages purchased at a vender in Dogshead for just this purpose.

The moment I'd been waiting for came with the onslaught of items being chucked at us from all directions. Tomatoes splattered like mini bloody heads against the chain-link, the heads of lettuce making the metal jingle like the necklace of a proper lady.

This distracted the Bear for the heartbeat of time that I needed.

She was a top Dog, after all, a known champion. She was not used to having things thrown at her.

Me, on the other hand... I'd had the opposite experience.

So as the enormous black she-beast glanced down at an over-ripe tomato that had strained through the cage to land in a red mess at her paws, I moved.

Every ounce of power I owned went into my forward lunge. My eyes locked on the target of her thick neck. My jaws stretched wide.

I clamped them shut on her throat a second before I felt her mouth snap shut around my back.

Searing pain shot through me. Hot and bright like lightning from above.

I almost lost my grip on her neck as the world bounced in and out of focus. For the very life of me, I hung tight.

My body was whipped from side to side as the Bear tried to shake free. She'd removed her teeth from my spine, but the fire of her bite still ravaged there. I could taste her blood in my mouth while my own blood wetted my fur.

My teeth had sunk deep. She should be dead already. A smaller Wolf would have been.

A terrible thought rocketed across my mind unwanted: *Maybe she can't be killed.*

My body whipped to the opposite side, my grip slipping.

One more good shake, and I would be thrown free.

My back and thigh were burning like the fires of hell, my energy waning.

Finish her, little Wolf said a familiar voice in my head. I was not entirely sure I hadn't imagined it.

But I summoned the reserves of my strength and closed my jaws entirely.

Hot blood filled my mouth. A swirl of rabid hunger filled my soul.

I lost my grip a moment before the Bear collapsed over sideways, her throat a gaping mess of meat and fur and her dark eyes wide as though she just could not believe it.

From the shocked silence that befell the crowd, I knew she wasn't alone in the sentiment.

14

Getting back to the mud hut where I slept was a blur of happenings.

The announcer had made some stupid joke about a twist ending, and finally, the chain locking up The Ring was removed and the door opened.

People continued to throw food at me as the Bear was dragged from the cage. It took Murphy and two other Dogs to carry her. The crowd hissed and booed, the most vulgar of names bouncing off of me the same as those rotten tomatoes and brown heads of lettuce.

But I was allowed to pass.

I'd made it. I'd survived. I'd killed the Bear.

There was no pride in the knowledge. With the injuries to my back and leg, I would be lucky if I lived through the night.

Just make it back to the hut, I thought. And thought and thought until I stumbled through the arched opening of my muddy home and promptly collapsed on the pile of horse blankets and hay that was my bed.

From there, the world darkened and disappeared.

~

I knew before I opened my eyes that I was still in my hut. The smell of the muddy clay was unmistakable, but what I didn't know was how much time had passed.

Or who was with me.

I placed the scent a moment after my gaze settled on him, and I tried to sit upright, but a wheezing hiss escaped me and I lowered my head again.

"Easy, little Wolf," Ryker the Hound said. He nodded his golden head toward my back. "You took quite the beating."

I was still in my Wolf form, and since I didn't feel like speaking directly into his mind, I said nothing. Instead, I scanned him for a weapon, wondering with a jolt if he'd come here to kill me since the Bear had failed at completing the job.

He was crouched near the entrance to my space, his forearms resting casually over his knees and his sapphire eyes gleaming in the darkness. He carried no knife or blade that I was aware of, though I suspected he didn't need either to kill me. Especially in my condition.

"You won," he said.

I only lowered my ears and looked up at him.

He nodded toward me again. "I put some salve on the wounds. You're welcome."

Growling, I adjusted myself until I was lying mostly under the horse blankets, and shifted back into my human form. I laid on my side, as lying on my ruined back was not an option.

Despite my injuries, it still only took a few moments.

From his crouched position, Ryker grinned. "Magnificent. How did you learn to shift so fast?"

The pain was much worse in this form, and I spoke through clenched teeth. "What do you want?" I snapped.

His head tilted in a very Wolf-like manner. "To be your friend, little Wolf," he said.

"Liar."

He laughed. "Why are you so sure? Perhaps you intrigue me."

"Whatever game you're playing," I said, "I don't want any part of it. Either punish me for my crimes or leave me be, but make up your gods damned mind."

He moved so swiftly that I blinked and he was before me, his face inches from my own and teeth bared in a terrifying expression that was not a smile.

"Males cower before me, little wolf," he said, his tone so even that goosebumps rose along my forearms. "And, yet, there you lie, injured and entirely at my mercy... and still you speak so brazenly. Have you no care what happens with your life?"

Though my stomach had clenched with his proximity, my spine tingling at the threat behind his words, I bared my teeth right back at him and met his gaze square. "My life has never been my own to care for," I spat.

And though it hurt to do so, I crossed my arms over my chest.

Ryker the Hound remained very close, his body practically hovering over mine, his clothes and the horse blanket the only fabric between us.

I decided not to notice when his azure eyes darted down to my lips... and back up to my eyes again.

When his hand came up and his callused fingers ran down the side of my face, tracing the silver scar there, I went as stiff as an oak board.

Before I could decide whether or not to bite his gods damned hand off, he moved, pulling away from me in a smooth retreat.

Ryker hovered by the doorway for a moment, staring down at me with an unreadable look on his handsome face.

"You cost a lot of people a lot of money tonight," he said. "If I were you, I'd mind the target on my back."

I snorted and rested back into my blankets. When I glanced at the doorway again a moment later, he was gone.

~

S leep claimed me again soon after, and once again, the sensation of not being alone in my hut woke me. Judging from the sound of the cicadas outside my hut door, I knew that it was the very middle of the night, the sunrise hours from arrival and the shadows holding fast to their corners.

The scent of lilac and honeysuckle filled my nose, and I slung an arm over my head, groaning. A wet cloth touched my forehead, and I hissed at the sharp smell of alcohol and the burn that seared across a scrape on my head I hadn't been aware of.

I made to bat the cloth away, but Goldie's delicate hand caught mine in hers. "Keep still, knucklehead," she said, albeit gently. "You want these cuts to get infected?"

Another groan slipped past my lips. I heard rather than saw Goldie retrieve a cup and fill it with water, the sloshing sound making my dry throat ache. A moment later, the metal cup was placed to my lips. I drank the cool liquid down so fast that I choked and water splashed down my chin.

In too much pain and exhaustion to care, I dropped my head again, and mumbled, "Maybe death by infection would be a kindness."

Goldie's tongue clicked in disagreement. "Don't talk like that. I hate it when you say things like that."

I inhaled deeply through my nose and let out a slow sigh. I resisted the urge to tell her she hated when I said things like that because they rang *true*.

Silence fell between us as my friend cleaned my wounds, washing the blood from my back and leg. Though I would heal faster than a mortal, the wounds from the Bear's bites had gone deep. These next few days would be a torment of pain as I healed.

And the scars were sure to be hideous. Then again, they'd have to compete for attention among the other scars already marring my back.

While she worked, I told Goldie what had happened with Amara, speaking telepathically because it took less energy and could not be overheard.

She looked as relieved as an old hen, and I asked her if she wanted to tell me about how her side of the plan had gone down.

"It went fine," was all she said of the matter, and I knew my friend well enough not to press. Part of me knew it was because Goldie wanted to spare me from the horrors that were her reality, the things she'd been forced to do to survive. Many nights we'd come together just this way; her smelling of strange Wolves' aroma, and me lying in a bloodied heap. Ours was a friendship forged in the fires of hell. None other ran as deep or as true.

We finished discussing the matter at the same time as Goldie finished cleaning my wounds. We decided we would not speak of it again, and that we would put our slave-smuggling days behind us.

We implored the gods to look after Amara. We thanked them for the fortune that had allowed us to get away with it all.

And we were far too hasty with our gratitude.

15

The summons came shortly after the sun had risen.

Goldie had left hours ago, needing rest after the last two nights she'd endured, telling me in much the same fashion as had Ryker that I needed to be on alert.

"A Wolf who loses money makes no friends," she'd said, and yawned before disappearing into the night.

I'd sighed, draping my arm over my forehead and closing my eyes. I fell back into an uneasy sleep, keeping one eye open for obvious reasons.

But no revenge-seeker came to my door, and I listened to the night bugs call out their presence as the night slowly seeped into day.

With morning, so came the order. I had just pulled myself into a sitting position, every movement a lesson in agony, when the Hound appeared at my door.

He pushed aside the ratty blanket covering the arched opening of my hut, crouching just to step into my place, needing no invitation.

Slaves did not make choices, including who visited.

The Hound was one of my Master's, Bo Benedict, as was

evident by the sigil (a single stock of lavender wheat) sew into the front of his uniform. His face was as hard as the earth on which I slept as he said, "Get up. The Pack Master wants to see you. You've got thirty seconds. I'll be outside." He turned and disappeared beyond the blanket-flap.

"Good morning to you, too, shithead," I mumbled, and knew I'd been heard when a low grunt sounded from outside the hut.

I was in too much agony to care. The wounds on my back and leg had clotted over, but it would not take much to reopen the new skin. My long brown hair hung in mats and blood-clotted chunks upon my head, and I panted through the process of pulling it up into a bun. Just this simple task gave the sensation of wildfire ravaging my back, but I managed.

Dressing was worse. Just the scratch of the fabric on my fresh skin was enough to set my teeth on edge. When I stepped through the flap of the hut at last, the Hound was glaring at me.

"That was forty seconds," he hissed.

I folded my arms over my chest, my clenched fists the only indication of the pain this caused me. "You kill a bear and then let me know how long it takes you to rouse in the morning."

The Hound's eyes narrowed, but I could see the respect last night's kill had earned me. If there was one thing Wolves understood and revered, it was the alpha-quality that made for a talented killer.

So when I told the Hound that I needed to relieve myself, and turned on my heel toward the creek where the Dogs did such business, I wasn't surprised that he didn't stop me.

I needed to evacuate and wash, yes, but I also needed the precious few moments to accept the probability of the serious shit I was in.

∾

I n my eighteen years of living on Bo Benedict's plantation, I had never been inside the main house, where the Master himself stayed and slept. In fact, I'd only ever seen the place from a distance, a sea of lavender wheat between me and the imposing structure that it was.

All white sides with red clay shingles on the roof. Pillars framed the front of it, large and imposing, flanking duel doors of thick red mahogany. The structure itself was u-shaped and rectangular, with more windows than one could count in a single sitting. The grounds surrounding it were pruned to perfection, the grass thick and emerald, the flowers vibrant and plentiful in varying shades of blue, violet, fuchsia, and marigold. A grand fountain graced the center as the focal point.

My Hound escort and I crested the hill on the eastern side of the estate, and it was an effort to keep the pace of my heartbeat in check. The Hound had not told me what the subject of this summons was, but I could think of a few actions I'd partaken in lately that might be the cause of it.

As the main house loomed before us, an invisible axe seemed to be looming over my head.

We crossed the grounds quickly. At the large double doors of the entrance stood two more Hounds sporting Benedict's lavender wheat sigil, sewn into their uniforms just above where their hearts beat. The two guards hardly spared me a glance as they nodded to my escort and held the door open for us to enter.

Looking into the house from the outside felt oddly like staring into the gaping maw of some terrible beast. I must have been hesitating, because rough hands shoved me from behind, and my dirty, bare feet stumbled over the threshold.

The marble floor of the foyer was cold against my skin, but I could pay the sensation no mind with everything else there was to look at.

Two wide staircases framed the entryway, leading up to a

landing where paintings that were likely worth more than my existence hung in ornate frames upon the walls. A large circular table sat in the middle of the foyer, a ceramic vase placed atop it and exploding with an array of colorful flowers. The real centerpiece was the crystal chandelier hanging from the ceiling, glittering like the diamonds in the Southern Mines. The ceiling itself was mostly glass (save for the part that supported that enormous chandelier) and the light from the morning sun cast twinkling bits of gold in every direction, like the night sky in reverse.

My teeth ground together hard enough to make my jaw ache and the fresh wounds on my back throb as if in answer. All of this. Paid for with the blood of Wolves like me. Every crystal hanging from the ceiling and thread making up the violet runner covering the marble floor.

If I hadn't already hated them all, this would be reason enough. I quite literally slept in the mud while these people lived like royalty.

Before my gawking could get me into any more trouble, I was led to the rear of the foyer, beneath the left hand, curving staircase, and down a long hall where more art adorned the walls. The thought of one of these paintings hanging in my mud and straw hut caused a laugh to bubble up from my belly, but my nerves were such that it died before it reached my throat.

There was another set of double doors, not as imposing as the archway at the entrance to the house, but ominous with their dark cherry exterior nonetheless. Without having to be told, I had a feeling that fate awaited me on the other side of those doors.

And I was right about that.

~

M y heart stopped dead in my chest.

The room beyond those double doors held thick carpets and furniture made of dark, aromatic wood and leather. Bookshelves lined three of the four walls, but not a single tome adorned them. Instead, sculptures and trophies and framed pictures held quarter upon them. The space was large enough to fit ten huts and a trough or two. Before three sets of imposing bay windows, plush chairs and daybeds had been arranged. Near the eastern side of the room, a huge shiny wooden desk clear of clutter dominated the space.

And behind that overcompensating desk sat the Midlands Pack Master, Bo Benedict.

But this was not what made my heart stop its humming. I'd expected to see Benedict here; this was his house, after all.

The person I had not expected to see was Goldie.

She met my gaze for the briefest of moments before looking away. It felt as though my tongue had swollen to three times its size in my throat.

The urge to grab my friend by the arm and hightail it out of there hit me hard in the gut, but a glance back at the Hounds still hovering by the doors reminded me that escape was futile. And even if we made it out of this room, there was the matter of the collar around my neck.

It was surely just my imagination, but standing there just then, that collar seemed to constrict around my throat like a noose.

We'd been caught. And we were totally screwed.

What other reason could there be for Goldie to also be here?

My friend was not the only unexpected guest in the room, however. Also present were Reagan Ramsey and his Head Hound, Ryker. Beside the Head Hound stood Mekhi, still sporting some of the injuries I'd given him in our scuffle.

And then there was the red-eyed male I'd glimpsed in the

shadows before my fight, and then again in the crowd during the match. My gaze lingered on him a moment. Despite the tension that had filled the room like a noxious gas, it was difficult not to stare.

Whoever this red-eyed male was, he was utterly captivating. Skin as pale as snow with high cheekbones and a strong jaw. Tall and lean with a muscular build. Those ruby eyes were framed with the darkest of black lashes, and the thick ebony hair atop his head was coifed up handsomely. He noticed my attention and stared back at me with amused indifference.

My mouth got the better of me before I could subdue it. "What's going on?" I asked.

This earned me glares from the Hounds in the room and utter dismissal from the others.

It was Reagan Ramsey who spoke next. His lip curled in distaste as he looked at me. "This is the one? This is the Dog that beat my Bear?"

I hadn't noticed his presence before, with all of the other distractions in the room, but Benedict's Overseer stepped forward now. His name was Wesley. I knew it well. He'd once tried to spell it on the skin of my back with his whip.

"This is Rukiya," Wesley drawled, his accent reflecting his Midlands origins. "She don't look like much, but she gives 'em hell in The Ring."

"How many wins does she have?" Ramsey asked, as though I were not standing right there in the room.

"The Bear made her eighteenth," answered Wesley. "We suppose that's about how old she is, but we can't be sure, since she didn't come with papers."

Ramsey looked at Benedict, who was lounging in his large leather chair behind his big desk, boots propped up on the edge as though he hadn't a care in the world. For once, his wide-brimmed hat had been removed to reveal his bald head, and it rested atop the desk beside his boots.

In his fine slacks and button-up shirt, Ramsey could not have looked more the opposite. "Were you planning on sending her to The Games this year, Ben?" Ramsey asked.

Bo Benedict sucked at his teeth, looking me over disinterestedly. "I wasn't gonna... but seeing as how she just took down the West Coast champ..." He shrugged.

It was an effort to keep my brow from furrowing. Why were they talking about these things? What did they matter if Goldie and I were going to be put down for helping Amara?

I dared a glance at my friend, but her gaze was steady on the carpet.

I looked again at the red-eyed male, but jerked my gaze away when I saw he was still watching me.

A moment of silence fell before Ramsey said, "How much do you want for her?"

Now there was nothing I could do to keep my brows from reaching the ceiling. Whatever I'd been expecting, this was not it.

Benedict shifted so that his boots returned to the floor. "If she's strong enough to take down your champ, I'm not so sure I'm looking to sell her at all, my friend."

From the look that flashed over Ramsey's handsome face, I would wager the two were anything but 'friends'.

Ramsey gained control over himself within the next breath. "As I'm sure you're aware, Marisol is hosting The Games this year," he said slowly. "I need a strong female to stand in for the Bear." He pointed a finger at me. "My Head Hound says I should buy that one."

Benedict gave another lazy shrug and spread his hands. "Make me an offer."

"Three," Ramsey said.

Benedict scoffed.

"Five," Ramsey tried again.

Benedict only looked at him this time.

"Seven," said Ramsey through clenched teeth. "And I think

we can agree that seven is more than enough for a single female Dog, especially since I lost a pup to your land only yesterday and she still has not been recovered."

Through this exchange, I didn't dare breathe.

Benedict said, "My Hounds searched for your missing pup." A shrug. "If they haven't found her by now, she's likely become dinner for some untamed beast. Your Hounds should've kept a better watch on her. I don't see what that has to do with this deal."

The rage that flashed behind Ramsey's eyes was the only indication of his discontent. His fit body remained relaxed and unconcerned. "Seven," he repeated. "Do we have a deal?"

Benedict considered. "Eight, and she's yours."

The look on Ramsey's face spoke for him. That was more than he was willing to pay for me... but just before he could voice his refusal, Ryker leaned over and whispered something low enough for only his Master to hear. As he did so, Ramsey's gaze went to me, assessing.

When Ryker finished, Ramsey nodded once, letting out a slow breath. His eyes were cool again when they met Benedict's, and he held out a smooth hand. "Eight," he agreed.

The two Masters shook hands, and like that, I was sold.

Like a bag of grain. Or a spice for seasoning.

"It's settled then," Benedict said. "And why is she here?" he added, nodding toward Goldie.

It was Mekhi the Hound who spoke; the first time I'd heard his voice since our encounter in the alley a day prior.

Dear gods. Had it only been a day?

"I requested her," Mekhi said. "I've taken a liking to her." His tongue ran out over his lips, his ginger hair tied back and matching beard trimmed. "I'm willing to buy her with my own coin," he added.

Every ounce of restraint I possessed was employed in that moment. I bit down on my tongue hard enough to taste blood, my mind flying a mile a minute. The bruises this bastard had given Goldie the other night were just fading, and I'd be gods damned if I let this happen.

My Master spoke before I could manage. "You West Coast Wolves," he mused. "You make a habit of stepping into other territories and running off with the females?"

To this, Reagan Ramsey grinned. He was all the more handsome when he did so, but there was no mistaking the beast behind his eyes. He spread his manicured hands wide. "We are keen on valuable females, yes," he admitted, and shrugged. "If Mekhi wants to buy her, I see no reason you two shouldn't barter."

Mekhi's eyes practically gleamed. "How much?" he asked.

Benedict gripped his chin between a thumb and forefinger, considering.

I practically exploded under my skin.

I was going to kill them.

I was going to kill every gods damned Wolf in this room if Benedict sold Goldie to this sadistic bastard.

"Eh..." Benedict drawled, "Pay off her debt and add three and she's yours."

Mekhi's head tilted. "That's a bit steep for a common whore, no?"

Benedict smiled. "You're the one who wants her."

I could hardly hear the words past the ringing in my ears and the telepathic murmur of Goldie begging me to hold my chill.

Mekhi looked at Goldie... and then at me.

And grinned.

"It's a d—"

"Just a moment," a smooth voice cut in, severing the Hounds words like a slice through skin.

Every head in the room turned toward the red-eyed male, who batted those thick lashes just once—almost innocently.

"I also have need of another female," said the male, his scarlet gaze going to Goldie. "I've always had a thing for redheads, so I'll take this one."

"You dirty Mixbreed sonofabitch," spat Mekhi. "You just heard me say—"

The male's eyes had been on Goldie, but as they flipped to Mekhi, the Hound shut his mouth without finishing the sentence.

If it were even possible, I might have felt bad for Mekhi. The way the red-eyed male was looking at him surely withered most males.

But his voice was calm when he said, "I'll pay double what he said." He jerked his chin toward Mekhi, a lock of his ebony hair falling from the coif. He smoothed it easily back into place.

Mekhi looked hot enough to boil oceans. "I can't match that!" he all but shouted.

"Adriel," Ramsey said slowly, the tone mildly disapproving, though I got the feeling he found the whole thing amusing. "Why do you torture him so?"

The red-eyed male—Adriel—gave the slightest of grins, his handsome face like that of an innocent pup. "I'm an entrepreneur, Ramsey," he said. "You know that. And I recognize good product when I see it." He turned toward Benedict. "Double. Do we have a deal?"

Benedict offered his hand, and the two shook on it.

Mekhi stormed out of the room, slamming the door behind him.

The reverberation shook me all the way to my bones.

16

Sold.

To the West Coast Pack Master. And Goldie, to a male with eyes as red as a devil. A male who made Hounds like Mekhi tremble in their boots. Adriel, Ramsey had called him. A dirty Mixbreed, according to Mekhi.

Even as I was all but shoved out of Bo Benedict's house and ordered to be ready to leave by midday, I still could not process what had just happened.

I'd thought I'd been called to the main house because Ryker the Hound or Bernard the Bartender had betrayed Goldie and me, or perhaps someone else had seen us during our efforts. But this...

Never in a million lifetimes had I expected *this*.

I trudged back to my hut in a daze, hardly noticing the fields or Hounds or Dogs around me. I passed by the pup kennels, where the youngest Dogs were kept in rusty metal cages, (the fate we'd saved Amara from, no doubt) but did not hear their harsh barks or hollow whimpering.

When I reached my dismal living space at last, I pushed

through the blanket flap covering the entrance and stared down at my meager belongings.

A couple sets of raggedy clothes, a pair of shoes with holes, a knife I'd fashioned from a shard of metal. I didn't need until midday to get my things together. I could carry everything I owned on my back and hands.

"I came to see if you need help," said a voice behind me, making me jump.

I spun around to see Ryker the Hound standing just beyond the arched entrance, his handsome face outlined by the gold of the ascending sun.

"But I can see that you've got it covered," he added.

In a move that should've cost me my head, I shoved the Hound hard in the chest. To his credit, he did not stumble, only absorbed the impact.

"Is that supposed to be a joke?" I snarled. "You find all of this funny?"

"Not at all," he said, but otherwise did not react to my assault or outburst.

It made me want to punch him in his stupid handsome face.

"I'm not entirely sure what you're so angry about," he said slowly. "I kept your secret. I let the girl go."

I jabbed a finger at him, but didn't dare put my hands on him again. If I was going to commit suicide, I could think of better ways.

"And I still don't understand why you did that—Why you're doing any of this. Why convince Ramsey to buy me? Why let me go in the first place? And who the hell is Adriel?"

Ryker quirked a golden-brown brow. "I answered your first three questions the last time we spoke, and as for your last... Adriel is a bastard, but not someone you need to worry about."

"The hell I don't," I snapped.

"The whore?" he said. "She's a friend of yours?"

"Call her that again, and I don't care whose Head Hound you are, I'll cut your tongue from your mouth."

Anger flared behind his blue eyes at this, and his hand twitched at his side, so near to that coiled whip... but the Hound did not strike me. "I'll take that as a yes," he said.

Ryker took a step toward me. I stood my ground and refused to shrink away. He had to bend his neck to fit in the hut, his close-trimmed hair grazing the ceiling and his shoulders wide enough to block out the sunlight beyond.

"I wish I could tell you she's better off with Adriel than she would've been with Mekhi," Ryker told me, his voice low as though he was sharing a secret, "but your friend is not lucky in belonging to the Mixbreed. Adriel is as cruel and cunning as they come."

"Sounds like more than a few Hounds I know," I replied.

The Hound's hands clenched into fists but remained at his sides. "Are you determined to anger me, little Wolf?" he asked, his tone so deadly even that I chose my next words carefully.

"I'm determined not to be fooled by you," I said truthfully.

The Hound tossed up his hands, his handsome face exasperated. "Okay then, little Wolf," he said. "Good luck with that."

With an order to be at the tracks at noon, he exited my hut and left me standing in the mud, cursing his stupid face and that of the rising sun.

～

I had a little less than an hour to make my goodbyes, but it was more than I needed. There was only one person I cared enough about to bid farewell to, only one piece of this wretched place I dreaded parting with.

I found her waiting for me in a spot we'd shared many times over the years; near the tracks where the train cars rolled into Dogshead and out again, taking passengers from coast to coast.

The ground here was all weeds and gravel, the metal tracks cutting through the land like a giant stitched scar. The fields of lavender wheat rolled to the west, and forests of emerald trees stretched out to the east.

Concrete platforms had been constructed near the tracks, allowing easy access to the trains, and filled with travelers, (mostly from the west this time around, as they were Reagan Ramsey's crew) who looked tired and bleary-eyed and perhaps a bit ashamed from the prior night's festivities.

Goldie sat on a felled, moss-covered tree edging the forest, far enough from the tracks to be out of danger, and close enough to feel the earth rumble when the large carts sailed past. Her golden-red hair hung in soft ringlets down her back, which was sun-kissed, same as my own, from the summer rays. The dress she wore was an emerald that complimented the shade of her eyes, which were so full of emotion as she looked at me.

I took a seat on the log beside her, staring out at the tracks and the quiet commotion surrounding them. "This was a twist I wasn't expecting," I said. I was trying to make light, but my voice came out a tad too tight to convince.

No tears escaped her eyes, but the sadness was evident enough in her tone. "Only you would joke at a time like this," she said.

I leaned into her a fraction, the closest to an embrace we would share before departure. "We could still run, you know... I would still run... with you... if you asked me."

Her delicate throat bobbed as she looked down at her hands and smiled. "I know you would," she said.

"I would take an honest shot at killing them all... if you wanted," I added. I couldn't say why, but I needed her to hear it.

Goldie only sighed, her full pink lips pursing. "Yes, I know," she said.

I'd never really known what love was, but if this was it, I was sure I didn't want a damn thing to do with it. I hated the heaviness that settled over me, the pressure that built up in my chest. Most of all, I hated how small and weak my voice sounded when I told Goldie goodbye.

And I hated seeing the sorrow in her eyes as she told me the same.

~

We could not allow the farewell to last any longer, neither of us keen to draw out the woe. I watched her retreat with my shoulders square, my heart sinking, and my face a mask of stone. She was getting on a train headed east, while I would board one going west, and that was the end of it.

Deciding I could use a stretch before cramming myself in a train cart at Reagan Ramsey's demand, I wandered deeper into the trees, looking for a good spot to relieve myself.

What I ended up finding was not a latrine.

The sound of whimpering reached me first, and had I been less of a nosy little Wolf, I might have headed in the other direction and minded my own business.

As it was, I padded a bit closer and peered around the trunk of a large tree.

Glowing scarlet eyes stared back at me.

Though I immediately regretted my decision to meddle, I found myself rooted to the spot same as the tree beside me. It was not just the red eyes that captured me, but the scene as a whole.

Adriel stood among the trees, only he was not in his mortal form. He stood over ten feet tall, ebony fur covering the tip of his hideous snout and down to the claws that had replaced his hands and feet. If not for those ruby eyes, I would not have even known it was him. His head was that of an overgrown Wolf, but his enormous and muscled body stood upright like a man or a bear.

Before him, a dirty-looking male trembled and pleaded, terrified in his smaller humanlike form.

The male hardly got the chance to draw another breath before the beast named Adriel snapped his neck and let his body fall to the earth. When I blinked again, the beast was gone, and the handsome, pale-faced male with the stunning red eyes had replaced it.

And he was utterly naked.

If I'd been able, I might have gasped. Instead, I only stood there, gaping like a fish on the sand. My stomach lurched as Adriel stooped, his tight muscles contracting, and bent his head toward the dead body. Fangs pushed out over his full lips, and he grinned up at me.

"Are you just going to stand there, dearest, or would you like to join me?" he asked.

"Please be good to her," I replied, clearing my throat twice before the words would follow. I didn't elaborate. He knew to whom I was referring.

In answer, he sank to his knees and tore into the still-warm throat of the dead male before him, the sounds of his meal fading behind me as I exited the forest, more than disgusted.

Repulsed.

And this was the monster that now owned Goldie.

17

The train ride was as unpleasant as an itchy ass on a scorching day, a statement that was not a leap from reality. The metal carts trapped in the summer heat, and the smell of overcrowded Dogs dominated the spaces. The door to the cart I rode in was kept open, the land rushing by just to the left of me, the sun making me squint my eyes.

A thin, grated walkway surrounded the train cart, allowing for access to different parts of the train while in motion, and it was the railing of this walkway that I leaned my head upon, watching the world go by in a blur beside me.

I tried to push thoughts of Goldie out of my mind, to ignore the fact that I would likely never see her again, but it was a useless effort. My heart felt as heavy as an anvil within my chest.

Time passed, I'm not sure how much, when the train cart in which I was riding received an unexpected visitor. I felt his presence ripple through the other passengers before I opened my eyes and saw him. Every Dog in the cart had gone utterly silent.

I lifted my head from the railing where it had been resting, my eyes peeling open and settling instantly on Ryker the Hound. He stood only a couple of feet in front of me—*over* me, looking down with that ever-inscrutable expression on his handsome face, his muscular frame absorbing the wind that had been blowing back my hair only a moment ago.

"Come with me," he commanded, his blue gaze meeting mine before he turned on his heels and began crossing between train carts with nimble leaps, not waiting for me to follow.

There were a few snickers from the Wolves within the cart, a couple foul names thrown that had me baring my teeth at the other passengers before climbing to my feet and following after the Hound.

Leaping between the train carts was not a difficult task for an able Wolf, but my back and other various parts of me were still healing, and after jumping twenty or so times, sweat was clinging to me and I was pretty sure I'd ripped a few wounds clean open. As I made it to the final cart at last, the land speeding away on three sides of me, I had to lean against the metal to catch my breath.

Ryker stood there waiting for me, and seeing that I was in pain, he opened the small door that led inside the caboose cart. Then he wrapped a strong arm about my waist, supporting a good portion of my weight, and led me inside.

The last cart held only luggage and other various belongings too large for passenger stowage. The lack of other bodies made the air inside this cart infinitely more tolerable, and I breathed in deeply as the Hound rearranged a couple big suitcases and gently set me down on them.

My body was in too much pain for protest, and the situation was too weird for words, so I only sat silently and glared at the Hound, my eyes narrowed and untrusting.

"What. The. Hell," I said.

Ryker shook his head a bit while stacking a couple more suit-cases and using the stack as a table as he arranged various items which he removed from the pockets of his black uniform. "Are you always so pleasant?" he asked. "Or are you ever the feisty little Wolf?"

I said nothing to this condescending bullshit. Only sat there and glowered in his direction.

When he turned back and looked at me, there was amusement in his sapphire eyes. "Relax," he said. "I'm just going to clean your wounds. I have some painkiller as well, if you want it."

I resisted the urge to tell him that I didn't want shit from him, but I was pretty sure my eyes said it for me.

"What is it you're after?" I asked. "Sex? Because you should know I've killed better males for trying."

The Hound only exhaled slowly, dousing a cotton ball in a blue liquid that smelled of alcohol. "Take off your shirt," he said.

My hand struck out before I could think to stop it, aiming for the right side of his stupid face. Even though I was fast, Ryker was faster, and he caught my wrist easily in an iron grip, halting my hand before it got anywhere near its target.

As soon as he gripped my wrist, he stepped in closer, standing between my knees where they were draped over the stacked suitcases. The scent of him flooded my senses. He smelled like seaside and sunshine, no doubt remnants of the western coast we were now heading to. His handsome face hovered close enough to mine that if I tilted my chin up a fraction, I could have brushed his lips in a kiss.

Not that I would *ever* do that. The bastard was a *Hound*, after all.

I could scarcely draw air as his blue gaze held mine. There was a certain fire in those icy eyes that scared me... Or maybe *thrilled* was a better word.

"You should let me heal you, little Wolf," Ryker the Hound said, releasing my hand and returning to his setup as though he had not just paused the world with that last interaction.

I would not admit it, but I was so confused and drained and

disheartened that I didn't utter another word while the Hound proceeded with doing what he'd said.

~

The Wolfsbane was a blessing, and even if I had only been in half the pain I was previously in, I would not have been able to refuse it.

"The Wolfsbane is Sorceress-spelled," Ryker told me, rubbing the cotton onto my back. A cold, stinging sensation seeped into me wherever the cotton touched, followed by soothing relief.

The Hound proceeded in cleaning my wounds while I sat silently with my shirt clutched over my chest. I was more uncomfortable than I let on that he was seeing the ruined mess that was my back, the scars that were a timeline of my very life, but my pride was outweighed by the knowledge that many a Dog before me had perished from post-fight wound infections.

And spelled Wolfsbane was not an easy commodity to come by.

After he finished with my back and thigh, he turned away while I pulled my shirt back over my head. I watched the muscles in his back work as he repacked his things. When he turned to me, he handed me a green dried herb that I recognized as more Wolfsbane.

"Chew it," he said, "and it'll take even more of the edge off."

I stared down at what he'd placed in my hand. Then looked back up at him. "This is expensive stuff. Why are you giving it to me? What do you *want* for it?"

"Is it so hard to believe that I've just taken a liking to you? You're very pretty, you know?"

My jaw nearly hit the floor. "You're joking, right?"

"Or at least I assume you would be, if you had a bath," he added.

It was a mixture of anger and embarrassment that made my

cheeks flood red. "My apologies if I haven't had time for proper hygiene between fighting for my life in The Ring and being sold between males like a bag of fucking potatoes," I snapped.

The Hound grinned, flashing straight white teeth and making a dimple form on one cheek. "And don't forget helping a child escape Dogshead in the dead of night."

This response had me snapping my mouth shut.

As he'd known it would.

Bastard.

I popped the dried Wolfsbane into my mouth and chewed while I glared at him.

His handsome face lit up with a smile, and I hated him for it. "Feeling better?" he asked.

Reluctantly, I nodded.

I hated him for that, too.

18

Apparently growing tired of my grunted responses and glowering in his direction, Ryker told me that I could spend the rest of the ride in this rear cabin, rather than returning to the cart with the other Dogs. He said he had some matters to return to, and left me a meat sandwich and a bottle of water before he slipped out the door and disappeared around the side of the train cart.

I glared at the stupid sandwich for all of two seconds before tearing open the wrapper and devouring it in about three bites. Then I downed the entire bottle of water. And though the Hound would be receiving no thanks for it, I begrudgingly had to admit that I felt much better.

With the way my wounds had been festering before, this may very well have marked the third time the Hound had spared my life.

But to what end? For what gain? Those were the questions that haunted me.

Despite my total distrust of him, I took him up on the offer to remain in the rear cart rather than returning to the ass-smelling cart that held the rest of the Dogs. I spent so much time breathing in the sweat and stenches of other slaves that I often forgot what clean air smelled like.

Like seaside and sunshine.

I cursed that dumb thought as soon as it entered my head.

Hours passed, and I leaned back against a stack of boxes and suitcases to rest my head, but ended up passing right out. When I awoke, darkness had fallen beyond the small rectangular window set in the door to the cart. For a few stunned moments, I didn't know where I was.

Then it all came back to me.

I was just climbing to my feet to stretch when the door to the cart opened, and Ryker the Hound beckoned me.

"Come see this," he said, and again did not wait for me to follow.

I considered staying put, seeing as how the train was still in motion, but for whatever reason, I sighed and joined him out by the railing, the black sky stretching endlessly above us.

We were at the bottom of a hill, judging by the angle, but it was hard to tell, because no stars were visible in the dark sky. The only light came from the other side of the hill. I tilted my head back and noted the scent in the air. It smelled like...

Seaside and sunshine.

When I looked over at the Hound, I found him watching me intently. I cleared my throat to say something mean to break this tension that kept building between us.

"*This* is what you wanted me to see...?"

My words trailed off as the train crested the hill it had been climbing, and a place unlike any I'd ever seen came into view.

My gaze was locked on the sight, but I felt the Hound sidle a bit closer to me, could feel the heat of his muscular body almost touching my back. His warm breath at my ear.

"*That* is what I wanted you to see," he whispered.

And—gods damn me—but I had to clench my fists against a shiver despite the warm night air. I moved away from him and gripped the railing, the lights of the city no doubt glittering in my eyes.

The sight was breathtaking.

Of course, I'd never been outside of Dogshead, but I imagined even seasoned travelers would revel at this. The city was set into the cliffs that overhung the seaside, where the rolling waves of a night-darkened ocean played an endless soundtrack amidst the calls of the seabirds and rumbling of the train on which we rode.

Homes and buildings were crafted from some glasslike material that reflected the moonlight in shades of soft pink, violet, and emerald. They were all unique, as though each one had been crafted, rather than just built, and there were too many to count.

On the highest point of the cliffs, towering over the glittering ocean that was black and silver in the moonlight, was a magnificent castle made of gray stone, as if constructed from the sands of these very shores. Its terraces and towers were many, and Hounds patrolled the grounds surrounding it like ants crawling over a dirt hill. I would wager that this was the home of Reagan Ramsey, the seaside equivalent of Bo Benedict's enormous plantation.

Blue fire was the source of the light I'd seen leaking over the hillside, adding a luminescence that was fed by the sapphire flames of thousands of torches. I wondered how many people it took to light all those fires.

As if reading my mind, the Hound said, "The torches were blessed by Apollo many eons ago, and they burn of their own accord after nightfall. It's said that the sun recharges their energy, and that as long as the sun kisses these lands, the torches will never die...Welcome to Marisol, little Wolf." His handsome face lit up with a grin. "I think you're going to like it here."

S tepping off the train and into the city was like stepping into a
new world. At once I felt very small and very ignorant. Even
so, it was an effort to keep my eyes from bulging out of my head.
There was so much to look at, so much to see, smell, and hear.

I'd returned to the cart with the other Dogs after the Hound
had welcomed me to his city, remarking that I would be with the
other slaves if he needed me and expecting him to yank me back
by my collar for the snap in my tone.

But he did not.

He let me go.

Again.

I made it to the cart I'd been in originally just in time to be
herded into a line with the other Dogs and counted by two
Hounds whom I'd never met. They wore the embroidered blue
anchor crest on the fronts of their uniforms, marking them as
property of Reagan Ramsey. They noted my presence as they
moved down the line of slaves but did not pay me any special
attention other than one remarking to the other that *this was the
one that killed the Bear.*

His partner snorted as though he didn't believe it, and they
continued on with their roll call. Afterward, they called all of us
to attention and the shorter of the two said, "You'll be expected at
The Cliffs bright and early tomorrow. They're at the south end of
the city. Don't be late, or you'll be considered a runner and
hunted down... You're dismissed."

The Dogs began to head off in different directions, no doubt
either to drink or fornicate or both. I stood atop the platform and
gazed out at the foreign city ahead, having no clue what to
do next.

Someone bumped into my shoulder hard enough from
behind that I stumbled forward. "Watch what the fuck you're
doing," that same someone said.

I whirled around to see a beautiful young woman who was

probably a couple years older than me. Her skin was a light shade of chocolate, her hair long and black. She wore baggy black pants and a shirt that had been strategically ripped to reveal her shoulders and midriff. Her eyes were big and almond-shaped and as dark as her thick, flowing hair.

"Watch what the fuck *you're* doing," I corrected. "And who the fuck you're talking to."

She barked a laugh. "You don't scare me."

"Then you're not very observant."

There was a moment of tense silence where we just eyeballed each other, the results of this interaction hanging in the balance. Just as I was beginning to ready myself for a brawl, she reached into her pocket and removed a pack of squares.

In a decisive move, she offered me one. "I'm Kalene," she said. "You're new."

I took the smoke but didn't give my name, waiting until she lit and drew from her own square before lighting and drawing from mine. The stuff they rolled and smoked on this side of the world may be wholly different from what I was used to, and I needed to treat everyone like an enemy until they were proven otherwise.

It was nothing personal, nor was it a defect of my character. It was simple survival.

"So you got a name? Or should I just call you 'new girl'?" Kalene asked.

"Rook," I said. "You can call me Rook."

Kalene's red lips turned up. "Well, Rook, you smell like shit, so what do you say I take you to get cleaned up, and then you and me can go find some trouble to get into?"

"Why? Why are you even talking to me?"

She gave me a look like this was a stupid question. "Because we're Dogs, genius. That means every moment could be our last." She shrugged. "So we might as well act like it."

It turned out that I could not argue with that.

19

Kalene led me across Marisol. Down streets that were paved with cobblestone and flanked by ornate green lampposts that burned of their own accord, blessed by the God Apollo himself, if a certain Hound were to be believed.

Again my senses were overwhelmed with stimuli. Again it was an effort not to appear as wide-eyed and green as I felt.

We passed shops that sported wooden signs proclaiming their names and hanging by chains that creaked ever so slightly in the cool night breeze coming off the water. These shops sloped with the streets that rolled like the hills of a valley, selling everything from clothing to herbs and potions. Glowing insignias graced the windows of the storefronts, claiming that within wonders could be found and fortunes could be told. Every structure was built of that same multi-colored glass that I'd seen from atop the hill on the train.

"It's seaglass," Kalene told me. "Made from lightning striking the sand. It's a trademark of the Western Coast."

And then there were the people.

Wolves and Vampires filled the streets, more people than I'd ever seen gathered in one place outside of the crowds that hovered around The Ring on fight nights. Some wore elaborate clothing and gaudy jewelry—shimmering or gauzy summer gowns, dangling earrings or clinking silver bracelets. Others wore plain clothes, the men in hats of various shapes and short-sleeved collared shirts and the women in cotton skirts printed with seashells or flowers.

As Kalene and I moved down the street, our attire, gates, and demeanors giving us up for what life station we held, people moved a few paces away or even crossed to the other side of the street entirely.

This seemed to amuse Kalene, who tossed her long black hair over her shoulder and strutted along as though she had every right to do so. She even winked at an older couple in fine clothes, causing the female to gasp and clutch at her purse before the male took her arm and led her away.

We walked about ten blocks before reaching the end of the cobbled street, which was just a rocky cliff that dropped straight down to the dark water some sixty feet below.

Kalene smiled when she saw the look on my face as I peered over the ledge. "Don't tell me the Bear-killer is afraid of heights," she teased, confirming my suspicion that my reputation preceded me. Then she stripped off her clothes until she stood only in her undergarments.

"Not afraid. I just don't like them."

"Well, you better learn to like them," Kalene said, flashing all of her white teeth. "Otherwise you should get used to smelling like shit."

She told me she'd see me at the bottom, and leapt off the edge of the cliff.

∾

S urely there was a path or trail that led down to the water. This cliff could not be the only way one could reach the bathing area.

I'd lied about not being afraid of heights, because as a Dog, to admit fear of such a thing would be considered a weakness.

And so would a refusal to jump.

There was nothing I could to do keep my knees from wobbling a bit as I leaned over the ledge and gauged the distance. An instant sweat broke over my brow. Before my involuntary physical reactions could progress further, I stepped back a few feet and stripped down to my undergarments. Then I took a deep breath... and jumped.

My stomach rushed up, the sensation of untethered falling making me grit my teeth and curse the gods in a silent, unintelligible stream.

But it lasted only a handful of heartbeats, and then the dark water was rushing up to meet me—swallowing me whole.

It was surprisingly warm and endlessly deep as the downward motion of my fall propelled me deeper and deeper. A thread of fear wove through my stomach as I fought against the trajectory, paddling my arms and kicking my legs in an attempt to surface.

There was a moment between this and when my head broke through the water where terror tried to grab me, and the idea that I could paddle and kick all I wanted but might never reach the air almost took hold.

But then I was there, my head above the water, my lungs drawing in precious air. The salty water burned the wounds on my back, which were much better thanks to the Wolfsbane. I didn't mind the stinging, however. The salt would further disinfect my wounds.

And it felt incredible to be rinsing free of the filth that had been clinging to me for what seemed an eternity.

A throaty laugh sounded beside me. "You made it, Bear-killer," Kalene said. "I was beginning to think you'd chickened out."

"That's because you don't know me very well," I snapped, and began swimming toward the cliff's edge, where others were pulling themselves up and out of the water. There were several ledges below the one I'd jumped from, and water was spilling over one of them in a mighty rush that created cascading water-falls on the lower cliffs. In the spray of these various falls, Dogs were bathing and playing, the area clearly designated for our use.

And though I knew most of them were simple, instinct-driven brutes, I had to admire the hard, muscled bodies of the male Dogs who'd survived enough battles to be grown and bathing in the waterfalls of this western cliff.

"Like what you see, Bear-killer?" Kalene whispered near my ear.

"Stop calling me that."

Her small round nose scrunched up and she arched a dark brow. "Why? It's a good name, a title you should be proud of. Your victory over the Bear makes you the reigning West Coast Champion, and guarantees you a prime spot at The Games."

I lifted myself out of the water with ease, and then made my way over to an outcropping of rock that was unoccupied and boasted a small but strong waterfall.

As I reached the spray and stepped under it, I tipped my head back at the simple pleasure that was running water. Thoughts of the last shower I'd taken—before my fight with the Bear and after my fight with Mekhi the Hound—came flooding back to me. It had been in Ryker's hotel room...

I stayed under the rushing water until that thought had been washed clean away.

Afterward, when I ran my hands through my long wet hair, the smell of the Bear's blood had finally faded.

⤳

K alene decided the best place to live like we were dying was Marisol's drinking district. This part of the city was not too far from the cliffs, where I assumed Ramsey's version of a mud and straw hut awaited me.

Not at all eager to check out the accommodations, and still riding an emotional low point with all that happened, I was not about to protest the drowning of my sorrows. Add to that the fact that I was still reeling over the separation from the only friend I'd ever had in this world...and yeah.

The night was still young when I found myself absolutely shitfaced. All those pesky issues that had been taunting me had flitted away, the jade-colored glasses I always wore slipping free and leaving the world on a bit of a tilt, and yet, somehow, more manageable.

And I wasn't about to stop there. I stumbled out of a bar with a name I didn't know and onto a street with the same, Kalene at my side and somehow less annoying than she'd been about an hour ago.

"Bet they don't have smoke dens in Dogshead," Kalene slurred, taking my arm and dragging me further down the sloped street toward a two-story building that looked turquoise under the moonlight. Hanging around the pearlescent exterior was a cloud of smoke that smelled strongly of an herb I recognized.

I had to give it to her. The girl knew how to party.

I held the door open for her, and together we disappeared into the smoky haze.

20

I regretted that shit the very next morning. Hardcore.

Peeling my eyes apart took more than a couple tries, and I groaned and rolled over... Only to get a face full of sand.

Cursing, I sat up and spat out the grains that had gotten into my mouth, clutching at my head when the movement set it throbbing. Between that and the wretched twisting in my stomach, I struggled to recall where I was, how I had gotten here, and what exactly the events of the previous night were.

A snore on the other side of me had me whipping my head in that direction, and I bit back another groan as I saw that the noise had come from a rather large male who was still asleep only a couple of feet from where I now sat. I didn't recognize him, but from what I could see of his face he was ruggedly handsome, his head shaved on both sides but grown a little longer on top. From the various scars covering his body, I would wager my winnings that he was a Dog.

And I could see every single one of those scars, because the large, handsome male was stark ass naked.

A relieved sigh whooshed out of me when I looked down and saw that I had retained my clothes... for the most part. My pants and sports bra were present... but my shirt was another matter.

Mentally shrugging and mustering my strength, I pulled myself to my feet and had to grip my knees for a moment before I was steady.

Three deep breaths kept down the contents of my stomach, which I could only guess at.

"Well, you no longer smell like shit," said a familiar voice in front of me, "but now you *look* like it. What am I to do with you?"

It was kind of funny, but I didn't laugh. "Then I look like I feel," I said, my voice gravelly and deeper in tone with the early morning.

A glance in the opposite direction revealed that the sun had not yet broken over the horizon, but was not long off in doing so. Kalene noticed where my attention went and nodded.

"We have until exactly three minutes before sunrise to be at The Cliffs," she told me. "So if you like to piss or eat in the morning, you better get to it. You don't want to be late. Ryker can be a bastard if you're tardy."

"Ever so eloquent," said a deep voice, and I looked back to see the large naked male sitting up and rubbing at his eyes. The muscles in his stomach contracted as he did so, and I jerked my gaze away before it could slip down any further.

This made him laugh, the sound so genuine that it took me a moment to recognize it. "That's all right, Bear-killer," he said. "I'm not shy." He waved a large hand down the front of him, as though presenting a display. "You have my permission to feast your eyes upon me."

Kalene rolled her eyes while I had a hard time deciding whether to appear amused or indignant... Which only made him laugh again.

I looked at Kalene, a certain desperation coming into my eyes, and jerked my head at the male. "Last night...? We didn't...?"

Now it was Kalene's turn to laugh, and she did so as she linked her arm through mine as though we were the best of friends. "Gods no," she said. "If I wanted to kill you there are easier ways than letting you die from disappointment the morning after with Oren over there."

"I heard that," Oren called from behind us, though he didn't seem particularly upset.

We were already walking away from him, but Kalene glanced back over her shoulder to take him up on the offer to feast her eyes while he stretched as though being naked in public were as natural to him as breathing.

"He does have a nice ass, though," she mumbled.

"I heard that, too," he called.

As we walked down the beach, I saw other Dogs rousing from their slumbers and stumbling out of their small living structures, which were little more than shacks on the sand built from the leaves of palms and wood scavenged from the Western forest.

Kalene had informed me yesterday that each Dog had to build his or her own living quarters in their free time, or else sleep out under the stars. Last night, when I'd been drunk and toasted, I'd found this so wickedly efficient on the part of Reagan Ramsey, my new owner and Pack Master.

"Or you can take the home of a Dog who dies," Kalene had told me, "but you'll have to fight several others for it, and they'll be mostly males. Really, it's not worth the trouble."

This morning, I found this less wickedly efficient and more just dickheadish. Make the slaves build their own homes with material they gather.

"At least the drinks and drugs are still free," Kalene had added, clapping me on the shoulder and passing me the pipe.

I didn't bother telling her that though we didn't trade coin for those drugs and drinks, they were not at all *free*. If she didn't know this on her own, she was a willfully ignorant fool.

I shook these thoughts from my head as I found a spot behind some large rocks and relieved myself. Then I went to The

Cascades—which were near enough by that I could hear them when I first woke up—and washed up as best I could while dozens of other Dogs did the same.

This small part of the island, Kalene had explained to me, was designated for the Dogs. We were allowed to drink in the bars of the city, smoke in the dens, and fuck in the whorehouses, but we were not to wander into the other districts, where the Wolves with basic rights lived. And, of course, we could not leave, or either the collars around our necks or the Hounds on our tails would make us wish we hadn't.

So, basically, same life as it had been in the Midlands at Bo Benedict's plantation. Only the scenery had changed.

And scenery means absolutely nothing to a slave. The most beautiful of cages, after all, is still a cage.

If any single place in the world was a testament to this statement, it was The Cliffs.

~

The climb was taxing and treacherous. But everyone had to do it. It was the only way to get there. And it was a test of strength and a revealer of weakness. Just like everything else in the life of a Dog.

When I'd stood on the beach, staring up at where Kalene was pointing, fear had spiraled in my stomach, the same brand I'd felt staring over the ledge of The Cascades yesterday, but I was careful not to let it show.

As other Dogs—both males and females—began to climb the cliff face like spiders up a wall, I only gave Kalene a nod and leapt up to the lowest ledge, following the same path as a male who'd gone before me, ignoring the slight pain this caused in my still-healing back.

When I'd made it fifty feet up from the ground, I realized that if the wounds on my back had been any less healed, this climb very well may have killed me.

As it was, it almost did, anyway.

I was so concentrated on keeping my footing, on ignoring the pains in my wrists and fingers from repeatedly gripping small ledges and hauling myself up, that I didn't notice the female inching closer on my right side... Not until the bitch tried to kill me.

Sweat was dripping down the sides of my face, rolling down the spine of my back, and I was taking a breath, drawing in the salty sea air, preparing to reach for the next foothold above me... When something wrapped around my ankle in a tight grip.

And *yanked*.

My brain processed Kalene's shouted warning to watch out a handful of seconds too slowly.

I'd been mid-reach, only one hand gripping a hold of the cliff, one foot bracing my weight, and there was nothing I could do as those two holds were broken, as my body was jerked away from the cliff face and sent free-falling into the air.

As my stomach rushed up to my throat and panic bloomed inside me like a mushroom cloud, all I saw was a glimpse of a smiling female with golden blonde hair and large blue eyes. She wiggled her fingers in a little wave, as if to say *goodbye*.

Useless fury replaced my panic as I continued to fall, the earth rushing up to meet me with a speed that felt inevitable.

Then, there was a hand, extended, reaching, and I latched onto it with both of my own, squeezing as my body was yanked to a stop... and I dangled in midair.

Heart hammering in my throat, my gaze traveled up the arm that was holding me, and my eyes met those of Oren, the large naked male I'd met just this morning. He'd put on a pair of shorts before the climb, thank the gods, or else I'd have a front row seat to his ball sac just about now.

"I got ya, Bear-killer," Oren said, and with a strength I could only admire, he maintained his grip on the ledge while swinging me up and allowing me to quite literally climb up his hard body to reclaim my own hold on the cliff face.

I looked down to see that I'd only fallen twenty or so feet; the ground was some thirty feet below us.

"Thanks," I told Oren.

The male reached up and gave me a couple taps on my backside, and if he hadn't just saved my life, I might have bitten off his hand for it. "Get moving, little one," Oren said, nodding to the top of the cliff. "We have to beat the sunrise... On top of that, the Wolf who just tried to kill you is up there. Something tells me you're the type of lady that might have something to say about that."

He hadn't even finished the sentence before I'd resumed my climb, the fire now coursing through my bones moving me along fast enough that I heard Oren chuckle softly beneath me.

21

I was so high up that I could see across hundreds of miles of endless turquoise-blue ocean if I looked over my shoulder and glanced behind me.

The air was thinner up here, the sun brighter. Not even the seabirds ventured up this high, though I suspected more fearsome beasts lived in the caverns and crevices of this seaside mountain.

Despite the rather forceful breeze up here, my blood was boiling, and I hauled myself over the final ledge of the cliff exactly three minutes and fourteen seconds before sunrise—those fourteen seconds all there were to spare.

Because some *stupid bitch* had almost killed me.

As soon as I pulled myself over, sweating and panting from the ridiculous climb, my eyes were scanning the gathered Dogs for a certain blue-eyed, blonde-haired female.

They settled on her, and that switch within me flipped.

She saw me coming and tried to prepare, but a wall of stone would not have been able to stop me. I threw my entire body into her as I wrapped my arms around her middle and lifted her into the air. A heartbeat later I was body-slamming her on the unforgiving rock of the cliff's ledge.

In the next blink, I was atop her, my fists pounding down upon her face. The scent of blood in the air followed.

As it splattered my face, my chest, and my bared and gritted teeth, I knew I wasn't going to stop until I'd killed her. Only cold anticipation arose within me at the prospect.

My fists continued to rain down upon the bloody mess that had become her face...

And then I was yanked back and up by my collar, and found myself flying through the air.

Before I could process what had happened, I landed in a heap so near the edge of the cliff that for a horrifying half-heartbeat I'd sworn I was going to go over. I'd hardly skidded to a complete stop when I was moving back toward the female I hadn't finished with.

My tunnel vision was such that I didn't see the Hound until I ran smack into him, his wide chest making me stumble back, the impact with me leaving a smear of blood on the front of his shirt. I did see him reach for the heavy black baton at his belt, however, saw as he freed it from his belt and raised it.

I braced for impact.

It didn't come.

Blinking, I looked up to see what had halted the fall of the baton upon me.

Oddly, I wasn't entirely surprised to see that it was Ryker the Head Hound.

~

"Take a walk," Ryker told his inferior.

The Hound who'd been about to hit me (and had likely pulled me off the other female and nearly thrown me over the edge of the cliff as well) looked utterly confused. "She almost killed that other female, sir," the Hound said.

Ryker's blue eyes were hard as stone. "Do I need to repeat my order?" he asked, with too much calm and poise.

The lesser Hound scurried off like a mouse sighted in a pantry. I knew without checking that every pair of eyes present was watching this whole exchange. Feeling suddenly ridiculous with the other female's blood painting my hands and face, I waited for whatever was going to come next.

In Dogshead, the both of us would have been whipped immediately for our fighting. But I was not in Dogshead anymore.

Me and everyone else around me watched as Ryker barked for some of the other Hounds to come drag away the female whose life I'd nearly taken, as she was clearly in no condition to remove herself.

After this was complete, the Head Hound prowled over to where I was standing, looking as rabid in my bloodletting as my old nickname implied. His handsome face showed nothing but malicious boredom, so very different from the expression he'd worn when cleaning my wounds on the last cart of that train.

"You like to get in fights, little Wolf?" Ryker asked me. "Then let's get in fights."

Thus began the toughest day of physical exhaustion I'd ever lived through.

I thought it would never end, and before it did, I'd wished several times that I had just died making the climb this morning. Kalene informed me that many a Dog *did* die making that climb. Coupled with the intense training Ryker was putting us through, just the thought of having to climb that cliff face again tomorrow was enough to make me want to cry.

That is, if I hadn't run out of tears a long damn time ago.

We did not stop fighting, running, crawling, climbing, and fighting some more until after the sun had fallen, taking with it at last the lingering heat of the day. Ryker made it clear to the other Dogs that the intensity of today's training was due to the show I'd put on this morning by beating up the other female, whose name I'd learned was Peni.

I made a mental note to tell him I hated him the next time the Head Hound felt in the mood to mess with my head again with his false kindness. He was a bastard, all right, and he wasn't fooling me.

When he finally called an end to the day, it took more grit than I cared to think about to keep from collapsing on the spot.

If there had not already been a target on my back for killing the Bear, there was certainly one there now. Even the male Dogs (who usually were decent to me on account of my pretty face) were glowering in my direction as we hauled ourselves away from the training areas. Wondering how we were supposed to get back down from the cliffs, and praying to any god that was good that we did not have to climb back down, I followed the crowd of Dogs in silence, careful to keep my distance.

A small blessing was that everyone around me was as drained as I, and I had no doubt that it was this alone that afforded me undisturbed passage toward wherever we were going.

I'd almost escaped when a Hound I didn't know appeared at the side of me. "Come with me," he said, turning on his heel and not waiting for me to follow. There were snickers and nods of righteous approval from some of the other nearby Dogs, and Kalene shot me a sympathetic look along with Oren, who had been pleasant to me throughout the day.

Having no other choice, I bit back a growl of frustration and followed after the Hound, ever the compliant little Wolf at the beck and call of her masters.

I hated them for it.

The Hounds perhaps most of all.

~

I was escorted back across The Cliffs training grounds, and then toward a line of trees that rolled over the land and into the distance away from the sea.

"Wait here," the Hound told me, a certain sadistic gleam in his eyes. "The captain wants a word with you."

Your captain, my captor, I thought, but did not bother to say anything. I was too drained to correct this chicken shit.

Soon after, Ryker appeared, exiting through the flaps of a large green tent that no doubt kept the Hounds cool during the days when the Dogs were sweating on the training fields. In Dogshead, Benedict had us working the fields rather than training in hand-to-hand combat, which was likely why Reagan Ramsey's Western Coast produced so many champions. I recalled asking Kalene last night who did the work for Ramsey's houses and other various businesses if the Dogs were always kept in training. She'd said that there were other slaves for that kind of work. Lucky bastards, she'd called them.

I didn't disagree. Everything is a matter of perspective, after all.

"Ramsey owns more Wolves than anyone on the continent," Kalene had told me. "He's got his paws in everything, and is good friends with the Vampire Queen."

It was these thoughts that were riding my mind as I faced Ryker the Hound, a hand going to my hip despite the fact that lesser offenses had gotten me whipped in the past. The urge to ask him what the hell he wanted struck me, but I pressed my lips together instead.

I was sure my facial expression spoke for me anyway.

"Follow me," Ryker said, and began heading into the line of trees.

Wondering why the fuck I was following everyone around like a gods damned puppy as of late, I scrubbed my hands down my face and then clenched them into tight fists at my sides.

Then I followed after.

22

Ryker led me through the trees, and I cursed the stupid muscles in his stupid muscular back when he stripped his shirt off over his head and tucked it into the back pocket of his black pants.

Which made me look at his round bottom that sat so neatly below his trimmed and tanned waist...

I decided just then that when I went back into the city this evening I would find a handsome Wolf to help me relieve some of this... tension.

Because, seriously? What. The. Fuck?

Dude was a Hound. And not just a Hound, but a *Head Hound*. One that there were horrifying stories about. One that was rumored to be as sadistic as he was handsome. One that could slit my throat while I slept or string me up by a rope in the city square and not face a single consequence for doing so.

Beating Dogs into submission must be a good workout, I thought bitterly, and refocused my traitorous gaze on the forest floor beneath me.

He stopped when he reached a small pool that was fed by a waterfall just big enough for one person to stand under. Rocky boulders that were the perfect width and height to make good benches ringed the pool. The water was the same turquoise as that of the nearby sea, only lighter in shade for the shallow depth. The sunlight that made it past the thick green canopy overhead danced in dapples over the water, and a light mist provided by the short falls kissed at the clean air.

My eyes narrowed as they observed all of this and then fell on the Hound.

Who was now removing his gods forsaken shoes and pants, revealing muscular legs and absolutely no underwear beneath.

I gave him my back and folded my arms over my chest. "What is it with you West Coast Wolves and randomly getting naked all the time?" I snapped.

A deep chuckle sounded behind me. "It was a long, hot day," he said. "I thought you might want to take a swim." He paused. "Wait... Who else keeps getting naked around you?"

"None of your business," I grumbled.

"Come swim with me, little Wolf."

I gritted my teeth. "No."

"Why not?"

Anger flooded me at the ignorance of the question. I turned on my heels and stalked toward the pool, my fists bundled tight at my sides. "Why not?" I said. "You're joking, right? What is it that you're not understanding here? You're a Hound, I'm a Dog. Why in all the realms would I ever want to get naked and swim in the forest with you?"

Treading water, his shoulders and golden-brown hair shimmering in the sunlight, he said, "I didn't say you had to get naked, but you're definitely welcome to."

"I will never willingly let you touch me," I told him. "You're wasting your time if that's what your goal is."

The Head Hound held up both scarred and golden hands. "Okay," he said, his blue eyes serious... but not in the aggressive, mean way they had been with the others all day in training. "I got it," he added. "But it was a really long and really hot day... So... will you swim with me?"

I looked at him like he was stupid. "Are you asking me, or telling me? Do I have a choice in the matter, Captain Ryker?"

Without hesitation, he nodded. "Yes," he said. "You have a choice in the matter."

In answer, I spun on my heels once more and stalked away.

The Hound did not call after me.

∿

Of course, the easiest way back down to the section of seaside that was designated for the Dogs was to leap over The Cascades again. Fear still spiraled in my stomach as I approached the ledge, where I could see Dogs bathing below, but it was not as intense as the day before. Probably because I was too damn tired to care.

Without bothering to strip off my clothes, (which needed a good wash, anyway) I leapt over the side of The Cascades and felt my stomach rise before making impact with the blessed water.

As I kicked toward the surface, an image of Ryker's lean and muscular body glittering with the water of that pool flashed through my head.

By the time I'd finished bathing, I was able to stifle that unwanted image.

Mostly.

Kalene and Oren were waiting for me as I climbed out of the water. I'd shifted into my Wolf form because unlike everyone else around here, I did not particularly like to go around naked in my skin suit. Both the female and male laughed when they saw me.

Oren nudged Kalene playfully and nodded down at me, where I stood on all fours shaking out my thick brown fur. "Bear-killer is shy," said the male.

Kalene grinned. "Did you see the way she whooped Peni this morning, Oren?" she said. "I'd watch it if I were you."

"Bear-killer likes me," Oren argued. "I stopped her from splattering into Wolf-meat at The Cliffs this morning."

I gave them the Wolves' equivalent of an eye roll and padded away to get dressed and dried, deciding that I needed to take on the task of building myself a shelter as soon as possible. That, and I needed to take my meager winnings from my last fight and purchase some personal items and new clothing.

Until I had a relatively private place to stumble back to, I would not be repeating the behaviors of last night. Before my body could sustain any more physical exertion, however, I needed to sit my sore ass down. Drink some water, eat some meat, take a breather. Or two.

The night bugs were just starting to call out their presence as I crossed the beach and headed toward the base of a mountain where Kalene had informed me a small path led back into a palm grove that was good for collecting items for my shelter.

I made it up the path and found the grove. It was quiet here, no naked Wolves or cawing seabirds. The sandy ground had yielded to tall grasses, and I slipped into them, easily concealed there in my Wolf form.

I passed out just as soon as I set my head between my paws.

~

I awoke in an unknown location.

The air smelled different here. My body was no longer encased in tall, soft grasses, and when my ears swiveled around on my head, they could not detect the sound of the nearby ocean lapping relentlessly at the shore.

My eyes snapped open and I held very still, assessing my surroundings. Rather than smelling like sea and sunshine, the air

smelled damp and earthy, and was cooler than I thought it ought
to be given the season.

Once my mind was firing on all cylinders, I saw that I was in
some sort of cave.

A match struck somewhere in the darkness beside me, and I
was on all four paws in an instant, my teeth bared and a vicious
growl emanating from my throat.

"Easy, little Wolf," said a familiar voice, and the flare of a
flame lit up Ryker's handsome face. He nodded over my shoulder.
"I brought you some clothing if you want to shift."

In answer, I only lowered my head between my front paws
and made sure every fang in my mouth was on display as I
growled again.

"Or don't," he said, and shrugged. "You could always drop the
walls around your mind and speak to me that way... I actually
prefer it. It's much more... intimate."

Cursing silently, I shifted just so that I could tell him off. His
blue eyes watched every move I made as I yanked the shirt he'd
brought me down over my head, not caring that my body was
bare to him for a brief moment.

As the hem over the shirt fell down to my thighs, and I saw
his gaze go from blue to glowing Wolf-Gold, traveling the length
of me and back again, there was nothing I could do to keep the
blush from rising to my cheeks.

"How the hell did I get here?" I snapped.

Ryker the Hound's eyes glowed for a moment longer as they
lingered on my bare legs. "I brought you here," he said, and his
voice was deep, low. "You were very tired. You didn't stir
one bit."

I tossed my hands up. "Oh, okay, cool. For a second I thought
you might have done something *totally creepy*."

Ryker set about building a small fire in the center of the
cavern, and he looked back at me over his wide shoulder. "Are
you mad because I pushed you at training today?" he asked. "I

had to. You don't want the others to think I favor you... Even if I do."

"Really? And why is that? *Why* do you favor me?"

The Hound moved so swiftly that I hardly had time to draw a breath and he was in front of me. His scent wrapped around me with the proximity, an essence of sunshine and seaside. With his height and the wide muscles of his chest and shoulders, I felt very much like I was standing within the shadow he cast, a ring of space that I wasn't at all comfortable in.

And the seriousness of his handsome face, the intensity in his blue eyes.

It terrified me.

No, if I was being entirely honest, *thrilled* was probably a more accurate word. Terrified was just what I *should* have been.

"I find you attractive, little Wolf," the Hound told me, his gaze going to my lips, then back up to meet my eyes. "You must know that you're rather beautiful, and beyond that, there's this... *fire* within you. It seems to captivate me, and now, I can't stop thinking about what it would be like to have you as my lover. All that fire... How you must *burn*..." With this last word, his blue eyes flared Wolf-Gold once more.

And something akin to flame swirled duplicitously in my midsection.

I took a step back from him. Then another. Some small part of me whispered that I should run. Another, traitorous part of me, was again pulling up that image of his golden body wading in that turquoise pool, of the way his strong hands had felt working the Wolfsbane into my back, these thoughts causing that heat at my middle to stoke and spread.

Sensing my discomfort, (if that's what one should call it) the Hound retreated, returning to his work on the small fire he was building in the center of the cavern. I almost sighed in relief, but managed to keep my reaction to his words mostly neutral.

"I brought you here," the Hound told me as he kindled a

flame within his woodpile and blew air on it, making the embers burn and glow, "because I thought you might want a safe place to sleep. After today, I didn't think you'd want to build your own shelter. We're not far from the beach, but no one really knows about this place."

I glanced around, looking at the space but not really seeing it. At last, I found my voice. "I'll *never* be your lover," I said. "I told you, you're wasting your time."

The Hound had finished building the fire and now busied himself laying out several thick blankets nearby. Once he was done, he sat down atop them and began removing items from a burlap sack. "Okay, little Wolf," he told me, and smiled wolfishly, "but I brought food and wine, and you can join me in having some, if you want."

I almost stomped out of that cave. I really did. If I had, things might've turned out entirely different. But then the bastard pulled out a hunk of cured ham that was as large as my head and a loaf of fresh bread that was a delicacy to any Dog's diet. When he popped the cork out of a bottle that released the sweet smell of good wine into the air... I huffed out a breath and took a seat on the blankets beside him.

23

The next day, Ryker trained the Dogs to death again on The Cliffs, the playful and challenging expression he wore with me in private no where to be seen. That night, I found him waiting at the entrance to the cave again with another bag of food and wine, as well as some other items that might make my 'stay more comfortable', as he put it.

I thanked him very much, but informed him that his efforts were useless, as slavery was an inherently *un*comfortable situation.

To this, he'd only nodded and placed the items he'd brought along the cave wall, as if I would change my mind later. I'd narrowed my eyes at him, because I knew he was probably right. You'd be amazed at what a person would do for basic commissary after being deprived for so long.

When the Hound waved his hand for me to join him once more on the blankets, I only sighed and obeyed. I'd decided the night prior that if he was determined to let me eat his food and drink his wine then that was his own stupid decision. Despite the fact that my traitorous body might find his attractive, I vowed that

I would never let him touch me. Not like that. Not for all the cured ham and fine wine in the world.

They could force me to shift and fight for my life in front of crowds of people, but I would *never* allow my body to be used the way they used Goldie's. I'd kill and die before I let that happen.

Thoughts of Goldie made my shoulders slump a fraction as I shoved a piece of bread in my mouth and flicked a couple pebbles across the cave floor.

"What's on your mind, little Wolf?" Ryker asked me on the fourth or fifth day in a row where he'd trained the Dogs in the morning and visited my cave with food in the evening. The bastard was clever, because the food and wine he brought was as varied as it was delicious, and never in my life had I sustainably eaten so well. It had less than a week, and I was already seeing a change in my body. My curves were beginning to fill in more fully, my cheeks appearing less hollowed out.

Dogs ate the mush that was provided them, or hunted game in the rivers and woods. We drank moonshine that could singe the hair off a male's upper lip, and water from the streams and rivers that fed the earth.

We did not eat aged cheeses, flaky breads, and seasoned meats. We didn't sit on blankets in caves and sip wine from glasses that clinked when held together. We sure as shit didn't do these things with Hounds.

And, yet, here we were... Him, too stubborn or stupid to leave me be, and me, too gluttonous about food and wine to deny him the opportunity. Or that's what I told myself, anyway.

I realized he'd asked me a question, and opted for the truth. "I was thinking about my friend, Goldie," I said, and actually looked at him, which I'd been adamant about avoiding since we'd began this evening charade. "I was wondering where she is, what she's doing... If she's okay."

The Hound leaned forward from where he'd been leaning back against the cave wall. His handsome face was all fine angles and shadows in the dimness of the cavern, and the firelight beside us danced along his golden skin. His blue eyes were intense as they held mine, and his voice was unnervingly gentle. "I wish I could tell you she's in good hands," he told me, "but the male who bought her is... not known for his kindness."

My jaw clenched. "And neither are you," I countered.

The Hound held up both hands. "Fair enough," he said. "But not every rumor that's whispered is true."

I tried not to let his words crush me. Suddenly the fine wine and food in my belly felt rancid. "Then the same could be said of this Adriel," I argued, clinging to the thread of hope that Goldie had landed somewhere better than where we'd come from. "Maybe not everything they whisper about *him* is true."

But even as I said it, the memory of the red-eyed Mixbreed male standing in the forest in Dogshead, murdering that other male right in front of me and then drinking his blood, the revulsion and horror that had coursed through me at the thought of that *creature* owning Goldie... A shiver ran down my spine, and there was nothing I could do to stop the goosebumps that broke out along my skin.

When Ryker's warm but calloused hand fell gently on my forearm, soothing away some of the chill that had formed there, for all of two heartbeats, I forgot to hate him.

Then I jerked my arm away, angry anew. "How could you let him buy her then?" I snapped. "If you like me so damned much, why didn't you buy Goldie, too? Rather than let her be sold to that—that *monster*?"

And as soon as the words spilled out of my mouth, I knew that this was the real reason I hated the male beside me so fiercely. It was not the fact that he was the right hand of the Wolf who held the leash attached to the collar around my neck. It was not even the fact that he was apparently a bastard to every other Dog in the world save for me. It was that he kept pretending to be decent, but he had not stepped in when the person I loved the most was sold to a known sadist, and a *Mixbreed* to boot.

There was no stronger stereotype in all the realms than that of the shadiness and shiftiness of Mixbreeds. They were crooks, liars, cheats, and killers. They had no loyalty to anyone but themselves, and they fit in nowhere. It was said that the mixture of races had led to the deterioration of the Mixbreed's soul, and as such, not many of them were ever born. To lend to the creation of a Mixbreed was not just taboo; it was considered an abomination.

And this was the fate that had befallen Goldie. Whether or not her purchase by the Mixbreed was Ryker's fault, I still blamed him for it.

"First of all," the Hound said slowly, "I didn't know the other female—Goldie, meant so much to you. I also hadn't been aware that Mekhi was going to try to purchase her, otherwise I would have tried to stop him... And, third, you can at least take comfort in the fact that Mekhi would not have been much of a better owner than Adriel. They're both shitheads... Lastly, if I recall correctly, it was *your* interactions with Mekhi that put Goldie on his radar. I think we both know he tried to buy her to punish you."

He may as well have punched me right in the stomach. My mouth snapped shut. We ate the rest of the meal in silence. When he slipped out of the cave that evening, for the first time since he began these visits, he did not bid me goodnight.

∼

I did not expect him to return.

But he did.

Night after night after night.

We didn't speak about Goldie again, and I spent many moons refusing to even look at him or acknowledge his presence while I stuffed my face with the delicacies he brought. The fights in The

Ring were on an offseason at the moment, as all the Dogs in the realm were preparing for The Games at the end of the summer. Vampires and Wolves and other various creatures would travel from thousands of miles away, from all over the world, to come and take part in the festivities.

On top of that, Reagan Ramsey was hosting the event this year. The entire city of Marisol was preparing for The Games. Bets were already being placed and merchandise sold. This year, Ramsey had promised the world, The Games would be bigger and better than ever.

The only thing I cared about was what that meant for a Dog.

About a month or so into his visits, I worked up the nerve to ask Ryker.

He folded a hand behind his head, the muscles in his arm and chest flexing, leaning back against the cave wall, and grinned lazily at me. "She speaks," he said.

I gave him an unimpressed look and waited.

At last, he sighed, plucked a grape from the bunch he'd brought us, and popped it into his mouth. I watched indifferently as his fine jaw worked. "Ramsey is expecting a large turnout for The Games," he told me. "He's put a lot of money into assuring that it's so. But the fights... they'll be different this time around, too."

"Different how?"

"Some of you won't just be fighting in Wolf form. There will also be unique match-ups and pairings, and surely some unexpected surprises... That's all I know."

I rolled my eyes. "Sure it is."

The Hound moved so quickly and so unexpectedly that I had no time to defend against it. One moment, he'd been leaning lazily back against the cave wall. The next, he was hovering over me, having made me lay down on the blankets, my back flat on the cave floor, his large and hard body aligned with my own, poised only inches above me.

All I could see was the sapphire of his eyes, the intensity in them. All I could smell was the scent of sunshine and seaside. And all I could hear was the pounding of my heart within my chest.

"Do you enjoy getting a rise out of me, little Wolf?" the Hound asked me, his voice low and almost threatening.

I knew I should shove him away. But I couldn't seem to make myself lift my hands to his wide chest and do so. And with his thick, muscular arms braced on either side of me near my shoulders, my arms were pretty much pinned, anyway.

A warm feeling near the pit of my stomach also indicated that if I were to shift my waist upward even a half inch, I would experience firsthand just how much of a *rise* I got out of him.

"Get. Off. Me," I said.

The Hound grinned down at me, playful challenge appearing behind his blue eyes. His handsome face was deadly serious, though. "Make me," he said.

Anger flooded my veins and I let my years of training take hold. Before he even finished issuing his two-word challenge, I'd managed to shift my leg so that my knee wedged sideways between our bodies, and with a maneuver dependent on skill rather than size, I rolled the Hound's large body to the side, taking the dominant position above him.

My fist was flying the moment I had the advantage, and it connected with the right side of the Hound's jaw hard enough to echo up my wrist and forearm at the impact. My other fist flew in from the opposite side, while I simultaneously drew back the first swing for another strike...

But the Hound caught my right wrist in his hand, and then caught my left in the other. Holding both in an iron grip, he jerked them behind my back, and my body pitched forward, my chest coming down to press flush against his own.

My breath was coming in gasps, my teeth bared with the further damage I'd intended to inflict.

The Hound held me easily in place above him, my legs straddling his hips, and grinned up at me. A bit of blood rolled down the corner of his lip from where my first punch had landed, and a sort of wicked excitement danced in his blue eyes. On the most intimate part of me, I felt his excitement peak in a wholly different way. Heat spurred in my stomach and down lower, but my fists were clenched in anger.

The Hound's tongue flicked out and licked at the blood on his lip, his grin growing as my eyes followed the movement. His face was only inches from my own, his body hard and imposing beneath me.

"Did you like that, little Wolf?" he asked me. "Do like making me bleed?"

"I *hate* you," I growled. "I hate *all of you*."

In answer, he lifted his hips a fraction, nudging at a sensitive spot of me with the proud length of his rock hard manhood. The heat that was building low in my belly turned into an all-out inferno, and gods help me, but I had to bite back another growl that might have come out sounding like a moan.

"Your mouth says one thing," the Hound taunted, "but your body says another... Which is it, little Wolf? Do you hate me... or is it that you want to devour me?"

Both, gods damn it. The answer was *both*.

As if he could sense the truth of this, he shifted his hips once more, grinding himself against me, the rough fabric of our clothes the only boundary between us, his hands still gripping my wrists and locking them behind my back, holding my heaving chest flush against the hard, golden surface of his own.

His tongue flicked out once more, the tip of it grazing the sensitive flesh of my throat.

"Let me go," I said, and hated that my voice came out rough and husky... like a plea.

The pressure at my wrists released immediately, but it took me a second to realize I was free to get up. Shoving at his chest, I peeled myself away from him. Ryker tucked the strong hands that had been gripping me only heartbeats before behind his head, as if enjoying the view of me sitting up on top of him.

When the urge to tear off his shirt and pants and ride him into the daylight struck me hard and compulsory, I found my feet in a flash and ran out of that cave as though my tail was on fire.

I didn't stop running until I'd located some cold water to bathe in.

And then maybe drown myself in morbid humiliation.

24

I was a gods damned fool and whatever this shit was that was happening with Ryker the Hound needed to stop. Like, *yesterday.*

I could barely look at him at training the next morning. He'd worked out alongside the Dogs and chose not to wear a shirt to do so. Every inch of his bare, golden skin was a taunt and torture. I wondered at how I could dislike someone so thoroughly and still want to do highly inappropriate things to his sinful body.

I was not a virgin, and had not been one for a couple years. I'd found a partner, or three, in Dogshead and did what I wanted with them when I wanted. There was no shame in this in my eyes, though the females in our world were judged much more harshly concerning such things than males. If the trees grew tits and legs the males could go around fornicating whole forests and likely no one would bat an eye. A female having more than one partner, however? Or several partners? Oh, the horror!

I paid no mind to this patriarchal bullshit. If I could very well die for the sake of entertainment, I would go fornicating whole forests, too, if I saw fit.

But a Hound. A *Head* Hound, at that. The whole thing was absolutely ludicrous.

That evening, after training all day under the hot summer sun, (which had only grown more torturous with the progression of the season) I sought out Kalene and Oren, rather than returning to my cave.

Kalene lifted a brow at me. "You've been scarce this past week," the dark-haired beauty commented. Her almond eyes flicked toward Ryker, where the Hound was busy discussing something with one of the other Hounds I didn't know. "Pray tell where you've been running off to?"

"I found a magical rainbow and I've been busy chasing Leprechauns around while in Wolf form," I said.

Oren's deep laughter sounded behind me before the large male threw a heavy arm around my shoulder. "I've met a couple Leprechauns, Bear-killer," he said. "And you do *not* want to go chasing them... But if it's trouble you're looking to get into." He gave me a squeeze and grinned down at me. "Then I am at your service."

I didn't say so, but trouble was the *opposite* of what I was looking for. Trouble would likely be waiting back at that cave.

So after we'd all taken refreshing swims in The Cascades, and Kalene let me borrow a clean shirt and matching skirt, we headed into the part of Marisol where Dogs were permitted to indulge in their preferred poisons.

I hadn't really ventured back into the city since that first night after my arrival, and it seemed the sights within were never-ending. The sloping, cobblestone streets seemed to split off in every direction, the ornate green lampposts cradling the blue Apollo-blessed firelight flanking every block. The shops were interminable; as were the various people we encountered wandering about. It was obvious that life in Marisol was an indulgent one, at least for anyone who was not a slave.

We passed by an open theater and an art gallery, the purpose of both Kalene had to explain to me. I didn't say, but I found these things almost achingly intriguing. I could only imagine a life where such frivolous pleasures could be enjoyed.

"Have you seen the arena yet?" Oren asked me as we crested a particularly slanted street and rounded the corner of another block.

I told him that I had not, but that I would like to. It was always wise to at least glimpse the cage in which one would be fighting.

"Damn it, Oren," Kalene complained. "I want a drink, and the arena is on the other side of town." She gestured toward an enormous domed structure on the northern end of the city.

Oren gave her a droll look. "Then go get a drink. I'll show Bear-killer the arena and we'll catch up with you in a little bit."

Rolling her eyes and shrugging, Kalene sauntered off in the direction of the nearest tavern. Oren turned to me with a grin. His ruggedly handsome face gleamed with a challenge. "I'll race you there," he said.

"We literally just spent all day doing physical exercise, and you want to race?"

Oren rubbed at the short beard over his chin and eyed me. "Are you afraid of losing, Bear-killer?"

My eyes narrowed. "Wolf-form or mortal?"

His green eyes glittered with anticipation. "Wolf, of course."

"And the race starts at the shift?"

He nodded. "And I'm ready when you are."

I laughed, and the sound was so foreign it startled me. "Then you've already lost, my friend," I told him, and shifted as swift as lightning, gathering my clothing in my mouth before tearing off into the distance.

I heard his curse ring out behind me as he made his own shift, nowhere near as fast as my own.

To add emphasis to my victory, I sat on the street beside the wooden fence ringing the domed arena in human form, my ankles crossed casually and a bored look on my face.

A few minutes after I arrived, Oren came galloping up in his Wolf form.

If he was large in his mortal form, he was fucking *enormous* as his Wolf, his fur the same dark brown as the short hair on his head. When he spotted me, I almost laughed again at the annoyance that crossed his face after his realization that he'd lost.

"Did I forget to mention I'm an instant shifter?" I asked. "My bad."

The enormous Wolf before me bared his teeth around the mouthful of clothing he'd carried and shook his head. I waited while he returned to his mortal form, giving him my back out of respect for privacy, even though I knew that the male could not care less.

A minute or two later, Oren was yanking on his clothing and striding toward me. "Where did you learn to do that?" he asked. "I've never seen anyone shift so quickly."

I shrugged. "I taught myself. I was the runt—a Bait Dog, actually, so early on I knew I'd need every advantage I could get."

"That's a hell of an advantage," he said. "A Wolf is never more vulnerable than when in mid-shift."

I nodded, recalling a number of occasions when that advantage had saved my life... and turned around to face the wooden fence around the domed arena where we would be fighting again for our lives.

The place was enormous, surely capable of holding tens of thousands of visitors. Beyond the wooden wall, the structure itself stood nearly nine hundred feet tall, blocking out an entire portion of the sky with its imposition. A lump formed in my throat and in the pit of my stomach just looking at it.

"Do you want to go in?" Oren asked me, staring up at the

beast of a place along with me. "I like to see where I'll be fighting beforehand, to get a feel for the place."

"Are we allowed to?" I asked.

Oren's handsome face glowed with mischief. "Do you always ask that question before acting?"

I gave him a small shove. His muscular body did not sway an inch. "No, I don't," I said.

He held a hand out to me, the same hand that had saved me from falling to my death on The Cliffs that first day. "Then come on, Bear-killer," he said. "I know a way inside."

Placing my hand in his was easy. Perhaps easier than anything else I'd done as of late.

~

It was cold within the darkness of the dome. Oren had located a loose board in the wooden fence, and he'd held it aside while I'd slipped through. He was too large to do so, but he easily leapt up and gripped the top ledge of the ten-foot wooden fence, and then hauled himself over.

He landed lithely on his feet beside me a moment later. I was busy staring up at the death dome before me.

"I've never seen a Wolf-built structure this large," I admitted. "It's somehow..."

"Intimidating," Oren finished for me, nodding, his green eyes taking it in same as me, all the playfulness gone from his attractive face. "Ramsey likes to put on a show."

I debated for about half a second before deciding to share with him the information Ryker had given me. Out of everyone I'd met since coming here, Oren was the one Wolf I found the easiest to trust. There just seemed to be this... *goodness* about him that was so contrary to the rest of the world. Or the rest of the world that I was accustomed to, anyway.

"Some of us won't be fighting in Wolf form," I told him. "And the match-ups and pairings are supposed to be... more interesting."

I could feel his green gaze on me as Oren turned toward me. "What do you mean by 'interesting'?"

I spread my hands. "That's all I know. It's just what I heard."

"And who did you hear it from?"

I met his gaze for a moment and then gestured to the building before us. "Do you know a way inside, or what?"

To my relief, Oren let the subject drop. "Follow me," he said.

He led me around to the other side of the dome, where there was an entrance that was barred with another gate, this one made of vertical iron rods. When I saw it, I was about to ask how the hell we were going to get through that when Oren gripped one of the iron bars on the gate and bent it outward as though it were made of nothing more than wet clay. He gave me a cocky grin when I gaped at him.

"You've got your speed, Bear-killer," he said. "I've got my strength. All of us who've lived this long have done so for a reason."

"Amen to that," I agreed, and slipped through the bent iron bars and into the dark mouth of the arena.

The chill of the place struck me first. I was standing in a dark tunnel leading to the center, and I waited for Oren to make a hole in the gate large enough for him to slide through before venturing forward. Utter blackness and silence stared back at me from the nucleus of the ring in which we had stepped into. Utter silence... and soon enough, death after death after death.

It had been a total forty-one days since I'd arrived in Marisol. The Games were now only a moon cycle and a half away. Here, I would be forced to take life, or lose it. Here, I would live or die.

As Oren fell silent beside me, I knew he was thinking the same thing.

In the gloom of the tunnel, the light of the stars and torch-lights of the city offering the only illumination behind us, Oren's hand reached out once more for my own. I placed my scarred and calloused fingers within his, and together, we went deeper into the arena.

In order to see within the darkness, both of our eyes lit up Wolf-Gold, and the details of my surroundings focused into view.

The bleachers and seats for spectators stretched up high enough to scrape the heavens, making a complete circle around the center of the arena. The floor was flat, hard-backed earth, and around the edges at intervals there were other iron gates that blocked off escape from whatever might eventually be released from within. If Ryker was right about Ramsey's plans for this year's spectacle, any manner of beast or creature might pass through those barred waiting rooms come Games Day.

When Oren's deep voice broke into the silence, goosebumps broke out over my skin, as if I were snapping out of some trance.

"Are you afraid, Bear-killer?" the male asked.

I didn't consider lying. "Yes," I admitted. "Every time." I turned to look at him in the darkness, his glowing golden eyes scanning our surroundings. "Are you?"

His gaze met mine, and slowly, he nodded. "Of course," he replied, as if any other answer would be absurd, and I supposed he was right.

I found myself moving closer to him, our bodies wrapped up in the silence of the shadows. Then I was removing my clothes, the rustle of fabric echoing in the darkness. After a moment, I stood naked before him under the canopy of that sky-grazing dome.

His golden eyes flared a bit brighter, widening as they took me in. I reached up and removed the band that was holding my hair up, and shook my head so that my long dark locks tumbled down around my shoulders.

"Rook," Oren said, his deep voice a near growl as he spoke my actual name for the first time since I'd known him. "What are you doing?"

I took a step toward him, tentative, inquiring. "If you're interested," I said, "I think... I think I need some release. It's been a while."

Oren studied me a moment. "Does this have anything to do with the way that Head Hound has been looking at you during training everyday for the past moon cycle?" he asked.

"I hate him," I answered, because it was true. "But I don't hate *you*." Another truth. I shrugged. "You saved my life my first day here... Let me thank you."

Oren peeled his shirt off over his head, revealing a muscled chest that was marked up with scars, as the body of every Dog that made it to adulthood would be. He prowled forward and stopped inches before me, tall and towering, and then waited silently as I unbuttoned his shorts and yanked him down to the hard floor of the arena.

He laid back and allowed me to have my way with him, spending some of that fire Ryker kept mentioning, shoving away thoughts of the Hound even as Oren stood strong and erect inside of me.

25

The next day at The Cliffs, I could tell that Ryker was angry with me. Whether or not he had an inkling of what had happened between Oren and me, I didn't know, because it could just be that he'd waited at my cave the night prior and I'd never returned.

After leaving the arena, feeling decidedly more loose and relaxed than when we had entered, Oren and I had made good on our promise to meet up with Kalene. The female had sniffed at Oren and me a couple times and then given us a knowing look. The fact that it came without judgment made me like her a little more. She'd handed us a couple shots of moonshine and we had commenced in partying the night away.

After the tavern we'd visited a smoke den. After that, Oren had invited me back to his small hut on the beach, and I had taken him up on the offer, slipping out this morning before the sun rose to bathe and get an early start on the climb, which I had made a habit of doing.

I was the first to make it to the top, as usual, using the quiet of early morning to steel myself before what I knew would be a trying day. I typically had at least twenty minutes before the other

Dogs would begin pouring over the edge of the cliff, reporting for practice.

I was waiting for the sun to rise, sitting with my legs dangling over the ledge of the cliff face when my strong nose alerted me to his presence. Over the past month, I'd learned his personal scent very well, and so I was not startled when he spoke without greeting from behind me.

"I waited for you all evening," Ryker said.

I didn't turn to face him, but I was fully aware that a small shove from behind would send me careening off the edge of this mountain and to the rocky beach below.

"I wasn't aware we were on a schedule," I replied, my tone even. "I thought Dogs had the evenings to themselves."

He was silent for a moment, but I could feel the anger radiating off him in invisible waves. "I thought you were enjoying our time together," he said, his voice carefully contained.

Now I looked back at him over my shoulder, his handsome face as alluring as a devil. "I hate you. I've already told you that. Several times."

His blue eyes narrowed, and he folded his arms over his chest, making the golden muscles in his forearms contract. "And I told you, we both know that's a lie."

Sighing, I climbed to my feet and retreated from the ledge, coming to stand before the Hound. I stopped just before him, close enough to feel the heat of his ire. Tilting my head back, I met his icy blue gaze. "What do you *want from me*, Hound? Enough of the games."

Ryker took a step closer, nearly closing the gap between us— but not quite. My heartbeat picked up in pace at the proximity, and he was tall and wide enough that I now stood wholly in his shadow. But I stood my ground, waiting for an answer.

His head cocked in a very Wolfish manner, his demeanor becoming instantly predatory without movement. Rather, it was the stillness with which he held his muscled and imposing form that was chilling.

And, yet, despite that chill, a touch of traitorous heat spiraled somewhere low in my belly. It seemed my night with Oren had not quelled whatever this ridiculous attraction to the Hound was.

"I think you know what I want, little Wolf," the Hound told me. He leaned forward, his mouth coming so close to mine that I held my breath. "And I think you want to give it to me," he added in a whisper.

He moved away then, his presence leaving me so abruptly that I only stood where I was for a moment and stared at the slowly brightening horizon. A handful of heartbeats later, Dogs began hauling themselves over the cliff side, bleary eyed in the morning but ever ready for another day in hell.

∾

I wasn't sure how, but he knew. I knew he knew because of the way he treated Oren during training that day. Perhaps our mingled scents still lingered, and the Hound had picked up my scent on Oren or vice versa... but, yes, he *definitely* knew.

He taunted, tested, and tortured Oren to no end, made him do extra of everything; more laps, more pushups, more leaps, climbs, crawls and hurdles. He insulted him, shoved him around... and pissed me off enough that by the time practice finally came to an end, I was absolutely *seething*.

Ryker had no gods damned right to treat Oren that way. And I had no doubt in my mind that he'd done it because of *me*. As though I was *his*. As though he *owned* me.

Oren, to his credit, did not hold it against me, though I knew he understood why Ryker was behaving this way. I apologized to him while we bathed in The Cascades that evening and then practically tore through the woods to get to the little cave and give the Hound a good piece of my mind.

Ryker was waiting by the small entrance to the cave when I got there and stormed up to him, fuse lit like a bomb about to explode.

Then, because he seemed to enjoy doing so, he surprised me. Actually, *shocked* is probably a closer word.

"I'm sorry," Ryker said, and bowed his head in what could not be interpreted as anything but submission to a Wolf. "I overreacted this morning. I had no right." He lifted his golden-brown head and met my eyes with a plea in his blue ones. "Forgive me?" he asked.

My mouth fell open, but I struggled to get any kind of words out. I snapped it shut and opened it again, but words still failed me.

He bent and lifted a basket that I hadn't noticed upon approach, a sheepish but hopeful grin coming to his attractive face. "I brought you pork roast and wine... Will you share it with me?"

My head told me to turn on my heels and leave, but my body pushed passed the Hound and entered the cave. "It's your world, buddy," I told him. "I just live in it."

A moment later, he followed me inside.

He spread out our blanket, took a seat, and began arranging the food and drink. I stood looking at him a moment before taking a reluctant seat beside him. We ate in awkward, loaded silence for all of five minutes.

"You treated Oren really shitty today," I said. "He didn't deserve that."

Ryker plucked a grape from the bunch and popped it in his mouth, crushing it between his straight white teeth. "He's lucky I didn't just kill him," he said so casually that I had to turn my head and look at him.

My lips twisted in disgust. "The life of a Dog means so little to you, huh?"

"It's not that."

"Really? Then what is it?"

"I could *smell* you on him," he said, and his handsome jaw clenched.

A blush bloomed instantly on my cheeks. "What?" I said.

That anger that both terrified and thrilled me filled his sapphire eyes. "When I walked by him this morning at line up... I could *smell* your scent clinging to him and I became... a little jealous."

My brows arched up. "A little jealous? That's what you call 'a little jealous'?"

"Wolves are territorial creatures, sweetheart," he said.

I nodded. "That's true. But I'm *not* your territory. Or your sweetheart... And you should know, I've killed stronger Wolves for saying less."

The Hound only grinned, leaning back lazily against the cave wall. "Right back at ya... *sweetheart.*"

I huffed. He just had a way of making me want to behave like a damn puppy. "You're infuriating," I said through clenched teeth.

Ryker raised his glass of wine. "It would seem we share the quality. With time, I think you might learn to love me."

"That is absolutely *impossible.*

"Nothing is impossible, little Wolf."

The ugliest of instincts in me reared their heads, and I narrowed my eyes, weighing my next words and then speaking them anyway.

"You're a coward, Ryker the Hound," I told him. "You're a slave driver and an oppressor of your own kind. You make a living and a life off the backs of others, and then pretend that what you do has any honor. You're a follower who is weak, and nothing more than a pawn pushed around by the Pack Master, who is not a Wolf worthy of your allegiance... *These* are the reasons I could never like you, let alone love you. *This* is my truth to you. Feel free to share yours whenever you're ready."

For the first time since we'd begun this strange dance of ours, the burning fury that I'd often seen flare in him and directed at others was directed at me. Gone was his easy swagger and cool indifference, his playful yet challenging way of addressing me. Here was the Head Hound there were so many horrifying stories told about. Here was the alpha lesser Wolves cowered before.

"You speak about things you have no idea about," he said, his tone so flat that I had to tell myself not to shift in discomfort. "If you think Dogs are the only slaves in this world, you're as ignorant as you are self-righteous."

My temper hit the roof. "I don't beat, kill, and hunt down other Wolves because some prick with connections tells me to," I snapped.

"But you still kill other Wolves to survive. In fact, you've likely killed more of 'our own kind' than I have, *sweetheart*. How many is it? Fifteen? Twenty? You do what you have to in order to survive, and so do I. How the hell do you think that makes you any better than me?"

My fists were clenched tight enough to ache, my blood rushing in my ears. "How dare you compare the life of a Hound to that of a Dog? Without Hounds, there would be no Wolves to keep all the Dogs in slavery. Without Hounds, the Pack Masters would be nothing more than shithead Alphas who go around comparing their withered penises and beating the shit out of each other!"

"You sure have a simple-ass way of looking at things," Ryker said, shaking his head in exasperation. "Too bad you're not as bright as you are beautiful."

I launched myself at him.

My body slammed into his in a tackle that sent us both rolling in a tangle across the cave floor. I was determined to choke the life out of him, my hands clawing for his golden neck, my teeth bared in savage anger.

Ryker caught me at the wrists, same as he had the last time, managing to do so a second before I was able to claw his eyeballs out. He was so much stronger and bigger that it was not long before he had me pinned beneath him, using his massive weight to hold me in place, near-crushing me to the cold cave floor.

Which provided a direct contrast to the heat that radiated off of him from where he hovered above me.

He still had my wrists in his grip, and he brought them over my head and pinned them there with one hand so that he could use the other to keep some of his weight off me.

"All that fire," he mumbled, his blue eyes darting down to my lips. "If I let you go, are you going to try to kill me again?"

"Probably," I said, my eyes narrowed in ire.

This made him laugh, the reverberation traveling up through the tight muscles in his flat belly, which was still pressed closely against my own. As if sensing where my mind was, he shifted his hips a little, and something began to grow there, making my breath come short. Like the two traitors that they were, my legs spread open an inch or so of their own accord, allowing Ryker to settle himself more fully there.

His eyes lit up Wolf-Gold as his handsome face stared down at me. "Don't see Oren again," he commanded, his voice low and guttural and firm.

My arms were still pinned above me, his hold still at my wrists, my breasts peaked and nipples hardening against the fabric of my shirt. His gaze drifted down to them, and his devilish tongue flicked out over his wicked mouth.

"Don't tell me what to do," I said, but the words came out weaker, softer... *throatier* than I'd intended.

When Ryker lowered that wicked mouth to my neck and ran the tip of his tongue over the sensitive skin there, his teeth grazing over the most vulnerable part of me, I was helpless to do anything but hold utterly still beneath him.

"Tell me to stop," he said, mumbling against my neck, his tongue darting out and tasting me again. "Tell me to stop... and I will."

I opened my mouth to say it, but the pressure around my wrists disappeared as one of his rough hands came down to grip my breast, his thumb rubbing slow circles around the middle. At the same time, his mouth had traveled higher up my throat, where he planted small, tongue-swirling kisses that seemed to blaze a trail of fire over my skin. His other hand went to my waist, where his strong fingers dug gently but insistently into the soft flesh of my hip, pulling me toward him at the center.

The word that he'd promised would cause his retreat got stuck somewhere in my throat, failing to make it out fully past my lips. My lips parted slightly to loose a small sigh as the hands of the Hound traveled expertly over me, as his skilled tongue explored my flesh.

My body arched upward into his, my hands finding their way into his short, thick, golden-brown hair, holding him to me, begging silently for him to continue.

Because he was a bastard, he lifted his head a little, pulling away from me. "Which is it, little Wolf?" he asked. "Do you want me to stop?" He leaned in, nipped gently at my neck. Pulled back again. "Say it. Say you want me to stop and I will."

Even as the words were spoken, his hips were thrusting forward, forcing my legs to spread apart further still, nudging at my center with the impressive tip of him. My legs wrapped around his trim waist and squeezed, my body opening up, the movement as good as an invitation.

Ryker separated himself from me and sat up on his knees before stripping his shirt off over his head. Then he unbuttoned and kicked away his pants in a smooth motion. After, his strong hands gripped my thighs and parted them so that he could reclaim his spot between them. Naked as the day he was born, he sat crouched on his knees before me, every muscle and inch of golden skin on full display.

My eyes took it all in; there was no use in even attempting

resistance. I yanked my shirt off over my head in the same swift fashion as he had, my breasts laid bare before him.

His eyes blazed like tiny golden suns, a growl rumbling somewhere deep within his carved chest. When he dipped his head and took the tip of my right breast into his mouth, scoring it gently with his teeth, I reached down between us and took him into my hand. A feral growl rumbled in his chest and vibrated against my nipple, which he held captive with his teeth and tongue.

He was smooth and strong and impressive, and I slid my palm along his length while my other hand gripped the back of his neck, keeping that wicked mouth held close to my flesh. Then I was flipping him, needing to take the dominant position, to maintain some control in this absurdly reckless situation.

Ryker laid down on his back without protest, cupping his hands behind his head while he watched me stand and kick away the skirt I was wearing. The *last* bit of clothing I was wearing.

Spread out like carved golden marble on the blankets covering the cave floor, the Hound watched me with predatory stillness.

Waiting.

I could still leave. I could still stop this.

Then Ryker removed one of the hands tucked behind his head and gripped himself at the hilt, his azure eyes locked on me. "Come here, little Wolf," the Hound told me.

And gods help me, I did.

I came to stand over him, a leg on either side, and then dropped down to my knees so that I could straddle his trim waist. I placed a hand on his muscular chest and held him down—a position of absolute dominance while I held his gaze. Then I shoved the hand he was using to hold himself away, taking him into my own palm again and giving him a less than gentle squeeze.

He arched up a bit, his eyes glowing gold as they held mine, another deep growl echoing up his throat. I kept one hand braced on his chest and the other between us, letting the tip of him rub against the now-moist part of me, making him hover at the entrance before granting admission.

Ryker's hands were at my hips, gripping tight enough to leave bruises, as if he were only just able to resist the urge to yank me down onto him. I knew it was the dominant, demanding look in my eyes that was stopping him.

He was letting me have control, though it was not easy for him.

So I eased down on him a little further, his impressive width forcing in deeper, making me toss my head back and sigh at the cave ceiling as delicious fire scorched me from the inside out. Beneath me, the Hound was practically trembling with forced reservation. So I eased back up again, freeing the tip of him, making his fingers dig even deeper into the womanly curves of my hips.

I leaned down and ran my tongue in a slow circle on the side of his neck. Still gripping him between us, I held him steady and guided him fully inside me in a single smooth motion while my teeth sank less than gently into his neck.

He let out a low snarl of pleasure as I moved my hips against him, never once yielding the dominant position. My own eyes remained hazel as his glowed golden, staring up at me, drinking me in as I exhausted myself atop him.

He came three times before I was through. Only after I'd rolled off him and lay staring at the cave ceiling, my heart galloping within my chest and a thin sheen of sweat coating my skin, did I acknowledge just how fucking stupid this whole thing was.

26

The Midsummer Solstice was upon us, the single day of the year where Dogs were not forced to work the fields or clean the latrines or train for The Ring. It was the only holiday still observed by our kind, the midway point between the beginning and end of the year.

In Dogshead, most of the Dogs (and everyone else, too) would head to the chapel in the early hours to pray to the Gods for a myriad of things. In the evening, these same Dogs would head to the nearest tavern or whorehouse to drink and fuck the night away.

I wasn't a woman of the gods, and I didn't pretend to be, so I usually skipped the morning festivities and took part in the evening's... but I was not in Dogshead anymore, and Marisol had its own way of doing things.

"You can't wear that," Kalene told me. "It's the Midsummer Solstice, you have to try a little harder."

I raised a brow at her, ever marveling at her obliviously blunt way of addressing people. I looked down at the brown woven shirt and skirt I wore, normal Dog attire. "I don't own any other clothes," I said.

She grinned. "Who said anything about clothes?"

Oren and another male named Ares had joined us, and if the former sensed any shift in me after what had happened with Ryker, he didn't comment. I did notice that he was careful to keep more of a distance, however, and I couldn't decide if that annoyed me or not.

Kalene and I walked side by side up a tilted street with the males trailing behind us. "So... I didn't see you around last night," she said, eyeing me with that dark gaze, red lips pursed in question. "What have you been up to as of late, my friend?"

I shrugged. "Sleeping, eating, being a slave. You know, the usual."

"You should be careful," she told me, her voice lowering. "Dogs have been disappearing from Marisol lately, vanishing without a trace."

We rounded the corner of the street and then crossed to the other side. "What are you talking about?"

"Haven't you heard?" Kalene asked. "Surely you've heard others whispering about it? Dogs are disappearing and no one knows where they're going. Puppies mostly... but there have been a few older ones, too."

Overhearing our conversation, Oren and Ares pulled up alongside us. Oren offered me his elbow, and I was relieved to lace my arm through his, glad that Ryker hadn't scared him enough into avoiding me altogether.

"That's right," Oren said, and pointed to the northern skyline. "Some claim there is a creature in the Northern Mountain, and that its been awakened and is stealing pups in the night to devour them in its cave."

"That's fucking morbid, Oren," Kalene snapped.

Ares chimed in. He was a quiet male with light brown skin and even lighter brown eyes. "And who says that they're being *taken*?" Ares said. "They could just be *leaving*."

From the look on Kalene's face, I could tell this was a possibility she'd considered as well. "But to go where?" she asked. "Where could they go where the Hounds or collars could not track them?"

The memory of the Halfbreed male dropping down from the sky and landing in the lavender wheat fields of Dogshead flashed through my mind, along with the image of Yarin scooping Amara up into his large arms and shooting back up into that star-flecked sky.

I kept this to myself, adding nothing as I listened to the others toss ideas back and forth.

"I've heard tales of the mountain creature," Oren agreed, "but I'm inclined to believe the tales of the one they call the Conductor."

I was still walking alongside Oren, and Ares wedged himself between Kalene and me, tossing an arm over both of our shoulders, more animated than I'd ever seen him at the topic of the conversation. "If there is a Conductor then where is he taking them?" Ares added. "I could believe the male exists if I could believe there existed a place beyond the reach of the Hounds and Masters."

Kalene snorted. "Who says the Conductor is a *male*? For all we know, it's a female. Males aren't exactly known for their generosity."

"That's sexist," Oren replied smugly.

Kalene arched a dark brow at him. "Just balancing the scales," she said.

"What are you guys talking about?" I asked, unable to maintain my appearance of indifference.

To my surprise, Ares was the one who answered, speaking more words than I had ever heard from him in a single moment. "It's like Kay said, for the past year, Dogs have been disappearing, several from right here in Marisol, most of them just pups... pups who haven't been moon burned and collared yet.

"But it's not just here that it's happening. Pups are vanishing all over the Territory, all of them property of one of the five Pack Masters... No one knows how it's happening or where these pups are going, but there are stories about a Conductor, a person at the helm of the disappearances. Someone who's leading all those young Dogs... somewhere."

"What about the older ones?" I asked, glancing between Ares and Kalene. "If someone is helping them escape, how is this Conductor getting the collars off?"

"Welcome to the mystery that has plagued our lives for the past twelve moon cycles, Bear-killer," Oren grumbled.

"Your guess is as good as ours," Kalene added.

The others mused a little longer while I turned the information over in my head, the subject finally pushing unwanted and inappropriate thoughts about Ryker out of my mind, for which I was glad. At last, we reached a side street where the buildings on either side were so close together that the males had to turn sideways to enter.

In this little alley, there was a single metal door with a covered and barred viewing window in the top. As Kalene rapped on it twice, the males informed us that they would grab some breakfast and meet us here in an hour.

I turned to Kalene, about to ask what the hell this place was when the covering over the little window in the metal door opened, and the face of a silver-haired old crone appeared on the other side. Eyes the color of thin milk stared out at us.

"What do you want?" she croaked, her voice as old as her face.

Kalene bowed her head reverently, an unusual gesture for the often brash female. "We'd like to be painted for the Midsummer Solstice, Madame," she said and held up a small bag, the contents of which clinked with the movement. "We have silver in exchange."

The window in the door slammed shut, and for a moment, I thought we'd been dismissed, but then the door swung inward, revealing shadows and darkness while a sickeningly sweet stench floated out from within.

I gave Kalene a look that asked without words if we really were supposed to go in there. The female only grinned and stepped over the threshold, leaving me to follow as she was swallowed up inside. Thinking that it would be damn ironic if I were to die in the chamber of some old, milky-eyed Wolf in sheep's clothing after having survived everything else life had thrown at me, I passed through the metal door and tried not to jump as it slammed shut independently behind me.

Kalene gave me another grin as I sidled up close to her, my eyes scanning the dim, stone-lined hallway we'd been let in to. Torches lined the arched walkway, and straight ahead, a steep set of stairs led down into darkness. Kalene chuckled lowly when she noticed my hesitation.

"I already told you, Bear-killer," she said, "if I wanted you dead, there are much easier ways to kill you."

I waved a hand toward the staircase. "After you, my friend."

Smiling wickedly, Kalene descended into the darkness, and I waited a breath or two for a howl of pain or death scream that didn't come. After that, I followed her into the shadows.

The stairway led down into a stone chamber that was cool and damp and smelled even more strongly of that sickly sweetness I'd caught on the way in. The ceiling was low, the only light cast by four torches that hung upon each wall, as if marking the four directions. On the floor in the center of the small space, atop a pillow that was as red as fresh blood, sat the milky-eyed crone.

A cloak was draped over her sagging shoulders, tendrils of silver hair spilling out of the hood draped over her head. Before her, a small, circular dais waited, and it was to this that she gestured with a wrinkled and impatient hand.

"Whoever is going first," she said in a raspy voice that sounded centuries old, "get up there. I don't have all day."

Kalene gave me a small shove from behind. "Bear-killer will

H. D. GORDON

go first," she said, and grinned innocently when I looked back at
her as though she was crazy.

The old lady waved a hand as though she couldn't care less.
"Then take your clothes off, Bear-killer, and step on up. Ten
others are going to show up wanting the same thing this after-
noon, and I don't have time to dally."

I folded my arms over my chest, and Kalene sighed and rolled
her eyes, whispering, "She's going to paint your body and it will
be magnificent enough that you won't want to cover it with clothing. She's the best Marisol has to offer, trust me. Even the wealthy
Wolves will admire us tonight."

I considered while the old crone snapped her fingers at me.
Shrugging, I shed my clothing, leaving only my thin panties
intact, and climbed up on the little wooden dais, feeling slightly
uncomfortable, though I had a feeling the crone was blind with
those milky eyes.

"I'm blind in the sense that you understand it, yes," the old
woman mumbled while she circled slowly around me.

My body went utterly still, and my mind fumbled with the
surety that I hadn't spoken that previous statement aloud.

"Madame Rama is a Seer," Kalene said from where she was
now leaning against the wall, picking at her nails with a small
knife. "Her gifts go beyond her artistry."

The old woman turned in the direction of Kalene. "You ruin
all the fun, sly one," the old lady said, and then returned to
studying me with those unsettlingly white eyes. "The one you call
Bear-killer is clever. She would have figured it out."

I leaned forward a bit and sniffed at the old female. "But you
smell like a Wolf," I said.

She grinned, revealing gapped and broken teeth, and tapped
her nose. "That's a keen nose you've got, Bear-killer," she said.
"Even for a Wolf."

With this, she turned toward a table pushed against one of
the stone walls, where vials and brushes and other various para-

166

phernalia waited. After arranging some on an old wooden tray, she set the tray atop a rolling metal table and pulled it over toward me. She looked down at her paints and brushes with those white eyes, and then back at me—her canvas.

"I'm going to paint you with wings of flame and a crown of thorny flowers, Rukiya," the old lady said, though I was pretty sure I hadn't told her my real name. "Flames and flowers," she repeated, "because those are the things that will bloom in your wake."

27

Madame Rama worked swiftly, her wrinkled fingers surprisingly steady and sure with paintbrushes clutched between them. Within twenty minutes, she'd painted every inch of me below the neck, and to my utter amazement, she'd done so using two hands at the same time, painting with both simultaneously and ambidextrously.

Then she'd taken extra care painting my eyes and lips, brushing a slight rouge over my cheeks as well.

When she was done, she jerked her cloaked head toward where a long, silver-framed mirror leaned against the wall, and I climbed off the dais in order to go stand before it. My jaw hung open at what I saw. In fact, I was still staring at myself in that silver mirror twenty minutes later when Kalene appeared in the reflection beside me, her body having gone through a magnificent transformation as well.

Rama had kept her promise about painting me in flames and flowers, but nothing could have prepared me for the masterpiece that she'd crafted upon my body. The flames began at my toes and licked up my ankles, their fiery beauty rendered in reds, oranges, yellows, blues and violets. These flames then yielded to vines of matching hues that laced, swerved, and crawled up the curve of my muscled calf, around my knees and up my strong thighs. The flowers sprouting from these vines were also flames, the petals like whirling licks of scorching fire. Around the curves of my hips, (which had filled out considerably in the past month and a half, what with all the fine wine and meats I'd been devouring) more of those multi-hued flames burned in the shape of a short fiery skirt. Around my muscled midsection, more vines and flowers. Over my breasts she had placed small stickers to contain my nipples, and had then transformed the impressive swell of them into matching, burning flowers, the embers of which licked all the way up my neck.

"One last thing," Kalene said, as she reached over and removed the band that had been holding my thick brown hair up off my neck. I gave my head a small shake, making my hair fall down over my shoulders in long, shiny waves.

"Gods be damned," Kalene commented, taking in her own body, which was no less magnificent with the vibrant orange fox colors the Madame had depicted upon her. "You and I are going to paint Marisol red tonight, my friend."

Madame Rama coughed from where she stood waiting behind us, and Kalene went to pay with the small bag of silvers it had likely taken her forever to save. Despite my astonishment at the old lady's artistic talent, I was eager to crawl up and out of this damp, smelly dungeon and feel the light of day fall over my skin.

We thanked her and I followed Kalene up the stairs, but before I had ascended fully to the top, the Madame called out to me in her crone's voice, her milky eyes pinning me and seeming to see something that most others were blind to.

"There are two paths before you, Rukiya Moonborn," the old lady told me, "and both lead to two very different fates. Your choices will determine which path you ultimately tread, so be sure that you choose wisely in the days to come... Your fate is not the only one that hinges upon it."

I had no idea how in all the holy hells one was supposed to respond to something like that, so I thanked her again and then scurried out of there as fast as I could without appearing too eager.

I emerged from the narrow alley and found Kalene, Oren, and Ares waiting for me on the sidewalk flanking the wide street. A flood of Wolves had begun spilling out into the streets of the city. Some wore mostly normal attire, but many were clad in getups as elaborate as my own, while others trotted and prowled about in their Wolf forms, as big as small horses that cut paths through the crowds.

"Good gods almighty," Oren said as his green eyes settled upon me, flaring Wolf-gold for a heartbeat before returning to their normal jade color. "You look good enough to eat, Bear-killer."

For what felt like the first time in forever, a small smile tugged up my lips. "I will be sure to consider the offer," I told him with a wink.

"Get a room, you two," Kalene said with a grin, pretending not to notice the intense way Ares was staring at her, taking in the remarkable form that was her body.

Somewhere up the street, drums had begun to sound, followed by the tinkling of bells and the blowing of horns. People leaned out of their windows in the apartments above the shops and rained flower petals down upon us, which then got swept up in the breeze that always flowed in off the ocean, making for a tornado of delicate blooms.

I marveled at all of it—at the Wolves atop stilts who towered over the crowd in their passing, at the musicians who all played independently and yet somehow in unison, making a sweet chorus of melody rise into the salty air. There were Wolves passing through the gathered handing out shots of fruity liquor, and sweet herb that was rolled up and passed from person to person.

And it was not just the street we were standing on. Every street in Marisol reflected the same celebration. In a total break from norms, one could not tell a Dog from a merchant from a Master. Wolves roamed and danced and made love against alley walls and in the corners, while children blew bubbles, chasing each other and howling down the avenues.

A hunt had clearly been conducted before this event, as various types of meat had been cooked and strung up in tents along the sidewalks. One only had to go in and rip off a piece of their preferred protein. Needless to say, by the time midday rolled around, I was feeling absolutely superb from no small mixture of contributors.

For the first time since I had come to this seaside city, I was actually glad to be here. Dogshead could never have provided a celebration the same as this, for shear lack of infrastructure and warm bodies. Every Wolf I passed seemed to be deep in the thralls of the same elation I was feeling... It was enough to almost make one forget—if only for a single rise and fall of the moon—that one was a slave.

Kalene, Oren, Ares, and I stayed together for the most part, partaking in the festivities like the oldest of friends. This made me wonder what Goldie was doing for the Midsummer Solstice, if that monster Adriel even celebrated the holiday. I sent up a silent prayer that my only real friend was at peace today... and then allowed thoughts of her to dissolve as I took another sweet shot of the numbing liquid.

We wandered from street to street, and I didn't fail to notice the way several Wolves eyed Kalene and me in our body paint. She grinned at me and tossed the thick locks of her ebony hair over a shoulder. "What'd I tell you?" she said. "You and me, we're gonna take our pick among the males tonight... We just have to choose one of the lucky bastards." She gave me another wicked smile. "Or two or three."

I couldn't help a small chuckle, because I always appreciated a lady who was confident in her sexual prowess. Our world tried very hard to shame females for this while encouraging the males, and as a rebel myself, I related to Kalene's sentiments.

This brought up memories of the way Ryker had looked while pinned under me... the way his eyes had blazed gold and his strong hands had gripped my hips.

I found one of the Wolves wandering through the street with a tray of shots and snagged yet another one, tossing it back in a gulp.

The day passed in a blissful haze, and soon, the sun was setting, sinking down over the ocean and creating vibrant streaks of pinks and oranges across the heavens. One by one, the green lampposts cradling the Apollo-blessed flame sprang to life, and the full moon rose grandly overhead.

Oren sauntered over to me and laced an arm around my waist, his large and muscular body swaying a bit to the rhythm of the sweet music and his green eyes glazed with the substances coursing through his system.

"Dance with me, Bear-killer," he whispered, and swept me into the center of the street, where others were also twirling, twisting, and gyrating in musical delight.

Kalene and Ares appeared beside us, the male having apparently worked up the courage to take Kalene into his arms. The four of us laughed and danced and grinned like fools as we passed around a joint of rolled herb and drank to our heart's content.

Never in all my life had I been part of a celebration so intoxicating, and I foolishly wished it would never end.

But despite all the things I'd survived, all the horrors I had seen and inflicted, I was still a young Wolf, and so I hadn't yet grasped the fact that all things have an ending.

And the endings of good things always come far too fast.

～

I'd wandered away for just a few moments, and I had lost my group of friends. Now I couldn't tell what part of this blasted city I was in, or even really which way was up. Every street looked the same, and everyone around me was as smashed as I was, so I headed toward the sound of the sea and found a bench beneath a tree. I took a seat and folded my legs beneath me in an effort to stop the world from spinning.

I was pretty sure I was going to be sick. Pitching forward, I gripped my midsection, sucking in slow and deep breaths, swearing to the gods I was never going to touch another drink again. I cursed myself more than once for being so damn indulgent.

When a small breeze came in off the ocean, I closed my eyes and tilted my head into it... A moment later my eyes were snapping open, my foggy senses perking to high alert.

It was not a shift in sound, or even in silence, but I felt it, nonetheless. It was the same feeling that had come over me in the days before I'd left Dogshead—an instinctual alarm bell that was both from the human part of me and the Wolf.

I was being watched.

My legs unfurled beneath me and I set my feet flat on the ground, my back going straight despite the roiling in my stomach. I studied my surroundings; the dark ocean was still churning straight ahead, the streets of Marisol still pulsing with partiers behind me. To my left and right, the beach stretched on endlessly in both directions, meeting with the mountain cliffs on the southern horizon.

There was nothing out of the ordinary to be noted... and yet...

The fog that was surrounding my brain was steadily lifting, my stomach settling, overridden with the adrenaline spurred by the instinctual alarm sounding in my system. When I stood, pushing to my feet, I found that my balance had returned.

One of the benefits of being a Wolf is that our blood runs

naturally hot, and when we get scared or excited, we can burn through lingering alcohol in our system in a matter of minutes.

Whoever or whatever was watching me had ignited this effect, and I focused on my ears, which were easily the strongest of my senses. A moment later, I'd shifted into my Wolf.

And in this form, I could hear it, some sort of serious struggle coming from the Northern Mountains. Clear-headed and fully conscious, I debated for all of three heartbeats before tearing off in the direction of those mountains, ignoring my own good advice when I silently pleaded with myself to turn back.

The words of Madame Rama echoed in my ears: *There are two paths before you, Rukiya Moonborn, and both lead to two very different fates. Your choices will determine which path you ultimately tread, so be sure that you choose wisely in the days to come... Your fate is not the only one that hinges upon it.*

And still I charged forward, as if I were tragically tethered to a life lived in danger, to a life of foolhardy mistakes.

28

I'm not sure what I had been expecting, but it was not what I saw.

I'd followed the faint sounds of struggle and the instinctual pull toward the trouble, and found myself on one of the several mountain passes that was ruled by shadows under the thick blanket of night. No Apollo-blessed lampposts stood here, and even the glow of the full moon could not penetrate the gloom created from the looming mountain faces.

And, here, upon this hidden pass, a wagon of puppies had been hauling into town, pulled along by two large and used up horses, and driven by a dirty-looking male with a worn whip clutched in his hand. Two other males were in the driver's company, and their appearances revealed them as hired hands, mercenaries paid to protect an investment—to ensure the transport of slaves.

But when I came skidding to a stop, taking in the scene, the wagon holding the puppies was on its side, the large horses still attached to it tangled and braying in panic. The driver was cowering on the other side of it, while the two hired swords clashed with a warrior as large as he was fearsome.

He reminded me instantly of Yarin, the half Fae/half Vamp warrior who had come to take Amara on the night before I'd left Dogshead. The gleaming black armor was the same, and though the two were opposites in coloring, their way of moving was also identical, as though they'd gone through similar training.

I went unnoticed, standing near the base of the mountain, crouching behind a bush that was just big enough to conceal my Wolf form, watching as the warrior took down the hired swords without even breaking a sweat.

In a handful of swift movements, he had them down on the ground, disarmed but cursing and spitting. From inside the barred wagon, at least half a dozen pups were yelping, pacing, and snarling as they watched the commotion. The wagon driver with the whip kicked at the caged pups but didn't go to help his two employees. Instead, he stood watching the scuffle as if waiting for something.

My attention was drawn away from the driver and back to the large male who had the other males pinned to the ground. The metallic sound of a sword sliding free of its sheath rang out into the darkness, and the eyes of the two males on the ground went as wide and round as the full moon hanging above us.

"Do you have any idea who you're stealing from?" hissed one of the males on the ground. "When he finds you, he's going to make you wish you'd never taken a single pup."

The large male with the sword grinned viciously. In a deep voice, he said, "Oh, I look forward to the day I get to meet your master face-to-face, rest assured about that." Then he lifted the silver sword and relieved the Wolf who'd spoken of his head.

Even from my vantage point some forty feet away, the irony tang of blood floated on the air. I remained where I was while the large male lifted the sword again, readying to remove a second head in the same spectacular fashion.

What the male didn't see was the cart driver as he nocked an arrow in his bow and lined up a shot, drawing back the string far enough to send the sharp tip of the arrow straight through flesh.

The large male with the sword heard the stretch of the bowstring and he turned, but he was not fast enough.

I, however, was.

I came charging out of the bushes without having the time to really consider my actions. In my Wolf form, my greatest strength was my speed, and it was one that had saved my life on more than one occasion.

With a snarling growl, I felt the power coil in my legs, and then I was springing into the air. My jaws yawned wide and clamped down on the forearm of the driver, misdirecting the arrow a split second before it had been fired.

My sharp teeth sank deeply into flesh and muscle, the curved tips of my canines snagging on bone as the sweet taste of blood flooded my mouth.

I bit and locked. The cart driver opened his mouth to scream, but the warrior with the sword had finally tuned into the interaction. He appeared before me as if by magic, and removed the cart driver's head before his cry of agony could even exit his mouth.

A bit stunned, I released the forearm that was clamped between my jaws, treading backwards as the headless body slumped to the ground.

From my position on all fours, the enormous warrior towered over me. Under the silvery glow of the full moon, his ebony armor gleamed, polished despite the many slashes and slices that no doubt told silent stories of the battles past. Just like Yarin, this male was tall and muscular, but unlike Yarin, he had skin that was a smooth caramel, and short black hair that was cut very closely to his head. His eyes were a chocolaty brown, and they commanded the same intensity as had Yarin's, though they seemed a bit harder—*colder.*

I stepped back a few paces, my head lowered and my tail held still and stiff. The warrior's brown eyes narrowed on me a fraction.

He took a step toward me.

I took one back while releasing a low growl.

He stopped, still staring at me. "Who are you?" he asked, and his deep voice was as imperious as his gaze.

I almost ran. In fact, a heartbeat longer, and I would've shot off down the mountain pass like a bat escaped from hell. And even with his supernatural speed, I doubt the warrior would have been able to catch me.

But then he said, "Rukiya?" A pause. "Is that your name?"

My flight instinct diminished with my surprise. I glanced down at the three headless bodies on the ground, and then at the wagon of pups... and then I shifted back into my human form.

"How the hell do you know my name?" I asked. And not just my name, but my *full* name. Less than a handful of people knew that.

A slow smile came across the warrior's handsome face, and I stared at him in confusion for a moment before glancing down at myself and remembering the way that my body was adorned and painted.

"Ah, now I see what all the fuss is about," he mumbled, more to himself than to me as his brown eyes travelled over every inch of my body. "Thank you for the help," he added, meeting my gaze at last.

"How do you know my name?" I repeated.

He hesitated a moment, as if deciding whether or not to tell me. I folded my arms over my chest and waited. The smile that had softened his features was gone, and I got the feeling that it was an expression that was rarely glimpsed upon the male.

At last, he said, "My name is Yerik. I believe you met my brother, Yarin, not too long ago."

My heartbeat quickened in pace. "So then you must know what happened to Amara?" My voice fell a fraction. "Is she okay?"

Yerik gave a solemn nod. "The child is well, of course."

"Where is she?"

"I can't tell you that?"

"Well who has her?"

The look he gave me answered for him; he couldn't tell me that, either.

I bit back a sigh of frustration. "I'm not going to tell anyone. I just want to know that she's safe."

His dark eyes were unyielding. "She's safer if the answers to your questions remain unknown."

Yerik turned away from me, heading over to the wagon of puppies and ripping off the bars caging them as though the strength of the titans coursed through his thick arms. Gently, he lifted out the puppies one by one, gripping them carefully by the scruffs of their necks and setting them softly on the ground.

I was beside him in a moment. "What are you doing with these pups?" I asked.

Yerik looked at me like this was a stupid question. "What does it look like? I'm freeing them. They haven't yet been burned and collared." His eyes went to my throat, where the magical black collar always hung, and then to my shoulder, as if he could see the crescent moon-shaped brand on the other side even beneath the body paint.

"They'll kill you if they catch you," I said.

The warrior shrugged. "I guess I better not let them catch me."

"What are you?" I asked, fully expecting him to tell me that he could not answer this, either.

But he said, "Vamp and Sorcerer."

Just like his brother Yarin, he was another Halfbreed I had never encountered. So many questions were flying through my mind, but I could hear a clock ticking over our heads. Wherever he was taking these pups, they needed to go. And I needed to return before my absence was noted, though I was pretty sure the entire city of Marisol was as smashed as shattered glass just about now. Still, the longer we stood here, the more risky this precarious situation became.

I glanced at the puppies sitting around him, their pointed ears perked and their little tails already tucked in submission. They were so young, so small. If taken in somewhere safe now, they still stood a chance at a free and happy existence. They'd glimpsed hell, no doubt, but they were fresh enough that there was still time to wipe their slates clean and offer them a life of hope.

For them, it was not too late.

"May the gods travel with you," I said, and then thanked him earnestly for what he was doing, even if it made me feel complacent and shameful. At least *someone* was saving the youth of my kind. At least some of them wouldn't end up as slaves, Dogs, and working ladies.

Yerik hesitated, and I got the feeling he was trying to decide whether or not to tell me something, but then he sighed and looked down at the six pups waiting to be liberated, and gave me a single nod of goodbye.

For a moment, I expected him to gather up the pups in his arms and shoot up into the air, as had his brother. But then the warrior's brown eyes swirled like orbs of violet vortexes, and he waved a hand that left a purple swirl in the air.

I blinked, and the warrior and six Wolf pups were gone, having disappeared into thin air.

Mind reeling, I shifted back into Wolf form and raced back toward the glow and commotion of the city, which had carried on in celebration without me.

For some unsettling reason, no matter how fast I ran, I couldn't shake the feeling that I was once again being watched, and the only thing I could hope was that if my instincts were correct, the watcher was a friend rather than a foe.

Make no mistake about it—this last encounter could easily

cost me my head... or worse. It also made the second time in just as many months that I'd assisted in the escape of slaves. I was certain of only one thing: I was walking a fine line here.

And something told me that sooner rather than later, I would need to make the fall to one side or the other.

29

I was not surprised to find Ryker waiting for me outside of my cave when I returned not too much later that evening. I'd considered heading back into the city to search for Kalene and the others, but my head was spinning with so many thoughts and my adrenaline was pumping so hard that I thought only of some peace and quiet.

A stark reminder of my reality that had come with assisting the escape of those pups, wiping away any appetite for celebration, and I was not in the best of moods as I approached the entrance to the cave and saw the Hound standing there.

"Go away," I said, moving to shove past him... but he stepped in front of me, blocking the way.

His eyes roamed over me in a slow, proprietary manner, and I glanced down again as I remembered my appearance once more. Scowling, I wished I had not let that old lady paint my body this way. Who needed brutish males leering at them even more than usual? Not me.

Ryker took a few swift steps toward me, closing the distance between us, near enough for me to feel the heat radiating off of him. His blue eyes glittered as his handsome jaw clenched with restraint. "You're angry," he said in greeting. "You're too beautiful to be so angry all the time. You should try a smile."

This was the absolutely *wrong* thing to say. In a show of strength I usually reserved for The Ring, I shoved the Hound aside and stalked into the cave, barking at him over my shoulder once again to leave or risk losing his genitals.

Of course, the bastard ignored this and followed me inside.

I was busy lighting a couple of the lanterns that he'd hung upon the cave walls a few weeks ago when Ryker came up behind me, the shadow of his larger form swallowing up that of mine on the wall. His arms slipped around my waist, and I stiffened as his nose nuzzled at my neck.

Where my magical, binding collar hung.

I shoved him away from me again, that burning anger that always blazed within me awakening from its dormancy, matching the flowery flames that were painted all over me. He was a Hound, a slave driver, and an enabler of a vicious tyrant. I had lost my mind in ever becoming intimate with him, and I cursed myself for being so physically driven.

Ryker approached me again, his movements focused and predatory. My hands balled into tight fists at my sides, ready to swing at him should the mood strike me. I'd asked him to leave twice, so as far as I was concerned, he'd earned whatever violence befell him.

"I want lick all of that paint off your body," Ryker said, and his words slurred just a little, revealing that, like everyone else in this blasted city, he was fully intoxicated. Everyone else, but me, anyway.

I backed up a step. "I will literally rip your tongue out of your mouth if you bring it anywhere near me."

His handsome face fell a touch in disappointment, and I watched as his temper flared. "Why do you play these games with me, Rook?" he asked.

Despite all the time we'd spent together, it was a very rare occasion when he actually used my name, and as I studied the Hound in his intoxicated state, a small voice inside me whispered that I ought to tread carefully tonight.

But as usual, my mouth got the best of me. "Oh, *I'm* the one playing games? You can't be serious. I'm not the one who's knocking at your cave door every gods damned night, bribing you with wine and meats and forcing you to hang out with me."

His blue eyes narrowed to slits, that anger elevating ever so slightly. "I never *forced* you to do anything," he said.

That was fair enough, but I was in no mood to concede an inch. "Just leave me the fuck alone, then," I snapped. "Whatever you think this was, it's over."

In a voice as cool as the frost that had glazed over is gaze, the Hound said, "Is that really what you want? You want me to leave you the fuck alone?"

My response came as quick as lightning. "Yes," I snapped. "I don't know how many times I have to say it before it goes through your thick ass head."

For the smallest of moments, I was sure that the Hound was going to strike me, as he had surely done to many a Dog in the past. To his credit, he only shook his head and shoved past me, exiting the cave without another word.

He did not visit me again the next night.

Or the next.

Or the next.

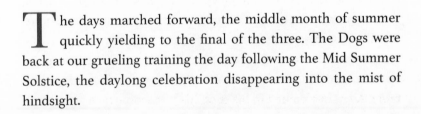

The days marched forward, the middle month of summer quickly yielding to the final of the three. The Dogs were back at our grueling training the day following the Mid Summer Solstice, the daylong celebration disappearing into the mist of hindsight.

But memories and thoughts regarding my last interaction with Ryker haunted me, no matter how much I cursed myself for even entertaining them. I'd done the right thing. I was sure of it. Well, *pretty* sure of it, anyway. The whole thing had been doomed from the start, an unsustainable and imprudent situation.

Kalene and Oren were quick to notice the alteration in my mood, as well as my evening routine, but they did not pry or question me on the matter, for which I was eternally grateful. The last thing I wanted to talk with them about was my unhealthy relationship with the Hound. I could just picture the looks of pitying incredulity they would give me.

The Games was the subject on everyone's lips, along with the mystery of the disappearing pups. Anytime the latter was brought up I would feign indifference while thinking about Yarin and Yerik, about the two occasions I had helped them in freeing enslaved Wolves.

There was no need to explain why this was information that I could not share with *anyone*, no matter how fond I'd grown of my few companions.

About a week after my breakup with the Hound, Kalene, Oren, Ares and I were sitting in one of Marisol's many taverns, tossing back cold ones after a long, hot, and grueling day in the sun.

Ares said, "You guys hear about that Seller that got robbed? Three dead Wolves and an estimated half a dozen puppies, vanished in the night... and not too far from here."

I did my best not to stiffen on my barstool, leaning casually against the tall, circular table that sat between us. Beside me, Kalene rolled her eyes. "Where do you pick up these rumors, Ares?" she asked. "They're all you care about lately."

Ares gave her a grin and a wink. "Not *all* I care about, darling," he said, and his voice lowered as he leaned across the round table. A spark gleamed in his eyes, his handsome face aglow with mischief. "Besides, we can't just ignore these things. There's too much talk, too much evidence, to just call these disappearances or random, unconnected incidents."

Oren gave me a droll look and then clapped Ares on the shoulder. "Thank you for the brief, Detective Ares. Sounds like you're on the case."

Ares made an exasperated sound in the back of his throat, and met our eyes one by one. "So you guys are telling me that Wolf pups—pups slated to become Dogs, specifically—have been disappearing in the dozens for the past year from every Pack, and you have absolutely *no* interest in why that's happening? Where they're going? *Who's* taking them?"

The playfulness that had been in Oren's expression a moment ago sobered away, and he met his friend's gaze with deadly seriousness. "Those kinds of questions will get you killed," Oren said, his voice equally quiet. He glanced around, making sure that no one in the tavern was paying our little group any particular attention. Then, he added, "If what you say is true, all we can hope is that whoever is taking the little bastards is caring for them properly, and that they'll get to live better lives than this..." He gestured around us, as if to encompass everything. "That's where my involvement in the matter ends." Oren made sure to look at each of us. "If there are brains in those heads of yours, that's where your involvement would end, too."

Ares held up a finger. "But not all the disappearances have been un-collared pups," he said. "Some of them have been branded, collared... *full grown* Dogs." His eyes darted around at all of us, looking as though he wasn't sure we were hearing him. "Don't you understand what that means? It means there must be a way to remove these damn collars, and to go beyond the reach of the Masters and Hounds."

Oren slammed his hand down atop the table between us hard enough to make Kalene, Ares, and myself jump an inch off our barstools. In fact, the whole tavern paused for a moment and looked in our direction. "There's no way and no place," Oren growled, baring his straight white teeth, his usually calm and handsome face twisting into something fearsome.

The other tavern patrons around us went back to their own business as utter silence fell between the four of us. A lump had formed in my throat, and I took a swig of cheap moonshine in an attempt to wash it down. The subject dropped after that, though it was obvious that Ares let it do so begrudgingly.

I understood both of the males' positions, and what it came down to was this; Ares was a slave who still held hope that there was a better life awaiting him, while Oren was a slave whose only remaining hope was taking the cards he'd been dealt and making the best of them. As a slave myself, I couldn't blame either for feeling their respective ways. Gods knew I'd fallen on both sides of that line at varying points in my existence. It was a hard life, and we dealt with it the best we could.

Still, the tense exchange had managed to spoil the mood, and since we had to be at The Cliffs bright and early the next morning, our group left the tavern shortly after. But when Oren and Kalene split off to go to their respective sleeping quarters, Ares hung back a bit. I noticed that he'd been watching me closely tonight, and I tried to slip away to my cave, but he stopped me.

"Hold up a minute, Rook," Ares said, jogging to catch up with me. He was one of the very few who called me by my name, rather than *Bear-killer*, and I appreciated this... but I had a feeling that whatever he wanted to say, I didn't really want to hear.

Or maybe it was more that I was *afraid* to hear it. Afraid of what I might do with whatever information he was going to share with me.

"I'm pretty beat, Ares," I told him. "So make it quick."

His light brown eyes studied my face closely enough that I had to remind myself not to squirm. "It's true, everything I said," he began.

I only looked at him, not sure what to say to that.

In a whisper, Ares added, "Someone is freeing those Wolves, and that means there must be a place beyond the reach of the Hounds and Masters... And a way to remove these collars."

Still, I said nothing.

Ares let out a puff of air, keeping his voice low with some effort. "The adult Dogs who went missing... it happened right here—*in Marisol*." He gripped the black collar that hung around his muscular, light brown neck. "That means the answer to removing these could be *here*. All we have to do is find it."

When still I remained silent, Ares tossed up his hands.

"Okay," I said. "I hear you... but why are you telling *me* this? What am I supposed to do about it?"

These were reasonable questions, and they served duel purposes. For one, I was curious as to why he'd continue this conversation with me, rather than Kalene, when I was pretty sure the two had been sleeping together. And, secondly, I needed to know if he somehow knew about my involvement in the disappearance of those six puppies a week ago; if he somehow knew my secrets.

"Because," Ares said, "you saw the way Oren reacted. I can't talk to him about it, and Kalene... she doesn't want to hear about it, either. She's afraid I'll just get myself killed."

I let out a short, humorless laugh. "So, what? Then you'd rather get us *both* killed?"

Ares sighed and shook his head, staring off into the distance for a moment, as if he could see all the way to this magical, free land he seemed so keen to believe in. "I'm talking to you about it because you don't strike me as a coward," he said, and there was such earnestness in his tone that my throat tightened a little. "Seemed to me like you were someone who isn't happy being complacent... Someone who still has hope. Someone who believes our lives were meant for more than... *this*."

With the next words that came out of my mouth, I felt something essential inside of me breaking. And, still, like the good little Dog that I was, I spoke them anyway.

"Then I guess you were wrong," I told him, and turned my back, heading toward the comfort of my dark, lonely cave.

30

Things were not the same between Ares and me after that, and I couldn't really say I blamed him. Despite the fact that I would step into a steel cage and fight another Wolf to the death, I was a coward. Teeth, fangs, and bloodshed may not scare me, but the belief that things could be different, the thought of allowing such hope to permeate in my consciousness... *that* absolutely terrified me.

A sense of melancholy fell over me as the days continued on, the end of summer and the beginning of The Games fast approaching. Beneath that enormous dome, where Oren and I had snuck in and enjoyed each other, the sounds of construction grew more and more frantic. A week before The Games were scheduled to start, those noises finally quieted.

In fact, an eerie sort of silence fell over all of Marisol. Until all the people began arriving. And when they came, they seemed to do so in droves.

Wolves, Vampires, and other various creatures began to flood into the city, filling up the inns, hostels, and hotels to capacity. Vendors selling every kind of item imaginable appeared as if from thin air, lining the streets with their carts, tables, and wagons. Musicians and artisans set up shop as well, wringing the influx of people for every bit of coin they could manage.

Meanwhile, the Dogs grew more and more restless. Fights broke out amongst otherwise docile Wolves, and the amount of alcohol ingestion increased tenfold. In a small mercy, the training on The Cliffs was on hold so that the Dogs could store up their strength for The Games just around the corner.

I found out where I was on the roster, the exact time and day of my first match up, when a Hound posted a flyer in the city square. So many people had flocked to see the lineups that the Dogs had to wait until all the others had cleared away in order to get a glimpse at our names on the list.

My heartbeat pounded hard enough that I could feel its pulse in my throat as I approached the post on which the flyer had been hung. Kalene stood beside me, the two of us having agreed without words that we would gather the news together. Over the past three moon cycles, I had slowly grown fond of the dark-haired, almond-eyed female, and her presence had helped to sooth the sting that had been caused by the loss of Goldie. I wished that the two females could have the chance to meet, as I suspected the three of us would get along wonderfully, but knew this was just another unanswered prayer in a whole sea of them.

The moon had risen over Marisol, darkening the ocean endlessly lapping at the shore and casting a bluish glow over the city. The ornate, green lampposts cradling the blue Apollo-blessed flames had sprung to life hours earlier, while Kalene and I had smoked away our worries in a darkened, underground den. In a rare show of solidarity and affection, Kalene's hand took hold of mine, and together, we read the words upon the flyer.

Silence hung between us as we took in the lineups. I located my name first... Then Kalene's, Oren's, Ares... This was not something the others could do; Dogs were not taught to read, only to recognize the letter combination of their own names. The fact that I knew how to read was one of my most guarded secrets.

For the first round, we'd each been matched up with Wolves from other Packs. Because I'd killed the Bear, who had been the West Coast Champion, my position was higher on the bracket, in a spot that would receive more publicity than some of the other fights.

"These are the names of the Wolves we have to kill or be killed by," mumbled Kalene.

Quietly, in a voice so small I barely recognized it as my own, I admitted, "It never gets easier."

Kalene gave my hand a small squeeze. "No," she agreed. "It does not."

"Maybe he was right," I whispered, more to myself than to her.

"Maybe who was right?"

"Ares."

Surprising me, Kalene gripped both of my shoulders and turned me toward her. "Don't talk like that, Rook," she said. "If Ares is bound and determined to get strung up by the Hounds in the street, don't let him drag you down with him. Everything he keeps going on and on about—it's suicide."

I shook off her hold, gesturing at the flyer. "And this is *better*?" I hissed. "Killing our own kind for entertainment. *That's* a better fate?"

Kalene only looked at me, and though I knew it wasn't really for her, I felt my anger rising. Before I could say something I didn't mean, I turned away from her and stalked off up the street, not stopping until I found myself in an entirely different neighborhood.

Overhead, the night sky was clotted with thick, gray clouds, and a silent electricity hanging in the air preluded a coming storm. The darkening weather felt like a reflection of my soul at the moment. I knew I would be apologizing to Kalene later, but right now, I felt on the edge of breaking down, and I wanted to make sure no one was around to see it.

After all, no one bets on a Dog who mopes around as if depressed. Everyone knew that it was much more preferable, and certainly more profitable, for slaves to be wearing smiles.

It made things more comfortable for everyone else that way.

~

The ceremonies that preceded the start of The Games were as arduous as they were elaborate. The part I loathed the most was always the showings, where they would line the Dogs up so that the betters could ogle us before deciding whom to place their money on.

It was the same process as before a regular fight, only the scales were ramped up by a thousand. There was so much preparation that I found myself growing angrier as I was shoved from one event to the next. Reagan Ramsey seem to love decorating all of his property, as could be gleaned from the various flowers, streamers, and garlands that now adorned the sloping streets of Marisol. The Dogs were included in this dressing up, and I was practically burning with ire when I was informed that Ramsey's Dogs would have their bodies painted for the first showing.

Painted, the same way I'd decided to have myself painted for the Midsummer Solstice. The difference was that on that occasion *I* had decided. This time, I would be forced to allow someone to paint me, and then made to parade that painting in front of everyone in Marisol.

I'd never been to any of The Games in the previous years, because only the top fighters attended, but nothing could have prepared me for the chaos surrounding them. As the hours ticked forward, drawing me closer to my first match, I found myself replaying all the things I'd learned and heard recently. Until just then, I hadn't fully realized all the ideas that had been subconsciously planted in my head.

How would you rather die? Goldie had asked me. *In The Ring, or in the attempt to commit a kindness?*

That means there has to be a way... a way to removed these collars, Ares had said. *There must be a place beyond the reach of the Masters and Hounds...*

And my own words, too: *Killing our own kind for entertainment.* That's *a better fate?*

These were the things haunting my mind as I was ushered into one of the tents that had been erected near The Cliffs, where the Dogs that would be competing had been sent to be "prepped" for the first showing. These were the things that made my fists clench in anger as I was told by an ugly, sneering Hound to strip out of my clothes and 'get my perky ass up on that stool,' so that the artisan could paint me.

The urge to rip his throat out with the flat edges of my teeth washed over me, and I was just barely able to resist. Instead, like a good little Dog, I removed my clothing, ignoring the leering way that the Hound looked at me, and climbed up on the squat stool so that the artist could start her work at my feet.

With every swipe of her brush, I had to remind myself that killing her would be a pointless, wasteful action. This young female with dark eyes and paint-flecked clothing was not the one I hated. It was not her fault that I was here.

And it was then, as the soft tip of the paintbrush licked at my body for the hundredth time, the paint now swirling up from my feet, all the way to my midsection, that a world-shifting thought struck me.

It was *my* fault.

The way things were, the life I was living, the things that had happened. I had *allowed* it. *All of it.* I'd been what Ares had called me—a complacent coward. Too busy blaming the world to notice my own share of the blame.

I decided instantly that I needed to talk to Ares.

I was done being afraid.

31

I was immediately ushered into a line of Dogs who were climbing into the back of a barred wagon, waiting to be transported to the center of the city, where all of Marisol and its visitors had gathered to get a gander at the performers.

Oren was also climbing into the same wagon I'd been directed to, but Ares and Kalene had been sent elsewhere. From the way Oren had reacted to the subject in the bar the previous night, I knew better than to bring up my most recent impulse with him.

The usually jaunty male was as reserved as the rest of us today, anyway. Oren's dark brows were pulled down low over his eyes, his hands resting on his knees as he rode alongside the others and me. Ramsey had not had the male Dogs painted, but instead, had dressed them in warrior's garb, complete with swords and shields, despite the fact that most of them would likely be fighting in Wolf form, and would have no need for such items.

There were seven males and three females in the wagon... and because the gods seemed to enjoy laughing at me, one of those females was Peni—the Dog who'd tried to knock me off

The Cliffs that first day, and whom I had subsequently beaten the shit out of.

Peni's long blond hair had been braided in a thick crown around her head, her body painted in a shade of blue that matched her eyes. She stared daggers at me when our gazes met, but I rolled my eyes and ignored her dumb ass. I didn't need to posture. I'd already whooped her once.

And as the barred wagon trundled closer to the center of Marisol, every Dog inside shifted their attention outward. The sounds and smells of the gathered crowds hit before the sight did, but even so, I was not prepared for what I saw.

There were more Werewolves, Vamps, and other various creatures here than I'd ever seen gathered in one place in all my life. I looked down at the ridiculous way my nearly naked body (I'd been allowed a small, stringy pair of underwear, and stickers that covered the centers of my painted breasts) and clenched my hands into fists hard enough to ache.

Then Hounds were yanking us out of the back of the wagon. Whips hung uncoiled at their sides, the handles gripped in their clenched fists, ever ready to strike a Dog who dared step out of line. To add even more insult to injury, two other Hounds waited outside the wagon with heavy iron shackles.

They barked at us to extend our wrists, and then clapped on the metal shackles. One set went around our wrists, and another around our ankles. With the amount of skin I was exposing, it was an effort not to knee the leering Hound who locked on the ankle restraints right in the face. He'd licked his lips while his gleaming eyes stared intently below my trim waist.

If I had not been shoved toward another line of Dogs a heartbeat later, I really might have killed the bastard right then and there.

I needed to get a hold of myself, before I did something *really* stupid.

The ankle chains made walking more difficult, and they were

heavy enough that they chaffed the skin of my bare ankles. Of course, the shackles were entirely for show (which only served to piss me off more) as there were hundreds of Hounds present and magical black collars around all of our necks.

It seemed the rumors about Reagan Ramsey being a showman were correct. The scene in the city center was nothing if not a spectacle. A large wooden platform had been erected in the middle of a green park, and spectators were gathered around it in a ring of people that stretched on as far as I could see. People were hanging from tree branches, out of building windows, and sitting atop each other's shoulders in order to get a better view of the stage.

The Hounds who'd been shoving us from behind a moment ago pushed their way to the front and now had to clear the way so that the Dogs could make it to our end of the platform. Hounds lined the entire wooden structure, some of them gripping batons, and others leather, metal-tipped whips. The people gathered all around shouted and shoved, many shitfaced drunk despite the fact that noontime was still a couple hours off.

Filthy bunch of animals, I thought, as I stood at the bottom of the stairs at the end of the platform, waiting for my name to be called so that I could step right up and be presented like a sideshow attraction.

Soon enough, I was being shoved up the stairs, and I turned my head and snapped my teeth at the Hound who kept feeling the need to put his hands on me. This earned laughs from the Hounds and taunts from the crowd.

But my eyes were already elsewhere as I crossed the wooden stage, the weight of all those gathered gazes falling upon me. On a balcony overlooking the square, shaded from the brilliant summer sun by a striped, cloth umbrella, and sipping amber liquid from a tumbler, sat my elusive Pack Master himself.

Reagan Ramsey.

I had not seen him since the day he'd purchased me from

Benedict, but he looked the same now as he had then. Dressed in fine slacks and a short-sleeved collared shirt, with sunglasses that likely cost more than I had perched on his straight nose, the Wolf appeared bored and unimpressed. Beside him were the other Pack Masters from the North, South, East, and Midlands. Bo Benedict stood out from the others with his ever-present wide-brimmed hat.

As the announcer read my name and stats, someone in the crowd shouted, "I'd rather watch this bitch fuck than fight!"

And this ignited a cacophony of howls, hoots, snarls and hollered agreements. My eyes narrowed to slits, scanning the crowd for the bastard who had spoken. An overweight, well-dressed Wolf who looked soft and pudgy like a man-child grinned back at me, assured of his safety with all these Hounds around.

I knew I was giving them what they wanted, but I bared my teeth and snarled at the gathered, thinking that perhaps there was a reason for the irons around my wrists and ankles, after all. If I were not in chains right now, I would certainly be able to do some damage before the Hounds could put me down.

When the name of my opponent was called, my eyes moved along with the rest of the audience to settle on a female who was at least six inches taller than me, though she was no where near the size the Bear had been. Black, tribal-like tattoos crawled over every part of her, and she wore clothing that marked her as belonging to the Northern Pack. Her hair was completely shaved off on one side, while the other had been allowed to grow long, and it hung in thick, golden locks over her shoulder.

"Rook the Bear-killer," said the announcer, his voice ringing extra loud beside me, "meet your opponent, Serilda the Sour!"

Bookies circulated through the crowd, taking the bets of people who thrust their money in the air, gazes gleaming with anticipation. The new nickname, *Rook the Bear-killer*, had taken me by surprise, though I supposed it shouldn't have. And I could see that the betters were impressed, though I couldn't give two shits less at the moment one way or the other.

From that comfortable, lavish balcony above us all, Reagan Ramsey and the visiting Pack Masters watched. Two females dressed in barely-there clothing had emerged from the double doors behind Ramsey. One now perched on his lap, while the other had settled on the thick arm of his chair. Even from the distance, I could see that he was looking at me, surely curious as to whether I'd been a wise investment or not.

The female perched on his lap slid down below the rail of the balcony, her head disappearing into his lap while his tipped back slightly and his lips parted. My anger flared as this brought up memories of Goldie, of the times Bo Benedict had made her do such things despite all the people present. Before I could do something even stupider than my previous inclinations, I jerked my gaze away.

And it settled on a pair of blood-red eyes that I recognized in an instant.

~

Adriel.

The Mixbreed who owned my best friend stood among the crowd in a suit of all black, his hands tucked casually in his pockets. He was just as lovely and just as terrifying as I remembered him, and had I not been shackled, I might have tried to reach him right then and there.

I needed to know what had become of Goldie... If she was still... If she was okay.

I didn't care how vicious they said his kind was; I would grip the bastard by the ball sac and shake the information out of him if I had to. Doing my best to hide my anticipation, I obeyed instantly when the announcer shooed both my opponent and me off the stage to make way for the next two Dogs. From there, I was herded back into a barred wagon, my eyes pinning the Mixbreed the entire time.

Adriel stared back at me indifferently, a touch of infuriating amusement playing around his lips. I gripped the bars caging me into the back of the wagon when he had the nerve to wink at me. This made him chuckle, his hands still tucked casually into the pockets of his black pants, his ebony hair falling forward a bit on his forehead.

I didn't drop his stare until the wagon rolled around the corner and out of sight, though it was easily the most difficult stare-down to maintain that I'd ever encountered—which was saying something. Wolves are dominance-ruled creatures by nature, and to avert one's gaze first is a certain submission. In fact, if I was being honest, had the wagon not turned the corner, I likely would've broken eye contact a few moments later, unable to withstand the weight of that scarlet gaze.

Scowling, I sat the rest of the ride in silence. When we were dropped back off near the area designated for the Dogs, I went to The Cascades first to wash off the ridiculous body paint that Ramsey had made me parade around in. The leap over the edge of the cliff and into the crystalline blue waters below no longer made me pause. Between The Cascades where we bathed and The Cliffs where we trained, my fear of heights had been slowly steeped out of me.

By the time I climbed out of the water and retrieved some modest clothing from the cave, the spectacle at the center of the city had mostly concluded. Dogs had been observed and bets had been placed. The people of Marisol and the visitors from various places had dispersed throughout the city. Some were having lunch in the street-side cafes, or buying memorabilia from one of the many stores. Others roamed to and fro, the city natives distinguishable from the tourists by their swift steps and the lack of utter wonderment in their eyes.

There was only one set of eyes I was searching for—an unforget-
table shade of red. But even as the sun rose to its highest point in the
sky, and then began making its inevitable descent, I couldn't locate
the Mixbreed anywhere. As the day inched closer to its close, I found
the fire within me dimming. My shoulders slumped a bit in weariness, and I decided that I ought to head back to my cave and get some
sleep. My first fight in The Games was only two sunrises away.

As night fell, the partying and chaos in the city only intensi-
fied. Every tavern, smoke den, and gambling hall was filled to the
brim with customers and hustlers. Not a single star could be seen
overhead for all the light pollution floating up from Marisol, and
even the constant melody of the restless ocean was drowned out
by the hoots and hollers and the festive music playing through
the streets.

I was finally able to put some distance between me and most
of the revelers as I approached the sanctioned Dogs' grounds
nearby the small woods that housed my cave. Some of the
tension left my shoulders as the sounds of the city faded behind
me, and I saw I was not the only Dog who had decided to stay
away from the ruckus tonight.

By now, I knew most of the other Dogs, and I nodded to a few
in passing as I headed toward the cave. I was almost within the
shadows cast by the trees when a voice spoke from behind me,
loud enough to ensure that I heard the words.

"She's probably sneaking off to bang the Head Hound again,"
said a female voice I couldn't place.

I stopped in my tracks.

Another female snorted. "Why would Ryker's sexy ass want to
fuck her? He knows he can come see me whenever he needs to…
exhaust himself."

That voice I did recognize.

Peni.

A small voice that sounded painfully similar to Goldie's

pleaded in my head: *Just walk away, Rook. Just walk the fuck away. You don't even give a shit about that Hound.*

And, yet, my fists were clenched hard enough for my short nails to pierce the skin of my palms, my body already having decided without consulting me that it was in no mood to just walk away.

I drew a breath as I went to spin on my heels and brawl for the hell of it... but just then, from within the shadows beyond the trees, I saw a flash of unmistakable, glowing red eyes.

32

Whatever bullshit I was about to fight over slipped out of my mind like water through fingers. Peni muttered something or other about me being too afraid to fight her without the advantage of using a sucker punch, but I was already moving away.

Toward the trees, where the red eyes had disappeared. I assured myself that I had indeed seen them as I went crashing through the brush near the point where they'd been. The moonlight could not penetrate the thick canopy of the woods, and soon, I found myself standing amongst shadows layered upon shadows. My eyes adjusted to the gloom... but Adriel was nowhere to be seen.

But I could still pick up his faint scent hanging in the air. I knew for certain it belonged to him because I had never encountered another like it. It was crisp, clean, and masculine, and yet, a little bit sweet as well.

"You've been looking for me."

The statement, spoken so slickly from within the darkness, almost made me jump. In fact, years of suppressing reactions were the only reason I didn't. Still, I had super strong senses, and

I should have detected him before he'd snuck up on me... But he had moved without making a sound, without so much as stirring the air that separated us.

Slowly, I turned to face the direction from which his voice had come. And, sure enough, there stood the Mixbreed male, as motionless as a statue. His skin was smooth porcelain, his face as handsome as a devil's. One side of his mouth pulled up in a grin that revealed straight white teeth and a single sharp, fanged canine. His eyes were that captivating, glowing ruby, and I felt as night bugs must just before flying straight into the alluring light of a torch fire and burning to ashes from the heat of the flames.

Around us, the woods had fallen silent, as if also under the spell of this unholy creature. Realizing that I was just standing there, staring into his beautiful face, I cleared my throat and said the first thing that came to mind.

"What did you do with Goldie?" I asked, and cringed internally when it came out sounding more like a gasp.

He was silent a moment. "Who?"

Whatever fear was incited by his mere presence was dampened by a healthy dose of anger at this response. "Goldie," I repeated, struggling to keep my voice down. "The female you bought in Dogshead about three moon cycles ago."

Adriel's head tilted, the only movement he'd made since I'd set eyes on him. His stillness was uncannily like that of a serpent poised to strike. In his otherworldly, smooth voice, he said, "You'll have to be more specific. I've bought many females in the past three moon cycles."

My fist almost threw itself at his lovely face for this, but my survival instincts won out over the impulse. "A female Wolf with ginger hair," I said through clenched teeth. "Slim and dainty and undeniably beautiful?" When he only stared at me, I threw my hands up. "How do you not remember? You bought her from Bo Benedict before Ramsey's Hound could buy her. You said you've always had a thing for redheads."

"Did I, now?" He asked, and the smirk he gave me made me think that he knew exactly who I was talking about, and had the whole time.

I'd never met a creature more infuriating in all my life... but I was also no fool. I'd seen what Adriel had done to that Wolf male in the forest near Dogshead, the way he'd murdered him and then drank his blood. The number of tales about his kind, about Mixbreeds, was endless... but not a single one ended well. Murderers, thieves, crooks, and sadists... and these were the polite adjectives others used to describe them.

"Please," I said. "Just tell me what became of her."

His tall, muscular body still didn't shift in the slightest, but those red eyes ran the length of me, making a blush crawl up my neck and my stomach twist itself into knots. "You speak of her as though she was your lover," he said. "Is that the reason for all your inquiries? Did you find yourself bewitched by the fire-haired workingwoman?"

The question was asked so plainly that I found myself answering honestly. "No," I said. "I love Goldie, but like a sister, not a lover." I met and held his scarlet gaze. "And, for me, that's a bond that goes much deeper. So, *please*... tell me what's become of her."

Adriel slid his hands into the pockets of his black slacks and leaned back on his heels a touch, considering. "And what will I get in return for this information?"

The pleasure of doing a good deed you fucking heartless bastard, I thought. What I said was, "What do you want?"

"Your blood," he said casually, as if he were commenting on the weather.

"What?"

"I'll take some of—"

"No, I heard you, but I'm sure you must have misspoken."

The Mixbreed lifted his wide shoulders in a shrug and turned

coolly away from me, pushing some of his black hair off his forehead as he did so.

It took enormous effort not to launch myself at his back.
"Wait," I said, scowling. "Fine, I'll... I'll give you some of my gods
damned blood, but you have to give me your word you'll tell me
about Goldie." I thrust my hand out before I could change my
mind. "Do we have a deal?"

Adriel's blood-red eyes glowed bright in the darkness. "We
have a deal."

When he took my hand into his own, a shiver went down my
spine. Blood was a powerful totem, and there was any number of
ways one could use it, things that could be done with it. The
warmth of his skin surprised me; for whatever reason, I'd
expected him to be cold to the touch.

With his proximity and the pending fulfillment of my end of
the agreement, there was nothing I could do to keep my heart
from skipping into a gallop within my chest. When I spoke, my
voice came out stronger than I'd been expecting, what with the
tightness in my throat.

"Are you going to... bite me?" I asked.

Adriel's mouth ticked up in one corner, making his beautiful
face all the more handsome. "Not unless you want me to,"
he said.

Before I could think of how to respond to that, he dropped to
his knees before me and gripped my right thigh with a warm,
strong hand. I had just formulated a protest when he drew a
finger lightly over my skin with his free hand, the touch not actually making contact. Whatever I was going to say died in my
throat as a thin line of scarlet followed in his finger's wake. The
hand that had been gripping my thigh released me, and a small
vial appeared between his ivory fingers. He collected some of my
blood in the little vial and capped it. It disappeared again in the
same fashion that it had come. With a wave of his other hand, I

watched as the laceration he'd made stitched itself back together, not leaving a trace.

Adriel rose to his feet smoothly, his lean, muscular body uncoiling with ease. His red gaze held mine, and his lips gave a small but wicked twist. "I can still bite you, if you want, Rukiya dearest," he said, that lulling voice of his like melting butter on fresh bread.

"Tell me," I said, my voice coming out slightly breathless.

He pushed a few locks of ebony hair off his forehead and smoothed a pale hand down the front of his finely woven black shirt. "Your friend is fine," the Mixbreed said... and then he vanished like smoke on a wind.

~

The bastard *literally* disappeared, which meant that he was likely part magic user... but I didn't give a rat's rotten ass about that. The son of a bitch had taken a vial of my blood, and in return, he'd given me... *fine*.

I cursed myself as I made it back to the cave, thinking that I should have known better than to trust a Mixbreed. Swindlers, cheats, and liars, they were. That's what everyone said, and in my experience, most stereotypes were stereotypes for a reason.

I was so wrapped up in my anger at Adriel that I didn't notice the Hound leaning against the cave wall until I was damn near right beside him. For the second time tonight I had nearly jumped out of my skin with surprise arrivals, and I heaved a sigh when I realized who it was.

I bit my lip, half of my brain telling me to say something mean and send him away, and the other half not allowing my mouth to actually do so. I would *not* go so far as to say I'd missed spending time with Ryker this past moon cycle... but I guess I'd gotten... used to having him around, and when he'd so abruptly stopped coming...

"Hey, little Wolf," the Hound said.

I nodded in greeting, my arms folding over my chest, waiting for him to explain the purpose of his visit.

Instead, he said, "Did you miss me?"

"I see you all the time."

"Yes, but not privately." He took a tentative step forward.

For whatever reason, I did not back away. "What do you want?" I asked.

He took another step closer, the movement more aggressive this time. "I wanted to make sure you were okay."

I gave him a look like this was stupid, because it was, and said, "Really? And why wouldn't I be okay?"

Ryker shrugged, the muscles in his strong shoulders rising and falling. His blue eyes were locked on my face. "Because people have been disappearing lately," he said slowly. "Vanishing without a trace... I'm sure you've heard rumors about it among the others."

I schooled my features into careful indifference and chose my next words wisely. He had not asked a question, but he was waiting for an answer.

"You mean *Dogs* have been disappearing? Of course I've heard about it, but I thought it was mostly pups going missing. Why would you think I'm in danger?"

The Hound studied me, his sapphire eyes searching. I'd told him no more than what all the other Dogs knew; that puppies were disappearing and no one knew how. Purposely, I had not revealed what Ares had shared about the few exceptions—the older, collared Dogs who'd also disappeared.

And, of course, I did not tell him about Yarin or Yerik. He'd have to beat that information out of me, and even then, he'd have a tough time.

Just when the silence had gone on too long to be anything but awkward, Ryker sighed and ran a hand down his handsome face. For the first time since I'd met him, I could see the weariness behind his blue eyes, and I chastised myself silently when I felt a little bad for him.

"You're right," he said, rather than *grown Dogs have gone missing, too.* "You're likely not in any danger. I just... I wanted to make sure you were all right."

"In two sunrises and a moon fall I'll be forced to step into a metal cage and fight another female to the death just so that wealthy people can have a bit of amusement on a summer night," I said. "So how could I be 'all right'?"

Then the Hound said something that floored me, something that left me standing in that cave with my mouth all but hanging open.

"I'm so sorry," he said.

And I wanted so badly to believe that he was lying, that he was just saying the only thing that would keep me from biting his head off... but I couldn't, because the look on his handsome face was so sincere.

Hound or not, there was genuine remorse in his eyes, in the slight droop to his wide, golden shoulders. When he turned to leave, I did not call out to him. Despite my physical attraction to him, I did not ask him to stay.

Because in all the histories of all the realms, *sorry* made about as much difference as *almost.*

33

The next morning marked the last day before my first fight in The Games, but the subject on everyone's lips at The Cascades that morning was not the upcoming fights.

Another shipment of Wolf pups had gone missing last night; another Seller left dead beside his empty, slave-trading wagon. The pups, of course, had vanished. Gone without a trace.

Every Dog I passed by was whispering about it, a certain electric energy floating in the air. The theories about what was happening, who or what was killing the Traders and Sellers and taking the pups, were as creative as they were endless.

But I knew none of them were right.

It was not rival Packs or mountain creatures or conspiracies between the Masters that was causing the disappearance of those Wolf pups. It was two handsome Halfbreed males, brothers named Yarin and Yerik. For whatever reason, this information felt like a burden inside me, something that both begged to be ignored and demanded to be acted upon.

I sought out Ares as soon as I was able, finally catching him alone so that I could ask him some questions that could easily get us both killed if overheard by the wrong ears. I found him outside the squat, old building the Dogs referred to as the Kitchen, where a Dog could go and get bland but hunger-staving food three times a day. The Wolves working inside the Kitchen were also Dogs, of course, and everyone took turns pulling their share of the labor. Should I survive until then, my shift would begin with the changing of the season.

Before I approached the handsome, brown-skinned male, I made sure that Kalene and Oren were not around... and then I had to break the awkward ice that still lingered between us from our last conversation, when he'd called me a coward and I'd told him I wanted nothing to do with rumors of escaping slaves.

I could tell this exchange had left as bitter a taste in Ares' mouth as it had mine, and I couldn't really blame him when he gave me a look that was speculative. Nonetheless, I asked him if we could talk, and he nodded his agreement as we carried matching bowls of Dogs' mush toward an old picnic table that was unoccupied and further away from any of the others.

We ate for a few moments in silence before Ares said, "What's this about, Rook?"

It was now or never, I thought. Keeping my voice low, I said, "What would you say if I told you I know what's happening with the disappearing puppies?"

Ares light brown eyes narrowed a bit, and he leaned forward on the table between us, setting down the spoon he was holding without taking the bite. "I would ask you what exactly you know, and how you know it," he said slowly.

I swallowed hard, glancing around us again just to be sure. "How about I answer the first part of that, and depending on your response, I decide about the second part?"

Ares nodded once, his eyes weighing on me as he waited for me to continue.

I started with what had happened with Amara, leaving out names, places, and even my involvement, calling the story a rumor I'd heard while in Dogshead. Ares listened intently, his bowl of mush forgotten along with my own. Then I told him about another "rumor" regarding the missing puppies from a week and a half ago, about what I'd "heard" might have actually gone down on that mountain pass, where the three headless bodies of a Seller and his two mercenaries had been found.

When I was done, I felt somehow lighter, having not realized the burden I'd been carrying with me these past months. The knowledge had been weighing on me, and it felt good to share it, despite the fact that I was well aware that I may live to regret it.

Letting out a small puff of air I hadn't realized I'd been holding, I waited for Ares to respond. After a few loaded moments, he said, "But where are they going? One male flew away with a pup in his arms, and the other just, what? Portaled with all six pups? Who are these males? Where are they taking the pups?"

"Somewhere better," I answered. "Somewhere safe... free."

"How do you know that?"

I bit my lip for a second, then took a leap. "Because I believed both the males when they promised me it was so."

I watched Ares closely as realization slowly crossed his face. "So *you* were the one who helped that Wolf pup from the woods? You were the one who also helped the magic-wielding warrior on the mountain pass... Is that what you're telling me?"

Leaning forward so that our faces were only a half-foot apart, in a low voice, I said, "What if I was? What would you tell me in return?"

A slow smile pulled up his lips. "I would say I knew my instincts were right about you. I would say I'm sorry for calling you a coward and complacent. I would be excited enough to kiss you, Rukiya."

I dropped his gaze and looked down at my small, scarred hands where they rested on the table between us. "Don't apologize," I said. "You were right. I was afraid and I was complacent."

Ares didn't argue. He said, "What changed your mind?"

I shrugged, letting out a sigh. "I guess I finally came to the realization that there's no reason not to try. We're already their slaves. We're already at the mercy of their whims. I mean, what more could they do to us? How much worse can things get?"

The answer to that, as it would turn out, was *a whole lot*.

~

In exchange for the information I had shared with him, Ares shared some interesting things with me as well. I could tell that I had gained back some of his trust, and I could only pray that he deserved mine.

He'd told me that the number of pups being taken had increased heavily in the past few moon cycles, and that the loss in monetary form was high enough that all five Pack Masters were somewhere between trying to work together to stop the culprits and accusing *each other* of being the culprits. All five Masters swore and held that they had nothing to do with the disappearances, that they each had been affected themselves. To this, one had responded that *of course* they were all being affected because whoever was doing it wouldn't leave themselves out for fear of looking suspicious. Then they had all looked at each other suspiciously all over again. Or at least that was the rumor.

This had made a smile tug up my lips, the expression so foreign that for a moment it felt funny and strange upon my features. Ares had also said that he'd been able to confirm the stories about the few adult Dogs that had disappeared as well. When I'd asked how he'd managed that, all he'd said was that everyone—even those as lowly as Dogs—left trails behind them as they moved through life, and that he'd always been good at following those trails. Since I had kept some details about my stories from him, I decided this answer was good enough.

"That means..."

Ares nodded and touched a hand briefly to the thick black

collar around his neck. "That there must be a way to get these off," he finished for me.

And, figuring out how to do *that*, we agreed, would be our top priority.

Oren and Kalene had found us then, and Ares and I pretended as though we had not been discussing top-secret information only moments before. I felt mildly guilty keeping these things from them, but until Ares and I knew more, we agreed that there was no reason to bring anyone else into it. The more people who knew what we were searching for, the more risky the task was. So this was just the way it had to be.

As I watched the slowly setting sun paint the sky with bright pinks, oranges, and purples over the Western Ocean that evening, my legs dangling over the ledge of a cliff near The Cascades, I considered the possibility that this could be the very *last* sunset I ever got to witness. Unless I somehow found the answer to the collar removal mystery in the next ten hours and also figured out how to hitch a ride to wherever Yarin and Yerik were taking those pups, I would need to once again fight another Wolf to the death for the right of survival. If ever I'd been completely willing to take my chances and run, it was this moment.

I was so tired of the killing, so weary of the death.

About halfway through our conversation, after Ares and I had both told our respective stories, he'd made a comment that had made my face go instantly hot, a blush creeping up from my neck to my cheeks.

"You know who might have some useful knowledge?" Ares had said, slowly, carefully. Then added with just as much caution, "A Head Hound."

My jaw clenched, but I'd had to agree. "Yes, maybe... but why, exactly, are you telling *me* that?"

Ares had given me a slightly pitying look that had made me want to slap the expression from his face. "People seem to believe you and Ryker have... formed a certain relationship," he said.

I'd pursed my lips together and nodded. "And what kind of 'relationship' is that?"

Ares sighed, realizing I was intent on making him say it. "They say you share his bed."

Rolling my eyes, I let out a long breath, thinking that it was more like I'd shared his blanket on a cave floor. What I said was, "So you're suggesting I use my body to get information out of him?"

Ares recognized this as the loaded question it was and had only looked at me. After a moment, I'd let my ire drop and begrudgingly mumbled that I would see what I could find out. We'd left it at that.

So that evening, after watching the painted sky go from day to night and returning to my cave in the forest, it felt like fate that Ryker the Hound should be waiting there. He was not wearing a shirt, every inch of his carved, golden chest on display, and water droplets glittered in his golden brown hair, as though he'd just taken a dip in the ocean that his skin still smelled of. His gaze— the same color of the sea in the daylight—fell upon me as I approached, and I felt a bit of heat stir in my stomach at the idea of allowing him to touch me again. At the predatory gleam in his eyes and the incredibly short rope I seemed to be balanced on.

That was how it felt—as though everything were hanging in the balance, as if things had been set up specifically for a coming fall.

With a sigh, I stopped before him, but didn't say a word. I just couldn't seem to find any.

After a moment, Ryker said, "I know you told me to leave, and I told myself not to come back here..." He let out a huff of air and ran his hand over his golden-brown hair, which I knew to be one of his few tells when he was nervous. "But I couldn't stand the idea of not seeing you before... Before your first fight in The Games. If you want me to leave, I will." His sapphire eyes held mine as a shadow of pain crossed his face. "I just wanted you to

H. D. GORDON

know that I'll be routing for you... that I pray to the gods that you're victorious."

Still, I didn't speak. My throat felt too tight for words to get past it. I swallowed once, twice, and again. Ryker ran a hand over his short hair once more.

"Will you please say something?" he said.

So I took him by the hand and led him inside the cave.

34

I kissed his neck, and his hard body went utterly still beneath my lips. I paused, pulling back a fraction and looking up at him beneath dark lashes. His eyes blazed Wolf-Gold, as bright as duel rising suns over sapphire skies.

I leaned forward again and placed another soft kiss on the spot between his shoulder and throat. Then another, this time letting my tongue dart out and taste his golden skin. His unique scent of sunshine and seaside surrounded me, and I let it sweep away any reservations like a tide rolling out.

Taking a short, single step forward, I closed the gap between our bodies, and soaked up the warmth of him, letting it seep into me while I nipped at his neck.

A low, rumbling growl came as response.

I nipped again, my lips and teeth grazing his chest, and then cupped him in my palm with a firm grip. The big, scary Head Hound trembled beneath my hold.

I grinned and stepped back, watching him shudder at the loss of my touch, warning him with my eyes to stay put when he went to move forward. I stripped my shirt over my head and then slid out of my skirt just as smoothly, so that I stood bare before him. Then I removed the band from around my hair and shook it out, letting it fall in long, auburn waves over my shoulders.

Ryker was on me before I could blink, closing the gap between us, forcing my back to the cave wall and crushing his hard body against me, *grinding* his hard length against me.

With a very Wolfish snarl during which I was sure my eyes were glowing gold, I shoved him back hard, using a good portion of my supernatural strength in doing so. The Hound stumbled back, and a smooth sweep of my feet knocked his legs out from under him. He fell back and landed center on the blankets spread out over the cave floor.

Exactly where I had wanted him.

I pushed my hair back over my shoulders as I crawled up him, giving him a stellar view of the toned and curvy body all those exhaustive trainings had earned me.

"I could eat you right up, little Wolf," Ryker said, and his voice came out more beast than man.

In response, I took him into my hand again as I held my body poised over him. As I began in slow strokes, I leaned down and bit not quite gently at the golden skin of his neck. In his ear, I whispered, "I still hate you, you stupid Hound."

The contracted muscles in his toned midsection mesmerized me as he laughed. "And that's still a lie," he replied, the words coming out between clenched teeth.

Hyperaware of the fact that I may very well die tomorrow, I sat back, tightening my grip just a bit as I grabbed Ryker at the base of his impressive shaft. Hoisting up on my knees and arching my back, I eased down on him, savoring every inch as he entered me.

The Hound tipped his head back and growled while I tipped my head back and felt the ends of my long, soft hair brush the top of my backside. Delicious fire burned wildly through my stomach, and I placed my hand at Ryker's neck as I rode him, thinking about how I could rip his throat out right then if I so desired.

The challenging, hungry way he looked at me gave me the feeling he was aware of the general direction of my thoughts. I let my fingernails dig into his skin a little with just enough pressure to avoid drawing blood. This made him growl again, his handsome face flashing with unchecked pleasure.

I dug in a little harder, and his rough hands came up to my hips in a vice grip. He lifted himself deeper into me while using his hands to hold my hips hostage.

I took every bit of it, not allowing him to take the dominant position even once, just like the last time we had done this. When the carved muscles of his stomach and chest contracted with his climax, I slowed my body on top of him, watching as his handsome face contorted with his release.

After, once I'd reclaimed my clothing and tied my hair up off my neck, the Hound lay motionless atop the blankets, watching me. When I looked back at him over my shoulder, the look in his eyes revealed that if there was ever a time to attempt to gather sensitive information from him, it was right now.

I did not feel bad about this, because I knew that before all was said and done, every conscious creature does a shameful thing or two to survive. And, on top of that, Ryker was right about one thing: My hatred for him was a lie. In fact, in a different world, I thought I might even be able to learn to love him.

But this was not a different world.

And there could be no learning to love.

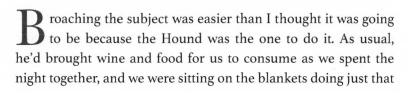

Broaching the subject was easier than I thought it was going to be because the Hound was the one to do it. As usual, he'd brought wine and food for us to consume as we spent the night together, and we were sitting on the blankets doing just that when Ryker said, "You never told me what happened to the pup from the woods. What you did with her?"

I had to tell myself not to stiffen, wondering how I'd gone suddenly from investigator to investigated.

I took a sip of my wine. "I have no idea what you're talking about," I said.

Ryker rolled his eyes, leaning back against the cave wall and crossing one ankle over the other. "If I was going to turn you in for it, I would've done so a long time ago... I'm just curious as to how the child is faring... if she made it somewhere... better."

Sipping more wine, I narrowed my eyes at him. "I have no idea how she's faring. She just disappeared into the night... like all the others."

Ryker's blue gaze pinned me. "What do you know about the others?"

I shook my head. "No more than anyone else. Just that pups are going missing." I chose my next words carefully and spoke them as casually as I could manage. "What I don't get is why they can't be tracked by their collars."

The Hound shook his head at this, still pinning me with his azure gaze. "The pups that are going missing have yet to be collared."

"Oh," I said, though I knew this, of course. I swallowed. "All of them?"

The look he gave me then could be called nothing but suspicious. "No... actually," he said, surprising me with his honesty, though I tried not to let that show. "Some of them have been adults, but they've been untraceable, as if they'd somehow..."

It was an effort to feign only mild interest. "Removed them?" I finished for him. "Is that even possible?"

The Hound gave me a smile that was handsome enough to break a heart were it not frozen over. "I suppose anything is possible, little Wolf."

"What are they going to do?" I asked, knowing my words were

dangerous territory. I cleared my throat. "The Masters, I mean. I bet they're not happy about losing their... assets."

Ryker was silent for a handful of moments during which I found it difficult to draw air. Then, he said, "Whatever it takes to catch whoever's responsible."

Despite the effort it took, I didn't drop his stare. "You're... so different than everyone says you are."

From the way his shoulders relaxed a fraction, I could tell this was an easier topic, though not by much. "And what does everyone say I am?"

"That you're as mean as they come, and that you... murdered your own brother for gain."

The Hound moved with a suddenness that surprised me, his handsome face twisting in anger as he brought it close to my own and spoke between clenched teeth. "I loved my brother, but I was left no choice. That's all I'm going to say about it."

I touched the collar at my neck as he eased out of my personal space again, and said slowly, "You can't be a good guy if you agree that some of us should be shackled and enslaved, if you continue to support the oppression of your own kind."

Ryker's eyes were as intense as the sea during a storm as he looked at me. "If you know something about what's happening with those pups, Rook," he said, using the nickname I actually preferred over all the others, "you need to tell me. If you don't, and Ramsey finds out, there won't be anything I can do to help you."

"Is it that there won't be any way to help, or that you *won't* help?" I asked, then added, "And if you knew of a way to remove the collars, would you tell me?"

Ryker folded his strong arms over his chest. "You answer first."

I spread my hands. "I already told you I don't know anything about what's happening with the pups."

He nodded, as if he'd expected me to say as much. "There is

no way for me to help," he said. "There's no way to help any of us."

~

A res had suspected that I would not get very far with Ryker, and he had planned accordingly. The next day, he met me at The Cascades, telling me that he might have a lead for us... provided I survive the day.

Because after months of preparation, my first fight in The Games was finally here. In a handful of hours, I would live or die, kill or be killed.

Kalene would not be fighting until the next day, and she surprised me by pulling me into a tight embrace as we stood watching the sunrise that morning. Her long, black hair had been left unbound, and though she did not cry, there was true sadness in her dark eyes as she looked at me.

I gave her a wry smile. "Don't look at me like that," I told her, and placed a hand on her shoulder. "I'm going to win, so there's no need to be sad."

Kalene shook her head. "I know you will," she said. "But even when we win... we lose, my friend."

I sighed my agreement, looking out over the ocean. "The life of a Dog... For what it's worth, I think you deserve better."

Kalene's red lips pulled up in an almost smile. "I feel the same about you, Rook."

A familiar male voice chimed in. "Well, you two should just have each other's babies," Oren said, swinging a beefy arm around my shoulder.

Kalene gave him a droll look. "If we could do that, Oren, my dear, we'd have absolutely zero use for you or any of your male counterparts."

If the weight of the impending fight had not been upon me, I might have laughed. As it was, I had to settle for a small smile.

When the two of them crushed me in a hug between them, they may well have been squeezing my heart as well.

Though I knew it meant death for three others, I sent up a silent prayer that the three of us be victorious.

What I didn't consider was the fact that some fates really were worse than death.

In some cases, death was a mercy.

35

Once again I was shackled at the wrists and ankles and loaded into a barred wagon. The streets of Marisol were quiet, because all of the citizens and visitors were already at the arena. Time took on the sort of pace that demands attention to every ticking second, like the flowing sand in an hourglass.

The beautiful buildings, all constructed of that multi-colored seaglass, the cobblestone streets, with their silent sentry green lampposts, passed by without me really seeing them. Before I knew it, the wagon was trundling into the shadow of a looming structure; so large it blotted out the sun. The roaring within the arena was enough to set the building shuddering, and I had to clench my hands into fists to keep them from doing the same.

The wagon stopped. The barred door was opened. My Dog companions and I were yanked out by the chains around our wrists and shoved toward a narrow passage that led into the arena. I followed the Dog in front of me, shuffling our feet due to the limited movement provided by the shackles. As we entered the dark, damp hallway leading us toward our fates, it felt very much like journeying to the belly of a beast.

And the sound within... The sound was *fantastic*. Absolutely world-shaking.

A mixture of scents bombarded my nose—roasting peanuts, spun sugar, flavored meats, sweat, and blood. Blood most of all. My heart began beating somewhere in my throat, my eyes glowing Wolf-Gold in order to pierce the darkness.

A hundred paces... one hundred fifty, and still we had not reached the center. The place must be even bigger than I remembered, a goliath of death and depravation. My mouth went dry, and I swallowed, which didn't help a bit.

Then a door opened on the right side of the small hallway we were traversing, and we were shoved inside. The room was just a small cell that was likely built right under the stands where thousands were waiting to be entertained by the spilling of blood.

There, we waited. Now that I had a mind to, I counted and found I was with three other males and two other females, none of whom I knew, though I had seen them at training and in passing. No one came to remove our shackles or to see if we had any last requests.

Time pressed onward, each second counted with the rapid beats of our hearts. Then the door opened, and a Hound barked a name that didn't belong to me. One of the male Dogs rose and followed the Hound out.

The male Dog did not return.

The crowd stacked over our heads roared and stomped and shouted, and bits of dust sprinkled from the cell's ceiling and drifted down upon us. The same Hound returned and called another name. This time one of the other females rose and followed him out.

An indeterminable amount of time passed.

The female did not return, either.

And on and on it went, until there was only myself and one other male left in the small, damp room.

When the Hound returned, *Bear-killer* was the next name on his lips.

I rose to my feet, finding them as steady and reliable as always, despite the fact that my stomach was tied into knots. The Hound slammed and relocked the door to the cell behind me, sealing inside the last male Dog that had been in my company.

Without a word, the Hound crouched down and unlocked the chains around my ankles, tossing them against the wall of the hallway, where they clinked against other shackles that had likewise been discarded. Next, he removed the chains around my wrists and tossed those as well.

The Hound gave me a challenging look, to which I responded with a wicked grin. It was not uncommon for a Dog to decide to kill the Hound about to throw them into The Ring. In fact, this job was the riskiest for a Hound to be assigned. My smile meant only that I knew this, and if I wanted to, I could likely kill this son of a bitch before any one was able to put me down.

In answer, the Hound placed a hand on the baton at his hip, and I rolled my eyes at his show of weakness.

He needn't worry. Killing a Hound in lieu of a fight was the act of a hopeless Dog. And I was not a hopeless Dog.

This thought struck me with such force that, for a moment, I forgot just where I was and what was about to happen.

I was no longer hopeless. If Ares was right, and if Yarin and Yerik were to be believed... There was the possibility of a life beyond this. Of a better future. Of... *freedom.*

Now it was not my nerves that were making my throat tight, but the unfeasibility that had always been attached to that word.

But time for thinking of such things was up. I followed the Hound down the hallway, where a red door waited at the end. Then I was at that door, and it was opening. Inside, a metal spiral staircase led up and up and up.

The roar of the crowd hit me as hard as the irony tang of Wolf-blood, and I was shoved through.

The voice of the announcer bellowed, "Help me welcome to The Ring, Rook the Bear-killer!"

∾

There was so much to take in that I didn't know where to look first. People stacked atop people surrounded me on every side, the stands in which they sat stretching up toward the heavens. The top of the dome had been removed, and was open to the blue sky above, where white, fluffy clouds drifted lazily by as though carnage were not taking place below.

And that was just the scene above me.

To my right, there was a rail-less walkway, about five feet in width, and it encircled the entire circumference of the place, coming full circle to my left. There was an identical walkway straight ahead, which let to the center of the arena—the area where death would be dealt. The center was also without boundaries or edges, nothing to keep Dogs from plunging right over the edge.

Over the edge, which led to a straight drop and murky, churning waters fifty feet below. Ryker had warned me that Ramsey was going to make things more interesting for this year's Games, but nothing could have prepared me for this. As I stared over the edge of the platform on which I stood, something told me that murky water might not be all that waited below.

"Shift!" bellowed the voice of the announcer, seeming to come from every direction at once, until the roaring of the crowd drowned it out.

I pulled my gaze away from the watery depths and saw that my opponent stood on an identical platform on the exact opposite side of the arena. Serilda the Sour stared back at me before stripping her clothes off so that she could shift into her Wolf form. The crowd's response to this had me baring my teeth as I made my shift instantly and *then* wiggled out of the clothing.

227

Something struck me hard in the head, and I stumbled sideways, the soft pads of my paws sliding over the walkway. Just as I righted myself, I was struck again on the other side, my jaws snapping at the open air in that direction in frustration.

Something whizzed past my head before spiraling away into the distance, and I finally got a look at what had struck me.

Heads of lettuce. Some of the people in the crowd were throwing *heads of fucking lettuce.* And that first one had nearly sent me over the edge of this ridiculous walkway. I guessed they didn't appreciate the fact that I had shifted before getting naked. I snarled at them, my ears flattening on my head and the fur on my back rising.

Across the arena, Serilda was finishing her own transformation. In Wolf form, her fur was as white as a fresh snow, her eyes like glittering chips of ice.

"Fight!" boomed the voice of the announcer.

The white Wolf prowled forward, and I went to meet her. The narrow walkway straight ahead led to the center, which was a larger, circular platform where the blood of Wolves already fallen still stained. With every step I took, the world around me faded further into nothing. Then I was running full tilt, and the white Wolf was doing the same.

We collided at the center, fangs flashing and snapping. My jaws closed around her flank but could not keep purchase. At the same time, I felt her teeth scrape over my back, though I did not feel the pain if there was any.

No, pain would be felt later.

If there was a later.

We snapped, lunged, and rolled, both of us searching for that deadly opening, that soft spot where the teeth could sink deep and sever something essential. The taste of her blood filled my mouth, a sampling that I needed to swell. I did not fight the sensation of the blood lust coming over me, though it was not a state I savored stepping into. On the contrary, it was simply necessary.

I danced back as the white Wolf darted in... and miscalculated my movements just a fraction. That was all it took. Her iron jaws clamped down on the back of my neck, making me howl out involuntarily. I was vaguely aware of an uproarious reaction from the crowd, but they may as well have been a million miles away.

Bucking, twisting, and thrashing with every ounce of strength I contained, I managed to free myself from her hold. But it cost me. The white Wolf was no fool; she knew there were other ways to claim this victory that just spilling my blood.

As her grip began to slip, she whipped her head to the side and sent my body flying, all the things around me merging into a blur. In this form, I was almost entirely unable to halt my momentum. My heart jammed itself into my throat as that rail-less edge came into view along with the murky, churning water below.

I hit the platform a half handful of inches away from that ledge, watching in horror as my tail slid over the empty space... and then one of my hind legs. For a terrifying moment that could only have been a heartbeat, but felt infinitely longer, I was sure that I was going over.

But then I was scrambling for purchase, clawing my way back onto the platform as quickly as I could manage. Behind me, in the spot where my tail had been only a moment ago, something enormous broke the surface of the water.

The crowd screamed in brutal pleasure.

I stared in absolute stunned horror as I watched a scaled, serpentine sea creature burst out of the murky water, maw yawning wide enough to swallow three of me whole. It's green, diamond-shaped eye pinned me where I stood, just out of its reach, promising that should I make the mistake of dangling a limb over the edge again, it would not miss a second time.

This was almost enough to make me forget the more immediate threat. In fact, I'm pretty sure that if Serilda had not been as astonished at the sea monster's appearance as I was, she could have easily taken me out during the distraction.

As it was, we both seemed to remember each other at the same moment. I darted away from the edge of the platform, charging toward her as if my tail were on fire. I needed to end this. Now. There were too many variables to let it continue much longer.

Apparently, Serilda was thinking the same thing. This time, however, when she attempted the same move that had cost me before, I was ready for her.

A secret that I guarded with my life was that I never gave myself fully to my beast in these fights. Most fighters did surrender fully to their Wolves, and while this had many advantages, it also had a way of dampening the human cognitive skills. The power of the human brain was something I held in the highest regard, and so I was always careful to cling to it, keeping at least a thread attached at all times.

I twisted my body in just the right way so that Serilda completely missed her target, which had been the soft spot under my throat. She came so close that I heard the click of her fangs as they snapped shut, felt her brush past me, stirring my fur like the kiss of a sweet summer breeze.

That moment occurred to me in slow motion, the vivid details of the scene jumping out in sharp relief. I saw my opponent, Serilda, with her snow white coat and her blazing blue eyes. I watched the way her body twisted, her fluffy tail held close behind her hindquarters. I met her gaze as I rotated so swiftly that I became a blur, using a speed that would not be possible with a Wolf any larger.

Serilda had not even finished her sail past me, had just only realized that she'd missed her target, when I dropped my head down low and charged forward... *fast*. So incredibly fast.

The top of my hard head made stunning impact with the side

of her strong and solid body, buckling it in a way that was not natural for a canine. A high-pitched, gut-wrenching whine was ripped out of her as I hit her with every ounce of strength I contained.

Serilda's ivory body took to the air, her four paws leaving the platform and her lupine face taking on a note of true terror. The moment was over in an instant, but I saw every second of it.

The blood of those who'd come before me beneath my paws. The looming edge of the platform, where that murky water with its enormous sea monster waited below. The moment the white Wolf realized that there was nothing she could do to stall her momentum. The absolute *thundering* of the crowd as Serilda went over. The spray of the water as that sea serpent breached the surface, with it's scaled head and diamond-shaped eyes. The outrageous width of its yawning maw, and the terrible swiftness with which it swallowed Serilda's falling body, snatching her out of the air and snapping its jaws shut before plunging back into the murky, churning waters below.

The massive crowd began to chant my name.

Bear-killer! Bear-killer! Bear-killer!

But all I could think about was the look that had captured Serilda's features in those final moments. A look—that I knew from experience—would lend itself to the legion of ghosts that haunted my dreams.

36

Among the Dogs who had survived the day, there was no celebrating on the wagon ride back to our designated area. Still covered in the blood of our opponents, we returned in silence, each of us feeling as much the losers as we were the winners.

Kalene was waiting for me near The Cascades, and I could tell that it took all her strength not to run to me. When I reached her, we clasped hands, and then she pulled me into a tight hug that hurt my sore body more than I would ever let on.

Or perhaps it was just the ache in my heart from which I was suffering. I could scarcely tell the difference anymore.

Kalene did not congratulate me. What she said was, "I'm glad you made it back."

I gave her a ghost of a smile. "I told you I would, and tomorrow, you'll do the same."

"Gods willing."

"Those bastards have nothing to do with it."

Kalene's red lips tilted up in a sad smile. "Careful, my friend. You'll sound jaded."

"And gods forbid," Ares said, joining us. Oren arrived back

from the arena not too long after, and the four of us washed our sins away in The Cascades before heading over to the Kitchen for sustenance.

While Oren and Kalene were getting seconds, I leaned forward and whispered to Ares. "So, what's the plan?"

Ares' light brown eyes met mine. "You still want to move forward? After today?" he asked.

I sighed. "I appreciate the consideration," I said, "but after today, *all* I want to do is move forward."

The image of Serilda being swallowed whole by that sea serpent flashed through my head, and I had to suppress a shudder. In a low voice, I added, "I'm done being complacent. I'm done sitting around waiting to die. Tell me what you need me to do."

So, he did... and I agreed that I would do it.

"This is dangerous, Rook," Ares warned. "They'll skin you alive if you're caught."

"Look around, my friend," I said. "We really can't get any more fucked."

That settled it. Tonight, when everyone was celebrating the close to the first day of The Games, I would sneak into Reagan Ramsey's cliff side castle and try to steal the secret to removing a Dog's collar.

It had to be me, and not Ares, because a strange male was much more likely to be recognized wandering through the castle than a strange female. According to Ares, Ramsey kept as many workingwomen around him as possible, which only served to make me hate him all the more.

If there was a way to remove the blasted collars, I vowed that I would try to help as many of those females to freedom as possible, because despite the events in The Games today, I still thought these ladies had drawn the shortest sticks of all. I didn't let myself think about Goldie, because if I did find the answer I was seeking, I knew locating her would be my next stop. Even if I had to go through that bastard Adriel to do it.

Knowing that I had my work cut out for me this evening I returned to the cave and rested for the remainder of the day. My sleep was deep and heavy, the world in my head nothing but darkness. In fact, if Ares hadn't come and woken me up, I might have slept right through the celebration.

Ryker was the only other person who had ever been to the place where I slept, and when I opened my eyes, I saw Ares tilt his head back and take in the scent of the Head Hound, but his face remained absent any judgment. I decided I liked the male a little more for this.

Ares informed me of the details of my mission, and then he pulled two lacy, mostly sheer items out of a bag and tossed them to me.

"What in the names of the gods is this?" I asked.

Ares' handsome face lit up in a grin. "That's what you'll be wearing."

I held up the garments—if one could even call them that—and looked back at Ares with narrowed eyes.

"Where did you get this?"

"I borrowed it from a friend."

My nose scrunched up, but I stripped down and donned the scraps of clothing, cringing at the way they left little to the imagination. The top consisted of a string that went around my neck, holding duel satin pieces trimmed with small golden coins over my breasts, and tying behind my back. The other piece was a satin skirt trimmed with those same golden coins that would jingle every time I walked and present a challenge in trying to remain silent and decent.

"One more thing," Ares said. He reached into his bag and handed me a gold mask that would conceal the top portion of my face. I stared down at the ridiculous item in my hand, tracing the gold whorls sewn into it with a finger.

After this, he wished me good luck.

Then I had only to wait until nightfall.

$\sim$

The Cliffside Castle perched above the city of Marisol as though the structure itself were a ruler upon a throne. The gray sandstone out of which it had been carved glittered silver in the moonlight, the many conch-shell shaped towers glowing with flames made green, pink, and royal blue by the seaglass in which they were cased. Water fell in shimmering, whispering waterfalls from many of the ledges and balconies, creating a fog of mist that kissed at the face of the castle unendingly.

Tonight, the place was even more spectacular than usual. The green lampposts leading up to the castle, with their blue Apollo-blessed flames, had been adorned with strings of flowers and twinkling little lights. The air smelled of salt and summer blooms, growing cooler the closer one got to the entrance of the castle.

The sounds of celebrations—gently playing music, the clinking of glasses, laughter and an occasional howl toward the heavens—drifted out only to be swallowed up by the revelry taking place in the city streets. The first day of The Games had been an exhilarating exhibition for most of the lucky bastards, and it would be followed by the type of debauchery that only seemed appropriate under the cloak of nighttime.

Carriages pulled by well-bred horses trundled up to the Cliffside Castle in a line as far as the eye could see, carrying the Wolves, Vamps, and other various creatures who were fortunate enough to warrant an invitation to Reagan Ramsey's personal after party. Instead of following these visitors, I went around to another route, where a service road blocked by a gate led to the rear of the castle.

Just as Ares had promised, there were other workingwomen filtering in through this way as well, along with various others who looked to be cooks, maids, and servants. Two Hounds stood at the gate, checking each caller who sought to come through. I swallowed down the nerves that were trying to wind in my stomach and managed not to jump when a hand landed on my shoulder.

"What do you call a Dog with no legs?" asked a sultry voice in my ear.

I spun around only to come face-to-face with a beautiful female with smooth brown skin and green eyes that were lined with kohl. Her lips had been colored a lovely shade of pink, and the outfit she wore concealed about as much of her fit body as did mine. Despite her stunning face, her hair was easily her most striking feature. It framed her face in tight, shiny curls that were full enough to sit in a dark cloud around her head and fall down her delicate shoulders.

One fine brow arched as she looked at me impatiently. "What do you call a Dog with no legs?" she repeated.

I cleared my throat. "It doesn't matter what you call her. She won't come."

Apparently having passed her test with the answer Ares had provided me, the female linked her arm through mine and said in a voice low enough for only me to hear, "Follow my lead. Smile. Do not look the Hounds in the eyes. Your name is Scarlett. Don't forget it."

I nodded my understanding, watching as she slid a mask similar to mine over her face. "And what do I call you?" I whispered.

"Angelise," she said. "Angel for short." She glanced at the gate where the Hounds were interrogating a fat Wolf with a chef's hat for what seemed like just the hell of it, and then back at me. "You sure about this?"

I tugged her toward the Hounds. "If we wait much longer, I might not be."

Angelise gave me a sympathetic look that was gone in an instant, replaced by the suggestive, sleepy-eyed expression that I'd seen Goldie use to her advantage many times. The two Hounds licked their lips as we approached, admiring all the skin revealed by our sheer, silky outfits. Just as it always had with Goldie, it made me want to knock the teeth out of the Hounds' mouth for looking at us the way they were.

There was a knock at my mental walls, a sensation that I hadn't felt in such time that it surprised me. When I looked over at Angelise, she showed no indication of what she'd done, but I lowered my shields and let her in, anyway.

Her sultry voice echoed through my head in the telepathic manner available to Wolves: *"Smile,"* she snapped.

My lips lifted at the corners and I forced my shoulders to relax, adding a little extra sway to my hips, the way I'd seen Goldie do so many times. The Hounds made a couple crude remarks, one promising to find me later if Ramsey wasn't "using" me at the time, and by the will of the Gods, I forced another smile to my lips and suppressed a cringe when Angelise blew a kiss back at them.

After this, the bastards allowed us to go inside.

Up the winding service road, and around and around to the rear of the castle. While Angelise and I followed the other workers, I kept reminding myself to smile and to hold my body in a way that was non-threatening. After so many years of constant fighting and posturing, it was more effort than I had anticipated, but I managed. With every step we took closer to the castle, the weight of my mission pressed down on me, threatening to sink me into the earth.

I shoved this fear away, reminding myself that this was no more deadly than a match in The Ring, and that my success here depended upon my ability to keep a cool head.

The service road ended at a stone wall with an arched entry-way, the castle itself looming directly behind. Here, we were stopped again by two more Hounds. More crude remarks from them and strained smiles from me. Once more, we were finally allowed to pass.

Scantily clad and scared out of my wits, I followed closely at Angelise's side as we at last entered the fortress that was Reagan Ramsey's Cliffside Castle.

37

The inside was as spectacular as the out. The air was much cooler within, the thick walls of gray sandstone slightly damp with sea spray, which gave the structure a clean, pure aroma.

Angelise and I passed through a servant's entrance and were directed down a long hallway toward another arched door. From beyond that door, the sounds of music, clinking champagne glasses, and laughter could be heard. I swallowed hard, and Angelise gave my arm a gentle, reassuring squeeze.

Silently, she told me, *"I know you're afraid, but your success tonight could lead to the liberation of thousands."* She met my gaze with those striking green eyes. *"Gods bless you, Rukiya Moonborn."*

That was the second time I'd heard that name, but I didn't have time to ponder it as we were shooed through the arched doorway and into a ballroom so grand that it took my breath away.

Silver chains with links the size of my hand descended from the high ceiling, ending in dancing green flames that licked downward, casting a mystical glow over the large room. In one corner sat a band of musicians, instruments poised on their shoulders and thighs, their lithe fingers plucking out a sweet melody on the strings.

People in masks and elaborate clothing were everywhere, and waiters with trays of foods I couldn't identify circulated the room. Beneath their jewels, makeup, and masks, the various people flashed smiles of perfect, white teeth, as if their only concern in the world was what they would wear to the next party. It was an effort to keep from gawking and scowling, instead keeping my docile smile in place.

"You see that crimson curtain over there?" asked Angelise, somehow managing to both flirt with a pudgy Wolf and speak in my mind at the same time.

I searched for and located where she'd indicated, affirming it telepathically.

"When you're able to do so without being noticed, you're to slip behind that curtain. There will be a door there, and to open it, you'll turn the knob twice to the left, and three times to the right. Do you understand so far?"

"Yes."

"Good. After you open the door, there will be three hallways leading off in separate directions. Take the one on your right. This will lead you to Ramsey's private study."

I listened carefully to all the instructions as Angelise continued. Then all I had to do was find my opening.

It came not too much later. When three fire-dancers claimed the center of the ballroom and began doing a dangerous routine that awed those gathered. While all eyes were on the dancers, I scooted over toward the crimson curtain and slipped smoothly behind it. Just as Angelise had promised, a door was hidden there. I turned its knob two times to the left, and three to the right.

There was a barely audible click, and the door swung open.

Holding my breath, I squeezed through and shut it gently behind me. Turning, I found a tiny chamber connected to three dark hallways, and as instructed, chose the one on the right. This led me to yet another door requiring another combination. Again, the passcode provided by Angelise proved true.

My heart was beating rapidly in my throat as the lock clicked open and the door swung inward to reveal Reagan Ramsey's private study.

Despite the cool air in the castle, and the fact that I was wearing barely anything at all, a sweat broke out over my forehead as I tried not to let thoughts of what would become of me if I were to be caught disrupt my concentration.

Recalling Ares' precise instructions, I ignored the plush carpet under my feet and the fine furniture scattered throughout the chamber and headed over to the west wall. Here, I found the real reason that this mission had to be accomplished by me. I had something most other slaves had never been afforded—the ability to read.

I'd learned secretly as a child, taught by one of the Gods-worshipers who'd stayed in Dogshead for a spell. For obvious reasons, this was a skill that I did not display, and Ares had only come to know about it by happenstance one day when we'd been in one of Marisol's taverns. I'd been shitfaced and had drunkenly read a few words that had been carved into a wooden table. When he'd revealed this plan to me, I'd realized that this was information he had tucked away.

The entire west wall was a bookcase, and on this bookcase there were countless tomes on varying subjects and stories. I had never seen so many volumes gathered in one place, and for a moment, I just stared at the letters, afraid that after all this time of being denied material to read, I had forgotten how to do it.

I took a deep, steadying breath and willed my mind to concentrate.

To my relief, it turned out that reading was like riding a horse; no matter how much time passed, once one was in the saddle again, it all came flooding back.

The letters on the spines of the books began to arrange themselves into words, and I scanned them as quickly as possible for the one I was looking for. My palms became damper with each passing second, aware that the time I was on was already borrowed. Nervously, I ran my fingers over a small totem of a Wolf that had been placed amongst the stacks.

Then my eyes settled on the book I'd been seeking, and I read the words on the spine to confirm. I pulled the ordinary brown book from the shelf and ran my hand over it while whispering the incantation I'd been given, which revealed the book's true color. Staring down at the Silver Codex, my heart thundered in my chest.

There was a small click behind me, and I turned to see that the main door to Reagan Ramsey's office had opened.

❧

There was no time to hide, or even to replace the book that was clutched like the color red in my hand. I could only stand like a big-eyed doe, staring at the open door in absolute panic as the person who'd opened it entered.

It was not Reagan Ramsey.

To my utter confusion, the person who walked through the door had crimson eyes trimmed with dark, thick lashes. His gate was so smooth and predatory that he did not even make a sound that my Wolf ears could pick up. He wore his usual black slacks and black shirt of the finest fabrics. As he saw me standing there before the bookcase, a wicked grin lit up his gorgeous face, and he ran a pale hand through his ebony hair, smoothing the shiny locks back to perfection.

On its own accord, the door he'd come through shut behind him, and I stood immobile, like a rabbit caught in a snare.

"Hello, Rukiya dearest," Adriel said. His red eyes darted down to my feet, running up my bare legs and hips, over my flat stomach and semi-concealed breasts, to my painted lips, and the gold mask covering my eyes… and then to the silver book clutched in my hand. He clicked his tongue. In his cool, collected, and alluring voice, he added, "Looks like I've stumbled upon you doing something naughty." His grin was all white, perfect teeth with long, pointed canines. "Lucky me."

"What are *you* doing here?" I whispered, saying the first thing I could think of.

In that even tone, he replied without hesitation. "Ramsey sent me to retrieve something. Your turn."

It was a wonder I could speak past the lump that was trying to lodge itself in my throat. I studied the Mixbreed with appraising eyes. "You're lying," I said.

Adriel's beautiful head tilted just so, the movement so slight as to be almost imperceptible. "Is that so?"

"Yes," I said, with more confidence than I felt. My eyes darted toward the secret door through which I'd entered the study. I weighed the odds of outrunning him, and came up devastatingly short.

After a moment of heavy silence, he said, "Maybe I am, but you still haven't told me what your business is in Ramsey's office." He nodded once at the book in my hand. "Or perhaps you've already retrieved what you came for."

Instinctively, I held the book behind my back, giving myself away in the process. Now I was considering my chances of taking out the Mixbreed if it came down to it… and was once again relatively sure Adriel could swallow me alive.

He took a step toward me, held out a pale hand. "Hand that over, dearest. Let's have a looksee."

My lips pulled back at little, flashing my teeth as I shook my head once. "No," I said.

This book could hold the key to not just my own freedom, but also the freedom of so many others. There was no damn way I was giving it to this shifty bastard. He'd already fooled me once after bargaining for my blood and telling me nothing in return except for that Goldie was "fine." I was not about to be fooled again.

Adriel took another step forward while I took one back. I held one hand out to him in a gesture that asked him to stay where he was. "I'm not giving you this book," I told him in a voice that was surprisingly steady. "This has nothing to do with you, so just let me be on my way, and we'll forget we ever saw each other here."

Adriel lifted a single dark brow, and for a moment, I thought he might actually laugh, but then his head angled as his attention was jerked elsewhere. He moved so swiftly that his strong, lithe body was standing beside me before I had a chance to even blink.

"Someone is coming," he said, and his arm moved to hover around my waist, pausing just before making contact with my mostly bare skin. And, then, in a wonder of all wonders, his smooth voice echoed telepathically in my head: *"I can shield you with my magic,"* the Mixbreed told me silently. *"But you need to keep absolutely silent, or you'll reveal us both. Nod if you understand."*

My brown eyes were narrowed down to slits, but I nodded.

Adriel placed a strong, warm hand at my back and pulled me gently toward him, pressing me against his wide chest, filling my nose with the clean, masculine smell of him. He flicked the hand that was not holding me in a deft twist of the wrist, and the air around us shimmered.

The door to Ramsey's office opened again, and this time it *was* the Master who entered... along with his Head Hound.

Ryker.

38

Adriel's skin was as smooth and flawless as porcelain, even this close, and for whatever reason, the heat of his body once again surprised me. I didn't know why, but I kept expecting him to be cold. Beneath my hand, which was splayed on his carved chest with our proximity, I could feel the steady rhythm of his heartbeat beneath.

"Because Mixbreeds don't have heartbeats?" He asked silently, a slight snap to his tone that I had never heard before.

Cringing internally, I realized that with the mixture of races in his blood, Adriel's abilities were as potentially limitless as they were unpredictable. A normal Wolf—or even a Halfbreed— would not have been able to speak mind-to-mind with me without my permission. Adriel had just waltzed right into my mental frequency as though he'd always been there, and now, he had rendered us invisible with just the flick of his wrist.

Which was a damn good thing, too, because Reagan Ramsey and Ryker the Hound were now in the room. Despite the fact that the creature who's arms were now wrapped around me terrified me, I held utterly still against him.

"I thought you said Ramsey sent you in here to get something," I said silently, recalling that little detail.

Adriel's sensuous mouth peaked at one corner. *"And I told you maybe that was a lie,"* he responded with a wink.

Reagan Ramsey stalked into the space with all the authority of a king, Ryker following obediently at his heels, shutting the door to the study behind him.

"What's the word on the disappearances?" Ramsey snapped without preamble.

For the first time since I'd known the Hound, he looked almost nervous. "We're working on it, sir," he said. "We're doing everything we can."

Ramsey moved so swiftly that had Adriel not tightened his grip around me, I would have jumped. The West Coast Pack Master flung the glass of ice and amber liquid he'd been holding against the far wall, where it shattered into a thousand glittering pieces, the amber liquid now running down the wall.

From the lack of reaction from Ryker, I suspected this was normal behavior from the Pack Master.

Spittle flew from Ramsey's lips as his handsome face went red, looking not at all like the gentlemen his fine suits attempted to portray him as. "Do you know how much gods damned money this fucking Conductor is costing me?" Ramsey growled. "My property is being stolen again and again, and all you have to say is that 'you're working on it?'" Ramsey prowled over to Ryker and got in the Head Hound's face. "Maybe you need more incentive, Ry... Doesn't your sister still work with the Healers?"

Whatever fear Ramsey instilled in the Hound, not a trace of it remained now. Ryker's blue eyes practically blazed, but he maintained his cool outwardly. "We'll find this Conductor and make sure he's brought to justice," Ryker said in a low, firm tone. "You have my word."

Ramsey rolled his eyes and retreated to the chair behind his desk, plopping down in it as if he had the most exasperating existence in all the realms. As he did so, Ryker wandered over to the bookshelf, pausing as he looked down at the small Wolf totem I'd brushed my fingers over moments before they'd entered. The Hound's handsome brow furrowed, and he sniffed once at the air, recognition passing behind his sapphire eyes.

Directly in front of me, his lovely face only inches from my own, Adriel looked down at me, one ebony brow arched high. I gave him a look that suggested I would chop his nuts off if he felt the absolute urge to comment on whatever stupid thoughts were currently passing through his dark mind.

The Mixbreed gave me a lazy grin and resumed watching the company. Shortly thereafter, Ramsey dismissed Ryker, who looked more than happy to leave. Then the bastard called one of his minions and ordered "two of the prettiest whores at the party" brought to his bedchamber immediately.

By the grace of the gods, Ramsey also took his leave at last, and once we were alone again, Adriel dropped whatever magical spell he'd been holding in place to shield us.

I stepped out of his arms and opened my mouth to say something, but the bastard beat me to the punch.

"If I were you," he told me, "I would make haste on my way out of here, Rukiya dearest."

Then he disappeared, his form blinking out of sight as though it were nothing but imagination. I stood for all of three seconds, alone in Reagan Ramsey's private study, before realizing that the silver book I'd been holding—the *key* to this entire fucking mission, was gone, too.

As I made my way out of the Cliffside Castle, I decided I'd kill myself a Mixbreed if I made it through the next few days alive.

∾

I didn't draw a deep breath until I'd made it beyond the thick gray walls of the castle. It was an effort to keep from shifting and running away from the place as though my tail was on fire, but somehow, I managed. So many emotions were roiling within me that it was difficult to process. I was furious at Adriel for tricking me once again, and also at myself for allowing the bastard to do it.

I was also disappointed, because I'd allowed myself to have hope, and I had risked my life, only to lose the book at the last moment.

On top of that, I was exhausted. It was difficult to comprehend that only this morning, I'd sent Serilda to her death and watched a sea serpent swallow her whole. This day had been absolutely never ending.

So when I ran into Peni on the way back, and the blonde female was clearly drunk and looking for a fight, I kindly told her to go fuck herself and continued merrily on my way. She'd slurred something about me looking like a whore and I'd flipped her the bird over my shoulder.

When I told Ares what had happened, he was nice about it, listening carefully as I relayed my story, but I could tell that he was disappointed. We mused about what Adriel could possibly want with the silver book that could hold our salvation, but ultimately decided that it didn't matter. What was most likely was that the Mixbreed would use the book for his own gain, as his kind did with everything else.

Ares had placed a hand on my shoulder, kindness in his light brown eyes. "We'll look for another way," he promised. "The answers are out there. We just have to find them."

But we both knew that with the loss of that book, our chances of ever being free of the collars were pretty much non-existent. While he was right about the answers being out there, time was needed to find them, and time was a Dog's worst enemy, the thing he or she had the least of in a world of scarcity.

By the time all of this conversation had been had, the sun was only a handful of winks away from rising, and I stumbled back to the cave intent on passing out as soon as my body hit the blankets. I'd chucked the mask and shreds of clothing and was shamelessly butt naked as I walked into the cave mouth.

The flickering light of a fire within made me pause, and I was not entirely surprised when Ryker the Hound stood from where he'd been leaning against the cave wall. His blue eyes travelled up my naked body as though he could not quite remember why he'd come here.

Then, he said, "I need you to give back the book."

My back stiffened, and I snatched a long shirt off the cave floor, shrugging it over my shoulders. "I have no idea what you're talking about."

He was in front of me before I could speak, blue eyes blazing. "Ramsey noticed it was missing an hour ago," he snarled. "I smelled you in his office."

I held his stare. "You're mistaken."

"Gods damn it, Rook!" Ryker said. "Give me the fucking book so that I can return it."

"*I don't have it!*" I shouted back, my voice breaking on the last couple words. I cleared my throat and tried to regain some calm before I repeated, "I don't have whatever you're talking about, and I think you should leave. Now."

"You don't understand," Ryker said in a voice that was almost a plead. "Rook, he already knows it was you."

When I spoke, my voice sounded strange to my own ears. "Who?" I whispered. "*Who* knows *what* was me?"

"I don't believe I've ever formally introduced myself," said a familiar voice from behind me, near the entrance to the cave.

I had only just made the connection of the voice to its owner when Reagan Ramsey stepped out of the shadows, his fine suit providing a stark contrast with the dark and dirty cave. Two Hounds the size of houses stood on either side of him.

"My name is Reagan Ramsey, and I'm your Pack Master," he said. He jerked his chin in my direction while staring down his straight nose at me. "Take her," he commanded.

The two house-size Hounds gripped me roughly by the fore-arms, one yanking tight on the collar around my throat just to be a dick... but I hardly noticed.

I was too busy staring at Ryker, wondering what this aching feeling in my chest was and why the hell it surprised me so much.

39

I was taken from the cave and dragged back up to the Cliffside Castle, only this time, we used the front entrance, where everyone could see what was happening. Ramsey had ordered me shackled again at the wrists and ankles, likely just for the element of show it added to my little parade.

Daylight had just broken over the horizon, but the only people up were the slaves who had not had the luxury of partying the night away.

The males stood in the fields, heavy plows attached to their backs, heads turning as we passed by. Females washing clothing in the waterfalls paused in their work to take heed as well. We walked by The Cascades and the Kitchen, grabbing the attention of every Dog we passed. Ares was busy grabbing an early morning bite when he saw us coming, and his usual lovely brown skin went so pale that he could have passed for a Vampire. I tried to convey with my eyes that he had nothing to worry about; I would not turn on him, no matter what they did to me, but I was shoved forward by one of the Hounds, continuing my death march.

Ryker marched right alongside us, but I didn't look at him. I couldn't bring myself to look at him. And I got the feeling he was not looking at me, either.

Once we reached the castle, I was led down a winding set of stairs. And then down another. And another, until at last we reached the dungeons, where not a trace of the opulence above existed. Without further ado, I was thrown into a small, dank cell, and the door was slammed shut behind me, locking me in.

No one had bothered to remove my chains, and there was no place to sit down in the cell, so I slid down against one of the damp walls and sat with my back leaning against it, not really seeing anything around me.

Hours passed, and despite my exhaustion, and the fact that I had not slept a single wink the previous night, I couldn't find sleep. So I sat staring, shackled at my ankles and wrists, at my throat and my heart.

When the door to my cell swung open later that morning, I remained unmoved in my position against the wall. I knew who it was by the clicking soles of his expensive shoes. He clicked his tongue as he came to stand over me.

"What did you do with the Silver Codex?" Reagan Ramsey asked me.

I raised my eyes to his. "I don't know what you're talking about."

Another click of his tongue, making me want to rip it right from his pretty mouth. "This is the last time I'm going to ask you," he said. "What did you do with the Silver Codex?"

I spat at his shiny shoes. "I slapped your mother on the ass with it as she was leaving my cave last night."

This earned me a backhand across the jaw. Brilliant, blinding pain shot through my mouth and up to my brain as my head whipped to the side. When the world seeped back into focus, I tasted fresh blood on my lip. Then the air was cut off from reaching my lungs as Ramsey's manicured hand shot out and gripped my throat, squeezing tighter and tighter until my vision began to blur at the edges.

"They told me you were a mouthy little bitch," Ramsey replied, his hot breath brushing my face as I clawed uselessly at the hand still restricting my airflow. It tightened further still. "Tell me where the gods damned Codex is."

Just when I was sure the darkness was going to claim me, Ramsey released his hold, and oxygen flooded back into my lungs in a rush. I gasped, sputtered, and choked. I tried to speak, but all that came out was a wheeze.

Ramsey knelt down in front of me, his head tilting in a very Wolf-like manner. "What was that? I couldn't quite hear you."

I waited until he leaned in a little closer, and repeated, "Go fuck yourself."

To my surprise, Ramsey only sighed through his nose as he stood, smoothing a hand down the front of his suit as if the bastard had some sense of propriety. "The truth shall set you free, sweetheart," he said, and held up his hands. "But if you insist on learning the hard way, so be it."

Ramsey sniffed and whistled, and in answer to his call, a short, bald male with a greasy face and beer gut entered the cell. Behind him, the male dragged a metal rolling cart, one of the four wheels squealing like a newborn sow. From my position on the floor the contents on top of the cart were out of my line of sight, but I could take a few educated guesses at them.

Following the cart, a Hound carrying a wooden chair came in. The chair was outfitted with enough thick leather straps to contain a Demon... or a Dog with information that was highly sensitive.

As the Hound yanked me to my feet and thrust me into the chair, I vowed not to betray a single secret that could lead these sons of bitches to Amara, Yarin, Yerik, Ares, or Angelise.

This would turn out to be the most difficult promise I'd ever tried to keep.

"Keep her alive, Gorsuch," Ramsey ordered, and then he was gone, the door to the cell swinging shut behind him, trapping me inside with the metal cart and the masochist.

～

Consciousness came and went like the tides just beyond the castle walls. When I was lucid, I was screaming so loud and so shrill that my throat burned like the fires of hell. Pain had always been a longtime friend of mine, but this was beyond that. *Agony* rode me like a careless lover, seeping into every atom I possessed and claiming a home.

The bald male with the gut and greasy face sliced, slapped, broke and burned, each time asking the same question: *Where is the Silver Codex?*

At some point, I began only answering in screams. Then darkness would claim me for what felt like only a flash of an instant, offering blessed reprieve for a blink before I was dragged back to consciousness once more.

Perhaps the worst part of all was that I kept expecting Ryker to come to me—not even to help me escape or end this madness, but just to be beside me for a moment or two.

But a day passed. Then two. The illusion of time marked only by the sound of the sea birds beyond the thick stone walls.

And the Hound did not come.

Miraculously, the pain that arrived with this realization was somehow deeper than the lacerations and charring. I wished only for it all to kill me. Prayed to Father Death like a most devote zealot... and received no answer.

Keep her alive, Ramsey had commanded, and so it was done.

By the third day, I'd forgotten my name and what color the sky was. I'd lost all memory of who and what I was and why any of it mattered. My only point of reference became the agony, the rest of it slipping away like dust on a wind, or droplets of blood down a fine-edged blade.

At some point or another, though it could have just been my imagination, Ramsey returned to the cell to check on the progress, asking about the answer to a question I couldn't recall. The male that brought the agony replied that I had not given anything up, that I'd gone mad already, and if he continued, he might lose me at any point.

Ramsey's answer was, *Well, we can't have that, can we?*

And then I was gone again, claimed by the blessed darkness.

When I came to once more, the male with the metal cart was gone. I was still in the dank cell, still chained and restrained, but I was laid out on the cold floor, and someone with soft fingers was probing at me.

Snarling, I snapped my teeth and thrashed against the shackles, held in such a way that left me unable to shift into my other form. There was a small squeal and the hands that had been touching me disappeared. Red ringing my vision, I snapped and snarled again at the female, whose eyes were wide in both terror and pity.

It wasn't until I passed back out and woke up again that I realized the female must have been a Healer, sent to patch me up just enough so that I could make it to whatever grand finale Ramsey had in mind for me.

With my physical form so weak, my mental shields were low enough that any Wolf could sneak past them and communicate, and the young female Healer did just that, speaking to me in a gentle voice no matter how volatile I became in my burgeoning madness.

"*Stay with me,*" *Rukiya,* she whispered into my mind. "*You have to fight now, harder than you've ever fought before.*"

"*Go away,*" I told her from the darkness. "*Or kill me and set me free.*"

"*I'm supposed to heal you just enough,*" she replied, "*but I'm going to do more than that.*"

"*I don't want to be healed. I want death. I'm tired. If you're here to help, please, end it now.*"

"*You did not kill a bear and feed a sea monster to die in this shitty cell. You need to fight. You need to survive.*"

"*How do you know this?*" I tried to peel open my eyes and take in her face, but they were swollen shut, and the heaviness of my body was so great.

"*Everyone knows this,*" came her reply. "*Slaves whisper.*"

"*What's your name?*"

"*Femi... And what's your name?*"

"*Bear-killer.*"

"*Wrong.*"

"*Rook the Rabid.*"

"*Wrong again.*"

The sudden, undeniable urge to tear the female's throat out flashed through my mind, but I couldn't see or reach her, because none of this was real. It was all just a dream. I was already dead.

"*Rukiya Moonborn,*" whispered a voice that sounded like my own, but did not belong to me.

"*That's right,*" Femi replied. "*You are Rukiya Moonborn, a slave only to your own mind. Break free of the chains that bind you, so that you can break the chains that bind us and free us all.*"

When I opened my eyes again an indeterminable amount of time later, the physical agony considerably less than I could ever recall it being, the young Healer with the gentle voice was gone.

And Ryker the Hound was standing over me.

At first, I thought I was still dreaming, but the world was in too much sharp focus, the aches and pains in my body too strident to be imaginary. And the twist in my chest—as though something jagged had been shoved through my heart—when I looked up and saw those familiar blue eyes... *That* was too real, too.

Pulling myself to my feet took enormous effort, but I could not stand the sensation of him standing over me. Before I could stop myself, I was lunging for his throat, aiming to tear it clean out with my teeth.

I was jerked backwards, and only after a couple moments of crazed struggle did I realize that I'd been chained to the cell wall.

Like a fucking *Dog.*

The Head Hound had the mind to jump backward out of my reach, his gaze flashing with a myriad of deceitful emotion as he took in my feral state.

There was a knock upon my mental frequency, a request to communicate, to which I responded with a deep, rumbling snap and snarl. I yanked against the chains, but they held firm, cutting into my bruised and battered skin.

Bearing my teeth, I gave the Hound a wide smile. "Come closer," I said.

The coward only stared at me. There was another knock upon my mental frequency, and I went utterly still. My head tilted as I studied him, and then acquiesced to his request.

"I'm so sorry," were his first words. *"It wasn't supposed to be like this."*

I laughed out loud, and didn't care an iota that the sound came out rather mad.

"Rook, just tell him what he wants to know... Please."

I met his blue gaze square, and saw him cringe under the undiluted fire that blazed behind mine. "You better hope I die in these chains, Hound," I whispered, straining against my bonds so that he could feel the promise in my posture.

"I'm sorry," he repeated, clearly not willing to even speak the weak words aloud.

He left then, and did not return again

And whatever love I'd been able to feel in my shriveled heart left along with him, also unlikely to ever return.

When two Hounds I didn't recognize came to retrieve me that evening, telling me that the arena awaited me, I was eager to go.

One last time, I told myself.

I would enter The Ring one last time.

40

There was the sound of thunder, rumbling and earth shuddering, but the night sky was clear, not a cloud hanging among the heavens. The noise was such that it sent vibrations into the ground, which travelled up through the wooden wheels of the barred wagon in which I rode.

One final fight, I thought, and then, I could rest.

As the wagon approached the looming structure of the arena, I said my goodbyes to the night stars. With all the light pollution from the Apollo-blessed lampposts and the enormous torches lit around the arena, the stars were not visible, but I knew they were there. They were my oldest companions, and I could feel their glittering gazes upon me.

We reached the arena, and I was dragged by my chains inside. Down a dark hallway, up endless spiral stairs, toward a door guarded by a Hound, the source of that thunderous sound just beyond. The Hound, easily twice my size, eyed me suspiciously as he removed the chains on my ankles. When he removed them from my wrists, I snapped his neck so fast that his face didn't change from the shocked expression even as his body slumped to the ground.

I stepped around him and pushed open the doorway to the center of the arena, ready to make my appearance in Reagan Ramsey's grand finale. Eager to have it done and over.

For the first time since I'd been forced to fight some fifteen years ago, I was not afraid.

In fact, I couldn't feel a thing.

~

A nd it was a Gods damned good thing I couldn't, because what waited for me on the other side of that door was a veritable nightmare. Had I been in my right mind, I might have soiled myself on the spot before deciding whether it would be wiser to just sacrifice myself to the sea serpent.

It was the same as the last time I'd been here. The thin, rail-less walkways leading to the circular platform in the center, which also sported no boundary to stop one from falling over the edge and into the churning, murky water below.

Except this time, chained upon that center platform, was a beast plucked straight from the mountains of some other, more feral world. Its enormous body was covered in large scales so dark a blue that they gleamed black under the torchlight. Its four powerful limbs were tipped in razor sharp claws that dug into the platform beneath it as it yanked against the chain around its long, scaly neck. Its wings were magnificent, midnight blue and membranous, with thick, corded veins spider-webbing through.

I'd only ever seen a Firedrake in pictures in old books, and only ever heard of them in old wives' tales, but unless I'd gone completely out of my mind—which certainly was a possibility—I was seeing one now. And its blazing red eyes were looking right back at me, as hungry as the sea serpent ruling the waters below.

The voice of the announcer rang out like that of a booming deity, breaking through the daze that had befallen me as I'd laid eyes upon the magnificent beast.

"*Now... we have a special treat sure to please even the most sour among us! Our very own West Coast Pack Master and host of this year's Games has handpicked the Wolves who will face off in our final match...*

Rook the Bear-killer has just entered The Ring, and she has been chosen because she is a traitorous thief and a liar."

The crowd booed. Tomatoes splattered near my feet, and I batted away more than a couple heads of lettuce.

The announcer continued: "*Rook the Bear-killer is also known as 'Ryker's whore,' because she is known to get very friendly with Marisol's handsome Head Hound.*"

There were more boos, and plenty of laughter. More food was thrown at me along with vulgar names and insults. They rolled off my shoulders like raindrops. I was almost free. Almost *free*.

Then the announcer called the name of my opponent, and the very blood flowing through my veins went ice cold.

A door on the opposite side of the arena opened, and Kalene was shoved through.

~

I f I hadn't spent almost every day of the past three moon cycles with her, I might not have even recognized the dark-haired beauty. She was still in her human form... but she was foaming at the mouth, her dark eyes glinting with feral madness, the human part of her gone in the wake of her beast.

Purple Wolfsbane, I realized. Ramsey must have had her dosed with Purple Wolfsbane. One hit of the stuff could turn the most docile of Wolves completely rabid.

I barely had time to process this turn of events when Kalene charged down the narrow walkway before her, headed toward the center of the ring, snarling and snapping like a starving animal. The sight was jarring, and my feet began moving before my mind gave them a conscious command to do so.

Kalene was almost to the center platform, and the Firedrake turned its slitted eyes toward her. I ran as hard as I could, afraid that in her altered state Kalene might get eaten by the winged beast simply because she was too out of her mind for caution.

Now I could feel again, and the emotion that filled me was utter terror.

I'd been prepared to die when I'd come here. What I had not been prepared for was watching a friend die. The panic that filled me was intoxicating, and I moved faster than I should have with my still-broken body.

The response of the crowd was *deafening*, eager to see the novelty of two females fighting in human form, the Firedrake pacing hungrily at the length of his chain in the center of the circular platform. The air smelled of blood, popped corn, and body odor. Time passed swiftly and in screenshots of action—the manner it usually reserved for dreams.

Or nightmares.

Kalene and I reached the middle in the same instant, and my crazed friend leapt into the air, fingers held like claws, ready to rip my throat out. The scorching heat of the Firedrake's breath washed over us, and I managed to grab Kalene by the shoulders and twist us out of the reach of the beast—but just barely. We went tumbling in a ball of limbs and dark hair.

Her fingernails dug into me deep enough to draw blood, but I didn't feel any pain as I used all my might to slow our rolling motion toward the edge of the platform, where the water and its monster waited below. I managed to stop us, but Kalene was thrashing so wildly that she gained the position on top of me. Her fists began flying toward my face in the following instant.

One of them connected square on my jaw, and stars burst before my eyes, the coherent thoughts knocked clean out of my head.

"Kalene!" I pleaded telepathically. *"You have to get control of yourself! It's me! It's Rook! I'm your friend!"*

But as she continued to wail on me, I caught another dream-like glimpse of her dilated pupils, of the furious, animalistic expression twisting her beautiful face into something horrendous.

I let the strength coil in my legs and kicked her off me with too much force, I realized, as Kalene's strong and slim body went sailing toward the Firedrake. Its snake-like eyes were glittering with anticipation.

The Firedrake opened its mighty mouth, huge fangs poised to devour my friend whole.

I was moving in an instant. As Kalene came within range of the mighty beast's yawning maw, I jumped high into the air, using every bit of supernatural strength and speed that I owned, and punched the scaly creature right in the face.

This bought Kalene the precious moment she needed to get out of the way, but she was too busy trying to attack me to think straight, so I sucker-punched the Firedrake and ran, crazy ass Kalene trailing after me.

The crowd roared with laughter... and suddenly another emotion returned to me.

I hated them for that laughter. *Gods* how I hated them for it.

I couldn't keep this up much longer. Kalene was drugged out of her mind. The Firedrake and sea serpent were flesh-starved. And my body was starting to fatigue, threatening to fail me at any moment.

For whatever reason, as I led Kalene away from the Drake like a mouse trailing a feline, I looked out into the crowd and spotted Reagan Ramsey sitting comfortably in the box seats, a smug grin on his well-groomed face.

And Ryker the Hound stood silently beside him.

Suddenly, as if the aspiration had struck me like a bolt of lightning, I wanted to live, if only so that I could watch those two sons of bitches die.

~

The idea came to me in the same lightning-flash manner as had the previous epiphany, and I decided to go for it before I lost the nerve.

Spinning on my heels in a full circle, I ran back in the other direction—straight toward the hungry Firedrake. The world rushed by around me in a blur, but I pinpointed my focus, preparing to spend my last reserves of energy.

I was at the bottom of my barrel, so I would only get one shot.

Darting into the Drake's range, I rolled to the side just as its powerful jaws snapped shut around the open air I'd just previously been occupying. I was bouncing up to my feet in the same instant, gripping the thick chain around the creature's neck and using it to swing one leg up and over it.

In a blink that I almost couldn't believe, I found myself sitting atop the Firedrake's strong, scaly back. I watched in stunned, adrenaline-fueled wonderment as my hands gripped the chain... and unlatched it from around the great beast's neck.

We were airborne so fast that my head spun.

The Firedrake shot up into the air like a dark star against an even darker night. I wrapped my arms around its neck and squeezed with my thighs for dear life as it spiraled and plummeted and rose again, trying to shake me free of it. I gritted my teeth and squinted my eyes against the rushing of air and the rising in my stomach. The creature let out a great, bellowing roar that echoed endlessly in the arena.

People in the crowd began to scream.

Over the cacophony of sound that erupted in the arena, I yelled into the Firedrake's ear, my finger pointing in the direction of a certain box situated advantageously within the stands.

"There is the one who has held you captive!" I told it, not at all sure if the beast could hear me, let alone *understand* me. "There's the one who has been your master! And mine, too. Let's go show him what we think of this."

To my utter amazement, the Drake twisted its magnificent body and shot off like an arrow...

Right toward that luxurious box seat. Right toward the incomparable Reagan Ramsey.

The fear in his eyes in the moments before we reached him— as the bastard saw us coming, and knew we were coming for *him* —was a thing to behold, a thing of absolute beauty.

The Firedrake slammed into those cozy box seats and snatched Reagan Ramsey, West Coast Pack Master and first class dickhead, right up into its powerful jaws, as easily as a bird of prey might pluck a fish from a lake.

The crowd that had been laughing, booing, cheering, and chucking food was in an outright panic. Their screams rose in a symphony that was music to my ears.

With Ramsey's mangled limbs still protruding from between the Drake's enormous teeth, the creature shot up and up and up into the air, aiming for the apex in the center of the dome, toward the stars that I'd bid farewell to only a handful of moments earlier.

With a deep breath, the creature opened its enormous mouth and shot out a scorching stream of brilliant blue fire, making me shield my eyes as an instant sweat broke over my forehead. Straight ahead, the cover of the dome turned to ash as though it were nothing more than burning parchment.

I watched the horror recede below me as the Firedrake sailed with mighty wings toward a future where nothing was certain.

41

The Firedrake landed on the ledge of one of the cliffs surrounding Marisol on its northern side, and I slid off its back already asking it to *please don't eat me.*

Everything had happened so fast, and now I was just numb, so I stood and watched the creature in stunned silence as it spat out the remainder of Ramsey's body, clawed it free of its fine suit, and tore into the flesh the way I might the bones of a chicken.

In the distance, the arena was still erupting with chaos, and I could see people spilling out of the doors like ants from a hill caught on fire.

The howls of the Hounds followed shortly after, and I knew, of course, that they were hunting for *me.*

I touched the magical collar still around my neck, and sighed. They would find me sooner or later, and then they would kill me for what I'd done.

I turned to the Firedrake, holding my hands out cautiously and noting that it had already finished devouring Ramsey's body... Which was a total mindfuck of a realization.

"You need to go," I told it. "You just finished eating an important Wolf, and they'll kill you for it. So go."

The beast only stared at me, tilting its scaly head to the side in a manner that reminded me of a puppy. I wondered how long Ramsey had kept the thing, how long it had been chained and locked up. The slave in me recognized the slave in it from the look in its big, snakelike eyes.

The Firedrake spread its wings, as if preparing to take flight... but then it turned back to me, and lowered its head. Without words, it seemed to ask if I wanted to come with it, to fly far away from here, to someplace where we would not be hunted.

When something wet slid down my cheek, it took me a heart-beat or three to recognize what was happening, and I swiped the tear away before it could leave a trail there.

I touched the collar at my throat once more. "I can't run," I told it in a voice that was barely more than a whisper. "They'd find me. This would lead them right to us." The howls of the Hounds were growing closer and closer, as if simply to punctuate my words. I sighed. "You have to go. *Now*."

The Drake stared at me a moment longer, and I could have sworn I saw sympathy in its strange eyes. Then, it turned and beat its enormous wings once before sailing over the edge of the cliff. I stood there watching as it disappeared into the night sky. For whatever stupid reason, another tear slid down my cheek, and I swiped it away as if I were offended.

The howls of the Hounds were close now, only a handful of minutes away.

I sank down to my knees, still staring after the long-gone Fire-drake, more exhausted than I could ever remember being in my short, miserable existence. I closed my eyes and waited.

When a voice spoke beside me, I almost jumped out of my skin with surprise. My head whipped to the right to see a pale hand had been extended to me.

"You should kneel for nothing, Rukiya dearest," said a smooth, familiar voice.

I looked up to see Adriel, his face so lovely that for a moment, I forgot I hated the bastard.

He wiggled his fingers. "Stand up," he ordered. "We don't have much time."

"Go away," I snapped, though my voice came out duller and more monotone than I'd intended. "You cost me everything, and if I weren't so tired right now, I'd kill you for it."

"The Hounds are coming," he replied, his voice taking on the affection of concern that I had never heard in it before. "They'll kill you on the spot when they get here, so *get up.*"

I struck out with my fist, but the Mixbreed dodged the blow easily by simply disappearing and then reappearing on the other side of me. "We don't have time for this," he said.

A hundred or so yards away, I heard a voice yell, "She's over here!" and the answering howls of at least half a dozen Hounds in Wolf form.

"Let them come," I said. "Leave me be."

Adriel made a disgusted sound in his throat. "The way they speak about you, Rukiya Moonborn, I expected more... fight."

"I'll show you fight if you don't leave me the fuck alone."

"Fine," Adriel said between clenched teeth. "We'll do this the hard way."

I had no time to defend myself or even blink before his fangs were sinking into my neck. I raised my hand to punch him, but felt my muscles go slack as absolute ecstasy flooded through me.

When my eyes fluttered open, I looked down to see what the Mixbreed held in his pale hands... and my own hands shot up to my neck...

Where there was no longer a Dog's collar.

I blinked, unable to believe it. "How?" I asked.

"Yes," said another familiar voice behind me. I turned on my heels to see Ryker. "How?" he echoed.

Adriel only tipped the Hound a wink and slipped a strong arm around my waist.

Then we were flying through time and space, having vanished into thin air.

~

When we landed—if that's what one would call it—I stumbled, and would have fallen flat on my face had Adriel not grabbed and steadied me. My head spun for a few seconds before I could orient myself, and when I did, I realized I had no idea where the hell we were.

Trees so tall I could not see the tops towered over us, the air thick with the clean scent of greenery. Early morning light filtered down in dapples of gold, and the clicks, chirps, and calls of the insects and forest creatures created a soft melody of sound. My strong nose told me there was a fresh water source nearby, and for whatever reason, I felt so blessedly small standing in the middle of it as I reached up and touched the place on my throat where that collar had always been.

"Welcome to Philomena, Rukiya," Adriel said, and though his voice had the same smooth cadence, there was something softer in it now, as if in reverence for the beauty around us. "We'll have to travel the rest of the way on foot, but this is a safe place... a *free* place."

My knees gave out beneath me with no warning, and I sank to the soft, plush floor of the forest, my hands gripping my thighs, my mind too shocked to catch up.

To add to my utter amazement, Adriel dropped to his knees in front of me, heedless of his fine slacks, and took my shoulders gently into his hands. "You're free," he whispered... and then said it again... and again.

At some point, it sank in, and my breath hitched in my throat. I covered my dirty face with my blood stained hands a millisecond before silent tears began to fall. Then the silent tears turned to sobs—shoulder-shaking, gut-wrenching sobs, and Adriel sat silently before me until I was able to gather myself.

Once I did, I felt like a dumbass. I sniffed, swiped a hand under my nose and beneath my eyes, and shot him a warning look. "You better not tell anyone you saw me do that," I choked out. "Or I'll kick your ass."

Astonishingly, he laughed, and it made his beautiful face all the more lovely. He held up a pale hand, as though he were taking an oath. "I won't tell a soul," he promised. Then added, "I mean, if I ever cried like a baby I definitely wouldn't want anyone to know, either, so I get it." He winked. "Your secret's safe with me."

My jaw dropped, and I gave his shoulder a little shove as I narrowed my eyes at him. "Where are we?" I asked.

Adriel's scarlet eyes twinkled, and a pointed canine poked out and bit into his lower lip. "This is my home. It's called Philomena."

I nodded slowly. "But *where* are we?"

"Philomena sits between realms."

I could feel my face slowly drain of color, a fear creeping into me that one would think I'd be beyond.

Adriel noticed my shift, and he stood in a smooth motion, moving away. "You shouldn't believe everything you've heard about my kind," he said. "It's ignorant."

Though he was right, I was offended. "I'm a slave," I snapped. "What do you expect?"

His red eyes blazed as they looked at me. "*Were*," he said. "You *were* a slave... Now, do you want to stand there yapping, or should we go see an old friend of yours? She hasn't stopped pestering me about you since I freed her months ago. I see why you two got along."

"Goldie," I gasped. "You're taking me to see Goldie?"

The Mixbreed turned back to look at me, his body preternaturally still and predatory. "Only if that's where you wish to go,

Rukiya dearest," he said. "I told you, you're *free*. Your choices are your own."

I hurried after him, fighting back more stupid tears. "You're going to explain all of this to me, right?"

He flashed me a look from the corner of his red eyes. "Do I have a choice in the matter?"

I considered. "No, not really."

He sighed, and through the perfection that was his physical form, for the first time since I'd met him, I could see the fatigue he was trying to hide, and it made me wonder what else he was hiding.

"How about I let Goldie fill you in?" he said. "We'll be there by sundown if we keep moving."

I almost asked why he couldn't just magic us there, or whatever the hell he called it, but another glance confirmed the fatigue I'd glimpsed. Perhaps he was too drained to do so.

"We can rest if you need to," I said.

This made him pause again and look back at me, amusement tugging up one side of his sensuous mouth. "After the past few days you've had, you're asking *me* if I need to rest?"

I shrugged. "I won't tell anyone," I promised. "If I ever had to rest like a baby I definitely wouldn't want anyone to know, either, so I get it." I winked. "Your secret's safe with me."

"Amazing," he mumbled, and turned around to continue on.

Once again I was running to keep up, my still broken body protesting despite my taunts. "What's amazing?"

"That you're still able to laugh at all."

I swallowed and held my peace the rest of the way, not bothering to tell him that I was only laughing because if I didn't, I would just keep crying and maybe never stop. Or that the tough façade I was clinging to was supporting the weight of it all by only a thread, dangling me over an abyss of the purest, deepest darkness.

Though I didn't know him well, and certainly didn't yet trust him, something told me I didn't have to say these things to Adriel, that perhaps he was intimately familiar with the mask one wears when pretending to hold it all together, while dangling only by a thread above the void.

According to Adriel, I was free, but so many others still weren't. Wondering what would become of Kalene, Oren, Ares, and so many others haunted every step I took through the forest, hung over me like a cloud formed solely to soak me.

The collar around my neck was gone, but the weight on my shoulders remained, and I feared I was too broken to carry it all, broken in a way that would never heal the same.

THE END

ABOUT THE AUTHOR

H. D. Gordon is the author of several urban fantasy novels. She is the mother of two amazing daughters, and a lover of kick-ass females, beautiful things, and nerdy t-shirts.

She believes our actions have ripple effects, and in the sacred mission of bringing love and light to the world.

H. D. spends her time with family, eating desserts, and taking strolls by the sea.

She resides in southern New Jersey—which she insists is really quite lovely.

For more information visit:
www.hdgordonbooks.com

Made in the USA
Middletown, DE
28 May 2018